WHISKEY AND OLD STOGIES

A Novel

Lisa Angle

Copyright © 2021 by Lisa Angle

ISBN: 978-1-7370474-0-7

Published by:
Humpback Books
809 East De La Guerra Street
Santa Barbara CA 93103

NOTE TO THE READER

The author tried to stay as true to Rufus's voice as possible without confusing the reader. Although, at times that became challenging. In order to prepare the reader for the immersive experience in this novel, the author offers some examples words the reader will encounter.

Bout = About
Round = Around
Ole = Old
Tuther = The Other
Ona = One of
Somma = Some of
Lotta = Lot of

The author hopes the reader will fall into the rhythm of Rufus's speech and not become hampered as they get to know him.

ONE

Back in them days I didn't knowed the first thing bout whiskey. How the mountain dew got you feeling so good everybody your best friend. How the corn squeezings turned your gut sour like the mash it distilled from. What the white lightning made you do to other folks. What the likker tricked you into doing to yourself.

I ain't nothing but a ole bootlegger what never so much as pissed off a fly in a outhouse. But cause I the only other living soul what knowed the truth bout that fire, reckoned I the best one to spin this here tale. I gonna do my darnedest to give it justice. If Jolene did the telling, the story'd come out like a overturned basket a eggs, all cracked and splattered.

Not that I didn't take the O'Hara side in any fight. Way I see things, the truth go way beyond the fate of that Harvey fella.

Last turnoff offered a carved sign on a post pointing one way, a hand-painted one sitting on a withered ole branch pointed tuther. I picked the branch cause I feel sorry for it. That way first passed a store not friendly enough to stop at then nother of them sticks with something stuck to the bark. Didn't knowed what the sign said. The words seemed to tease me like a worm wiggling at a fish.

The trees and creek whistled to me like a boy searching for a lost pup. At a wide spot in the road wood planks lay scattered like a wild storm blow through. What happened here? Something made a peculiar noise behind me.

Tsch, tsch, tsch. Tiptoed round the hole where the sound come from. Maybe a coon fall in there, trapped hisself. Tsch, tsch, tsch. I near the hole quiet as baking bread, careful not to scare him. Half a arms-length from the hole, I stopped. Didn't smell like no coon.

"Boo."

Jumped a barrel high, landed on my behind.

A boy climbed out, rolled on the ground, laughed hisself daft. Law, if he ain't scrawny. My blood sizzled like bacon fat. Watching him hold his sides, I give in to the fun, chuckled a bit too.

He catched his breath. "Got'cha good, sure enough."

"Sure did. What'cha doin in that there hole to begin with?"

He looked me in the eye. "Playin outhouse inspector. Reckon this hole where they aim to build the privy." He winked. "Name's Joe. I oughta be cleanin chicken coops, not playin child games. But Jole get mad, push over them boards then go off somewhere. I stay here in case a girl happen by. Beat all scarin you, even if you ain't a gal. What bring you to Cedar Springs?"

Nobody ever showed that much interest to ask me nothing like that before.

"Roamin round close on a month."

"Your kin must miss you."

"Ma got too many in the roost to keep track. Knowed Pa ain't missed me. If'n he shout out for a Rufus, onea my three cousins name Rufus likely pipe up. Pa don't knowed one from tuther. Most times he don't use no name, he grab the one standin handy."

"Don't sound like a nice fella."

"Learn me to stay outta reach."

Little Joe tell me to follow him way from the road, down a path lined with thick pine trees, to a homestead what looked over the creek. When we got in the yard, a hound-dog trotted up to sniff me, the sack in my hand too. "That there Tickle." Little Joe patted the dog on the back. "That there my brother Jack."

Some older boy set on the front porch, scraping taters and carrots. He tossed them in a pot with water. He ain't no giant but he looked like a oak tree next to Little Joe.

What in that pot do my empty belly some good. "How bout I throw this here quail I snare in with them taters. We share?" I offered the bag with my good luck of the day inside.

"Be nice to eat somethin besides chicken or fish this one time." Little Joe said. "Rufus ain't good as a female, but he company. How bout he stay for supper?"

"Best ask Jole."

"Jole get in one a them moods. Not gonna come back soon, sure enough."

"There plenty then."

To help I fetched water, stuck kindling in the stove. Little Joe keep up our spirits by running his mouth bout the gals he knowed, lotta them. Big Jack put in a nod now and again. Little Joe didn't seem to care if he hear or not. Them two seemed easy with each other like brothers oughta.

Glad to work in that kitchen. Never recollected spending time like that with nona my own kin. Then again ain't much I do remember bout my life as a young'un, least ways till I bout ten.

"You say you got lotta brothers, sisters, cousins. Sounds like a bushel fulla fun," Little Joe said.

"Things ain't always what folks think."

"Lotta aunts and uncles too, I reckon."

Ain't gonna bring to mind nona them.

"Smell like time to take the stew off the stove," I said.

The porch creaked. Door boomed open. Little Joe and Big Jack looked at one nother, Little Joe said, "Jole's back."

Jole stomped in the kitchen, snatched a cup off the sideboard. He pouring coffee before he laid eyes on me. Little Joe musta seen the chicken hawk stare cause he jumped to the quick. "Hey, Jole, meet Rufus. He visitin a spell."

"All I need, nother mouth to feed." Jole banged the coffeepot down on the stove. He a bit older than Big Jack, maybe a little stronger, more smooth-faced.

Big Jack and Little Joe like to melt into the wall. This place ain't atall like where I come from.

"I fend for myself. That there quail cookin what I put in."

Jole slammed down the cup, coffee splashed out. "I don't give a damn bout some quail. You not welcome here."

"Little Joe say I welcome." Used the name I called Joe in my head.

"Little Joe?" Jole planted fists on his hips. Muscles get tight under his union suit. He kicked a chair out from the table, plopped down. "That all I need after my trouble today. First them no-tail-bears try to take over O'Hara land. Then I go up to the Grady place for some lonesome time, find some Clyde."

"What's a Clyde?" Little Joe said.

"Who knows? Claim he kin. Say his name O'Hara, but I never hear of a O'Haras cept us three." Jole rub his face with both hands. "I gotta set out for town tomorrow, stop them negres from building on my land."

I meet a Cherokee one time but only seen colored folk in pictures. Hoped I get to spy some in the flesh soon. Hoped I get to learn from somebody important like Jole.

"I snare nother critter for supper tomorrow, if'n you want."

"You let Rufus stay, Jole? That quail stew smell right nice, sure enough."

Jole pulled a what-I-gonna-do face. He slumped to one of the two rooms on tuther side of the house. Whapped the door shut behind him.

My mouth hang open so I said, "Your brother one prickly fella."

Big Jack nudged me, shaked his head.

Little Joe said, "Jolene ain't our brother. She our sister."

TWO

Big Jack fetched me a real chicken feather pillow. Sleep better than ever before, waked up before sun-up, slipped to the kitchen door. Jolene jawed at Little Joe.

"What you thinkin, boy? Bringin home some little lost boll weevil. Like me catchin you with that one girl. Claim you don't know her ma a Harvey. What bout this one? If I find a Harvey on my land...."

"But Rufus ain't no boll weevil," Little Joe said. "And he not a Harvey neither."

"One and the same, boy, one and the same. When you gonna learn that?"

"Yes'm. But, Jole, Rufus not no Harvey."

"I don't give a damn. I want that varmint outta my house. Now."

Last word she snapped out like a hickory switch she gonna whip me with. I stepped in the kitchen. "Reckon I go outside then."

Stayed round the pump for a spell while Jolene hollered at Little Joe some more. After a bit, she come out on the porch with a straw hat over her short black not quite curly hair. She carried a shotgun.

"How many times I gotta tell you to git?"

"Oh, I gittin," I fall in behind her. She pulled some chicory from a bush, headed up the path. When she get to the planks scattered by the road, she spit, turned the way I come the day before. She carried that shotgun like she might stop short, take down a buck at a hundred yards. After a fair piece, reckoned to try swapping words with her. "Where we goin, Jolene?"

She spin round, jabbed the shotgun butt in the dirt like she breaking ground. My heart halted for a second. "Stop your followin me."

Shrugged. Go ahead, walking backward so as to look at her. "What the shotgun for, Jolene?"

"Boy, if you any greener, I stick you in my garden, see if you grow."

Stumbled on a rock, fall on my backside. She walked right on by. I crossed the road, run up ahead for a time. A peach tree stand behind a long turn. I climbed a fence under a low hanging branch, picked me a special treat. Spied her coming. "Hey, Jolene. Want a peach? This one nice'n sweet, just right."

She watched me bite a big juicy hunk. She take a piece a chicory from her pocket, stick that in her mouth, turned back on her way. We travelled long on different sides of the road. The sun get higher, the heat settle in round me. Didn't feel like doing nothing else, so reckoned to try her again.

Crossed the road, matched her stride. "Hey, Jolene, why don't you walk on the road? Or tuther side?"

"Grrrrr." She sounded like a mad dog when she growled. "Don't you know nothin?"

"Reckon plenty I don't knowed." Sure the truth. "But I knowed this road shadier on tuther side."

This get her to stop. She heaved a sigh like a man giving up on a mule. "From the Cedar Springs bridge to the Mill Creek turnoff, Harveys stay to that side of the road, O'Haras stick to this side." Her finger sliced the air like a knife chopping onions. "And if I catch a Harvey on this side, I gonna shoot him dead." She spit like what she said tasted bad.

How she gonna shoot a Harvey? That shotgun ain't loaded cause of no shell blast when she bang the butt.

"Well," I said, "Us Hollowberrys never run to feudin. But if'n I see me a Harvey, will sure say so. Will wrassle him down, sit on him while you shoot him, if'n you want me to."

"Now there's a boy with some ambition."

Long bout the time the sun hang highest in the sky we come on a honest-to-goodness town. The air hotter with all them brick buildings staring at me. Before we get to the middle I seen more folks than my ma got young'uns. One fancy lady strolled long with a pink parasol.

Law, if they ain't got automobiles too. Never seen more than one in a given place. This town got at least three.

I get so busy watching everything, I bout lose Jolene when she turned in at what I knowed the jail from the bars on the windows.

A sheriff with door handle ears said, "Leave that shotgun by the door. You know I ain't gonna let no Harveys in here."

"I got negres fixin to squat on my land. I wanna stop them."

"Fraida that. I come in the county clerk's office when this fella there, he talk funny, say he from France and he wanna invest in some land. Turns out that narrow parcel next to the road ain't O'Hara land."

Jolene let her mouth fall open. "Nah. That not true."

"He don't say nothin bout negres."

"You gonna let them get way with that?"

"That fella a lawyer. He ain't gonna do nothing gainst the law."

"That my land."

"For now. Seen your name in the County Clerk's notebook what list them that owe back taxes."

Look on Jolene's face turn so fiery I think her hat might start to smoke. Didn't wanna stay round when she blow. I run outta the door almost into nother lady with nother parasol. How I gonna help Jolene outta that there mess?

THREE

Wandered round taking in so many new sights my eyes set to swimming. Some folks called the town Swift River. The name fit cause the place set next to a river what run faster than a spooked pup. Bread and pickles ripe for the stealing out front of the mercantile. Eat a nice dinner while leaning back on a shaded post.

My fingers rubbed the smooth boards on the worned-out walkway, catched on something. I moved over, leaned in close. Law, if a coin didn't stick tween the planks. Take out my pocketknife, worked that coin like digging in a coal mine. Payed off. Got me a whole nickel to my name. Feel like a real man with honest to goodness money in my pocket. Waltzed round trying to figure out what to do with my find. Never got so much as a penny to my name before.

That coin gonna make Jolene like me more. Spotted her. Reckoned I try somma the new words I learned me on her. "Hey, Jolene. What'cha sittin on a sidewalk with your feet in the street for?"

If I a fly buzzing round her head, she might pay me more mind. Her chin rested in her hands. Her eyes never leave a store cross the way. A wooden Injun stand by the door, reckoned to get folks to stop in. Seemed to me that there Injun not too friendly, maybe a mite-a paint cheer him up. Didn't Injuns like to draw colors right on their hides? Jolene didn't blink the whole time she watched that store. A whole heap of folks passed by before she stand, ambled off with her gun, probably still empty of shot.

In the store the sweet smell of tobacco made me wish the stuff for eating. So many different kinds mixed in the air, one whiff get me dizzy. I plunked down my nickel.

Stayed under a chestnut tree on the edge a town to keep way from the thick afternoon heat till the sun ducked hisself behind a mountaintop. On my way back toward the Mill Creek turnoff, strike me that I on the wrong side of the road. Recollected Jolene watched that side like a bear might charge out from behind some trees. She got a eye out for Harveys, I reckoned. Harveys must be pretty dern ugly. I knowed in my bones if I met one, I hate him. With only one day and a night, I feel faithful to the O'Haras.

My wondering what a Harvey looked like got my brain to itching so bad I wandered into the woods near the turnoff. A path lead me up a hill while dark blanketed the sky, inviting the stars to come out to dance. Somewhere a creek crashed over rocks then I seen the cliff. Moonlight shine on the water. Reckoned I find me a piece a ground to curl up on for the night. Climb down at first light with the wad a line in my pocket, catch me a fish for breakfast.

In my dream I painted that wooden Injun, white feathers with red tips, yellow and blue stripes on his face, eyes so brown they twinkled like Jolene's.

"Wake up you lazy, good-for-nothing worm." That her yelling at me? My eyes cracked open. "Wake up, you worthless fool." Law, if that voice meaner than Jolene's. Come from behind a clump a rocks yonder. Dawn covered the mountains like a shawl. Pretended me a leaf on the bush I bedded under. Didn't move a stitch.

"Sorry, Pa. Just a quick nap." Sounded like a boy.

"Oh, poor Snake gotta get him a nap. Someone come long, pour out our mash, bust up our still. But Snake get him some beauty sleep."

"They busted our still?"

"Yep, come down the hill shoot your brothers and me. Killed us all dead."

"But you standin right..."

A scuffle stopped the boy's words. The fella said, "Now git to haulin up water and chop more wood, before I take off somma your toes."

What if that evil fella find me? Got a idea from the name he called the boy. Slithered like a snake out from under the bush. Made my feet soft like the dirt path. A twig snapped behind me. My blood stopped running, sure they after me. A deer dashed by, bout knocked me over.

Swear to never let my wondering trick me up that hill again. I knowed better than to get near a spooky ole still and a crazy moonshiner. On the road, I stayed on the right side, not crossing for a peach to fill my empty gut.

Back to the O'Haras' Jolene hoeing in the garden. "What'cha doin back here? Reckon I scrape you off my shoe in town."

Why she say that? She didn't wear no shoes.

She raised her hoe. "Now git, before I plow you under."

"Hey, Jolene. I bring you somethin."

She screwed up her face, looked round like she heard someone else talk. Them beans said nothing. "Somethin for me? What the hell for?"

Stepped over a watermelon, come closer so she didn't gotta yell so loud. "Hope you like it." Pulled the cigar outta my chest pocket.

The hoe clunked to the ground. Her eyes sparked.

"It name Stogie."

She carried my gift careful as a baby bird, cross the yard, up the steps, into the house.

Picked up the hoe cause I knowed what getting left in the dirt feel like.

Find Little Joe in the barn sucking a egg, his hound, Tickle, chewed a stick. "Hey, Rufus." Leastwise someone on this place friendly. "Where you get off to?"

"Me and Jolene go to Swift River." Seen a mule in a stall. Why Jolene not ride him to town? "She come back here, I get myself in a mess a trouble."

Little Joe said for me to wait so they all hear my yarn.

Jolene give me a plate at supper. After we eat, she take a lamp out on the porch to read to us from a newspaper. "Since Prohibition started on January 1st of this year, there has been a sharp rise in the making of moonshine whiskey in the inner mountain area. One North Carolina county alone, where the sheriff cut up forty-two stills in one year, had fifty stills cut up in ten days." She peered at them words like she didn't wanna miss one tiny thing. "Experts claim that a bushel of corn, which under normal conditions would bring only a dollar or two at the market, could be distilled into two gallons of whiskey priced at upwards of forty dollars a gallon...'"

My mouth boiled over. "That what my story bout too."

"Rufus, Jole readin. And this news fun, sure enough."

Jolene cut her eyes at me. "Hush up, Joe. I wanna hear this."

Spilled the story bout hearing the crazy fella and boy, throwed in a tall tale bout my getaway for good measure.

"What them folks look like?"

"Didn't draw no bead on em. But the fella call the boy Snake."

"Snake." Jolene jumped outta her chair. Me, Little Joe, and Big Jack scattered. Tickle scurried under the porch.

"Harveys." Her feet slapped from one end of the porch to tuther faster than a ax through a chicken's neck. "So the Harveys got them a still runnin up there."

FOUR

Yet nother day my eyes opened to some sorta ruckus before the sun showed his face. Big Jack rolled over, commenced snoring some more. Little Joe pulled a pillow over his head. I go to the kitchen where Jolene hitting the stove with the iron skillet. What she madder at, the stove or the skillet?

"Dern Clyde." She sat, hands over her head like the stove gonna whip her back.

"Morning, Jolene."

She didn't look up.

"What's the trouble?"

"Grrrrr." She jerked up from the table, go bout making coffee. "I shoulda got rid that Clyde fella when I first put eyes on him. Now I got me a problem to think on, no place to get way from them fool boys." She jabbered more to herself than on my count. "That our place, not some stinkin low-life Clyde's. I got a good mind to..." She tossed down the kindling. "That what I gonna do." Quick as a fish stealing bait she got her straw hat and a shotgun.

She didn't damn me for following. This time she walked tuther way, not towards town, crossed a bridge, then crossed the road. Now I knowed why she favored one side over tuther. We turned up a lonely path. The hill got steeper, the trail trickled out. Jolene trudged long like a hungry hound dog going home for his supper.

She cussed when she got a splinter stepping over a log. She sat down on that log. The shotgun she set close by not the one she bring to town. She picked at her foot. "Hear what I say. That there Clyde will get off my land or meet his maker. Say his name's O'Hara. Pig slop."

"How come this here your land when it so far from your house?" She wrong bout the piece next to theirs.

"This my ma's folks' place. She leave the parcel to us." A sliver come outta her foot.

"What happen to your ma?"

"Don't you talk bout my ma."

A rundown cabin, smaller than the O'Hara place, come in sight. Didn't look like much living go on there. Jolene stopped, raised the shotgun, take aim. Her finger on the trigger ready to spring. Her face turned hard. The gun boomed. A bucket fly off the porch. A nose peeked tween the curtains.

"Get your sorry self out here."

The door opened slow like sap running in a tree. A skinny fella slink out. His face pale as fresh milk, maybe from the gunfire, maybe from what nature gave him. Reckoned this Clyde. He didn't look like no O'Hara. Too tall, too blonde, his ears stick out from his head, little like that sheriff in town. Jolene lowered the shotgun, marched up to the porch. "Now I got the right weapon. You gotta listen this time. Get, or be got."

Clyde blinked. "Take me half a day to work my way outta that outhouse you tied me in."

Didn't find Jolene trapping him in a outhouse hard to believe. Wished I round to seen that.

"Now you loose. Be on your way." She shaked the gun with every word.

"How I know you got proper claim on this place?"

Two steps got her on the porch. "This how you know what's mine."

He got a year or two on her but she armed.

Leave them to their own business. In the yard weeds and dried leaves from many a fall past covered the ground. Dead branches hang low on the apple trees. "This parcel sure need some work," I said. Round the side of the house I spot a spade rusted darker than dirt. Ideas stirred in my head.

"Where that Rufus varmint get to?" Jolene come down off the porch, Clyde followed.

"A body make this a right nice place, if'n they got a mind to." I looked to Jolene, she looked to Clyde, he looked to the shotgun.

"Maybe I share crop for you, if you do got a claim on the land," Clyde said. "We both get some extra greenbacks."

She stuck the gun under his nose. "My claim to this land run in my blood. Don't forget that."

"Lotta cleanin up to do round here. Real hard chores," I said.

"I'll straighten things as much as I can." Clyde sniffed gunpowder, peered down the barrel at Jolene. "And this being your place, you might know about that whatnot in the shed."

At the shed, Jolene shake the open lock in his face. "Don't know how you got this open. My uncle never let us in. Whatever in there, it mine. You hear?"

He put up his hands. "Yes'm."

Jolene opened the door. We all stepped in. She stared at that thing like at that smoke shop in town. The contraption got a big black belly with one horn coming outta the top. Law, if a long, curly tail the color a dried pine needles growed outta that horn.

"What's that, Jolene?"

She squinted at me then at Clyde. "You two dumber than a couple owls hooting at the sunshine." She gone so quick I bout didn't catch what way she go.

Clyde watched Jolene skedaddle like a tomcat eyeing a rat sneaking outta his barn.

FIVE

Didn't knowed how I got down that hill with no Jolene to follow. Crossed the bridge, something wrong. I stopped, think. Then it hit me. I gotta cross the road. Sure didn't wanna butt heads with no Harvey.

On tuther side of the road, go on my way to the wide spot with the scattered planks. Jolene stand nose to nose with, not a gal, but a lady, likes of which I never seen before. Law, if her skin ain't dark like a log pulled from the creek.

That lady got tight lips, eyes what sparkled like crushed brown glass. "You welcome to the path. We gracious. Done matter you not."

Jolene stomp on home.

"That girl somethin else," dark lady said.

"Ain't gonna fight you on that," I said.

She tell me her name Glory. We talked a bit with the hot sun licking our faces. Asked Glory why her skin so dark.

"When I a baby, I stand under a hole in a cloud. God spill his chocolate puddin on me."

That made her seem special to me.

"Now you answers me a question," she said. "You knows dat Miz Jolene well?"

"Reckon I knowed a thing or two bout that gal." After three whole days.

"Bet you gots a good idea how to get on her good side." Glory winked, wiped sweat off her plump top lip, not tight no more now Jolene gone.

Wished I knowed myself. "Reckon if'n you ain't a Harvey, you got a good start."

"Mr. Comier gots us buildin him a store. My man, Jimbo, he doin the wood work." Reckoned that the fella with a hammer a ways off. "Hear the O'Haras gots excellent eggs and fryers. Wanna sell only the best here. That what Mr. Comier want. So I gots to get Miz Jolene to see my way."

"Wish you luck."

"You seems like a nice boy. Put in a good word for me, I's beholden to you. Gots a feelin you able to work some magic on her."

Find Jolene by the barn. "Glory say they buildin a store."

"I don't trust them sneaky no-tail-bears. She hidin somethin." Jolene clicked open the shotgun, checked on the shells. "I hate that woman more than no one else."

"But Glory ain't no Harvey."

Jolene looked at me like I kudzu choking her tomato plants. "I gotta scare some crows outta the field." She take her shotgun, swooped off to the corn.

Gotta show Jolene what I made of, how hard I work. Then she hear me better.

Spied a mulecart behind the barn. Thing looked like it sit out in the weather all winter. Pulled the cart outta the weeds. Got me a bucket a water, find some soap and a rag. Scrubbed that wood good. Wondered where to get me grease for the wheels, salt to rub off the rust. O'Haras gonna wanna use that there cart when I done.

"What the hell you doin?" Little Joe run at me, buck butt me down. "Why you touch that?"

"You gone daft?" Get my feet under me.

Little Joe clobbered me in the ear. "Don't fiddle with what ain't yours."

"Get way from me." Shoved him.

"Jole gonna whip you for this, sure enough."

"He don't know." Big Jack grabbed his brother by his overalls, turned him round. "Go get inside."

Big Jack pushed the cart back behind the barn. "Jole never see." He patted my shoulder, go on in the house.

All that for nothing. Jolene ain't gonna knowed bout my work. What get Little Joe all fired up?

Maybe Jolene get mad bout the cart too. Glad Big Jack keep his head.

We eat supper on the porch way from the steamy kitchen. Little Joe keep to hisself, ain't like him. Wanna ask what I do wrong but them boys glum as a graveyard.

Bout the time our forks scraped the plate bottoms Jolene come up the steps with a basket fulla greens. "Hey, boys." She showed her teeth.

"Jole, Rufus mess with the mulecart," Little Joe said.

"I clean it up good."

"Nobody tell him," Big Jack said.

"Never you mind," Jolene tell Little Joe. "Nother sign," she said to nobody in particular.

"But Jole…"

"From now on you wash what need washin, like these here greens." Jolene gave me the basket. "Y'all best turn in soon as you clean up them dishes. We gettin up nice and early tomorrow. I got a surprise."

SIX

Got up before the rooster to wait outside. Jolene lead me, Little Joe and Big Jack into the woods. She pointed at a haystack under some trees. "There," she said. "Get rid a that straw." She watched us work with crossed arms. We uncovered what looked a twin to whatever Clyde find in that shed. Cepting this one shorter and fatter.

Jolene thumped the contraption on the belly. "This here a still. Folks use this to make moonshine likker."

I laughed. Never think a still looked like that.

She cut her eyes at me, like I passed a stinker. "You boys listen up good. Do as I say."

Big Jack fetched corn meal from the barn. Little Joe bring water from the creek. I cleaned out barrels buried under more hay. Jolene go to Mill Creek, buy sugar.

While I mixed up clay to patch what she called the furnace I think on what that newspaper said. Lotta men go to jail for making shine. Reckoned jail hard work with nothing to show for it and bedding down with folks you didn't care bout. Pretty much like my pa's house.

By noon we sat on the ground grinned at our work. Little Joe said, "Say, Jole, what we gonna do once we get some corn squeezens?"

She pulled a face like Little Joe asked why the sky blue. "Sell it. We need the money to pay taxes on this place and the Grady place. And I not lettin that Harvey pack get head of me in business. What'cha think? We gonna drink it ourselves?"

She got to her feet. "Surrounded by fools."

"Sell it where what I mean," Little Joe said with his head down.

"Speakin a fools. I best get up the hill, set that Clyde on some chores." Jolene stuck a finger at me. "You comin too. Gonna need your help."

Sounded to me better than ice cream on Sunday.

SEVEN

"You never did tell me what this whatnot for," Clyde said.

"You and this here boy gonna run some shine for me, I gonna sell it, get rich. Do what I say, you might get rich too."

"Ain't you heard of Prohibition? That gonna bring the law around here."

"I know more bout Prohibition than most folks. Some lawman gonna do some catchin, they gonna round up them Harveys."

Clyde blinked. "Who the Harveys? They live around here?"

"Grrr." She go back to messing with the curly copper thing. "They shiners and they killers. But with us runnin two stills I gonna sell more whiskey than them no-accounts ever dream bout."

She tell me build a furnace like the one at the O'Hara place. She send Clyde to get sugar in Cedar Springs.

"I get it in Chimney," Clyde said. "Don't know how to get to Cedar Springs."

"This one goin for some in Chimney." Jolene jerked a thumb at me. "Don't want them seein us buyin too much in one place, folks figure out what I up to. Anybody say somethin, you tell em your ma and your aunties cannin some jam." She shaked her head. "Fools. Nothing but fools."

Reckoned Clyde best watch hisself or Jolene run him off. That tussle a sight I like to see.

When Clyde gone I said, "He sure fret a lot bout the law, talk back too."

"He smart to worry after gettin caught." Jolene snapped the rag she polished the still with. "Clean up the yard right nice. I check the house, he do good in there to boot. Make some flaky biscuits too. Don't see you doin no cookin."

In the weeks the stuff in the barrels take to bubble like white water in a creek, we tended to chores round the farms. Jolene tell me help Clyde at the Grady place. When Clyde fixed his vittles, I set on the porch, then go in get mine.

One night Clyde come in late, sat cross the table, looked me over like a mule he gonna buy. "You do everything that girl say?"

"What? Jolene? Reckon I got a mite to learn from her."

"You a O'Hara?"

"Nah. A Hollowberry."

"What'cha doing with them?"

Recollected setting with Little Joe, him whittling while I scratched in the dirt. He didn't laugh at my pictures, he liked them. And I liked his carvings. "Cedar Springs sure nicer'en the holler I come from. You kin to them?"

Clyde blinked a bunch of times. "That's what I say."

"Where you from?" He didn't sound like he come from the hills.

"Africa." He stopped blinking, swallowed hard.

"Folks like Glory from there, you a towhead."

"My parents killed going down a river so some apes raise me."

Never heard tell of no family with a name like Ape. Reckoned if any them Apes ever lived in Cedar Springs they likely side with the Harveys, not the O'Haras.

EIGHT

The night the O'Hara still ready for the first run a slow trickle filled a washtub. Tree shadows swayed on the ground from the moonlight shining behind them. Reckoned that why folks called this making moonshine. Jolene said the brew gotta run through the still nother three times.

Little Joe said, "How come?"

She dunked a cup, stick the likker in his face. "Think it done? You taste it."

He put his nose in the cup. His head popped up, his eyes full a water. "Believe you, Jole."

Come back down a few nights later for the fourth run to help with the jugs. Jolene said, "Reckon I take the first sip cause I the oldest." She bring the jug to her lips like medicine that might cure a terrible sickness she got. The muscles in her neck moved when the shine go down. We waited. A spark light up her eyes. "Not bad. Just gotta settle a bit."

"Let me try." Little Joe snatch the jug. His nose wrinkled over it. "Don't smell so bad like before, sure enough." He tipped the jug back quicker than she did. Half a breath later he looked like a pitchfork stick him. His face turned green, his knees give out. Jolene grabbed the jug before Little Joe dropped to the ground. Tickle licked Little Joe on his chin. Worried he might die, till he said, "That stuff devil piss."

Got my first taste when our fourth run done at the Grady place. Jolene said the likker go down almost as smooth as their batch. Clyde wanted a swig. Jolene waved the jar at me. "He go first."

Make me feel like a top dog. With both hands round the jar I take a pull. The likker go down fine enough. Turned to a red hot coal in my belly. Let my tongue hang out like a panting dog. Jolene chuckled. I shut my mouth, willed my innards to stop burning.

Little Joe and Big Jack take turns sleeping by their still. Me and Clyde traded off guarding ours. Jolene sat in when needed. One a them nights when clouds played hide and seek with the moon, I go up to take Jolene's place.

My feet fall soundless on the dirt. I rounded the bend. Law, if what I seen stopped me quick.

Jolene aimed her shotgun, the one that work, right at my head steady as stone with the trigger pulled back. She heaved, put her thumb on the hammer, eased it down gentle-like. "What you thinkin, boy? I bout shoot you clean through. Then where I be? Short one man to run this shine. That's where."

"You think me a Harvey, Jolene?"

"Grrrr."

She bout shoot me so I didn't take to her putting me off. "Girl, when you growl like that, you sound like some ole dog."

From the face she pulled, you might think I tell her a new way to make whiskey. "That's it. We gotta get a signal." She tossed back her head, howled as good as any hound I ever hear. "That the signal. Try it."

Answered her with my own howl. We both laughed like a couple younguns.

I the one what helped her come up with that signal.

Sat out with Little Joe at the O'Hara still, watched the mosquitoes swim in the dark blue, not quite black sky searching for skin to set on, suck. I tried to find stars peeking out behind the quilt of branches above me. Studied the shapes of them pines, trying to tell where one leave off, nother start. Little Joe whistled like night birds calling to each other. Tickle used to the noise cause he keep chewing grass.

A far off "Ooouuu" reeled my head back from somewheres else. Jolene showed herself in the firelight. "No good thieving bastard." She throwed a rock so hard it cracked bark off a tree ten yards way. "That son a bitch oughta get shot, skinned, fed to the hogs." She kicked a barrel. The lid fall off. She snatched up a paddle, stirred the mash. A syrupy smell filled my nose.

Little Joe hugged Tickle. "Didn't you sell the whiskey, Jole?"

"Sure I sell the stuff. Not for what I posta get." She hammered the lid on the barrel. "That cheat down in Mill Creek don't give me near what I know the price gotta be. I swear he got Harvey blood. Say he don't need a regular whiskey supply. Probably cause he buy from them stupid, pig shit Harveys."

"What's that jug there?" Little Joe pointed to one she carried in with her.

"I hold one back." Jolene picked up the jug. "Cause he don't pay the goin rate." She find a cup to pour some shine in, flopped down near us. After a sip or two, she get nother tin cup. Offered some shine to Little Joe.

He shake his head. "Not drinkin me nona that gut-rot."

I take the cup. With every drop the mountain dew go down easier. I learned how to do small gulps, throw them back so the front of my mouth didn't go dead. Like sliding in a cold bath that not so chilly once you in, the whisky needed getting used to.

"Tell us a story, Jole."

Jolene cut her eyes at Little Joe. "You more'n a pup now."

Little Joe groaned. "Rufus wanna hear you spin a yarn, sure enough." He kicked me. "Jole tellin us tales since Tickle no bigger'n loaf a bread."

"Never recollect nona my kin doin no storytellin." Didn't recollect nothing at all bout my life as a youngun.

Jolene tipped back her cup, swallowed. "All right then."

"Tell us the one bout Rupert Harvey stealin his pa's watch, leavin these here parts, never comin back." Little Joe looked happy.

"Nah, don't wanna think a them rotten Harveys."

Her words floated in my brain like smoke snaking up from a flame. She spin a yarn bout a tree that grow in some woods a long time ago. Seemed the twig started out real scrawny. He wanted to be big like the trees that towered over him. Three birds visited the sapling, an owl and a crow. I missed the third bird visit with my mind drifting in and outta Jolene's tale. Them there birds tell the tree how huge he gonna get.

Many winters with wind and rain come, blowing down big trunks, giving the twig water to grow on. Jolene's words got slower with the telling, like the whiskey dripping from the worm. When I think the story done Jolene throw in nother wild storm. I feel the gusts inside me swirling round.

"The now big tree prayed and said, 'Good Lord, why'd I ever wanna be big?' But too late. He got tore up and washed away."

Little Joe looked like he lost his best pal. "Reckon I stay small, be happy, sure enough."

Jolene peered off into the night sky. "Not me. I'm gonna be a big tree. Cept my roots gonna be so thick and deep no storm, or Harvey, gonna do me in. I know. The birds tell me."

If I got me money, I put it on them birds. Knowed they right, Jolene gonna be one big tree someday.

NINE

Helped Little Joe go egg trading. Some folks need more'n their own chickens lay. Tell Little Joe the mule and cart make the job easier, he said no we gotta carry the buckets of eggs.

Noticed leaves turning yellow and brown and red. Gawked at how nature make them colors go together so when you cut your eyes at them they blurred to one. Nobody ever mixed a dye that fanciful. Might give a try myself someday.

Eggs all gone, we headed back. Stopped to say hey to Glory. She touched up paint round the store windows. New paint smell teased my nose.

"What you boys up to?"

"Swappin eggs for this here bacon and flour." Little Joe hold up his sack.

"You wont be needin to do that if you sell at this store," Glory said. "Food all come from farms round here. Fresh more than no other store. So Mr. Cormier tell me to call dis Fresh Farms. We gonna sell Stewart milk and butter, and I wants to sell O'Hara eggs. Be lots easier for y'all."

Reckon Little Joe outta words for one time in his life. He put his head down, scraped his toes in the dirt. "Jole won't give in on sellin to you, sure enough."

"Dat girl gots her a mighty big spirit." Glory looked like she talking bout a child. "Wait here." She go in the store, come out with a yellow, red, and blue can. "Give dis to Miz Jolene. They don't sell dat canned pineapple in no other store near here."

"Reckon that ain't gonna change her mind much," I said.

"You takes dis to her, you see." Glory pushed the can in Little Joe's hand.

"Yes'm." Little Joe hold the can like lighted dynamite.

"We gonna sell fruits and vegetables too. Mr. Cormier say he hear y'all gots good apples. Some folks named Harvey in Mill Creek gots nice pumpkins."

By the look of Little Joe that dynamite go off.

Jumped in to help. "If'n you sell somethin from the Harveys, the O'Haras ain't never come round. Don't you recollect me tellin you they in a feud?"

"Oh." Glory looked befuddled. "No, I don't recall."

"Harveys won't come to this store, sure enough," Little Joe said. "Sits on the spot where Zeek Harvey get himself killed."

Wanna ask bout Zeek Harvey, how he get kilt.

"How I gonna pass this pineapple on to Jole?"

Seen in Little Joe's face his mind spinning like one a them fancy fishing reels.

"Reckon you best not. Me? I hide that can where she ain't gonna find the thing. Leastwise, apple from a pine tree don't sound like it taste worth a lick."

We headed to the barn to rustle up a hiding place. When we close enough to touch the barn door, the darn thing opened. Jolene come out with her shotgun, straw hat on her head. Her eyes fall on me. "What'cha doin here. You posta be up to the Grady place helpin Clyde."

"Clyde say he pull rest a them weeds hisself."

"I see bout that. On my way there now. I aim to do some duck huntin on Little Bear Lake." Her look turned to Little Joe's hand. "What'cha got there?"

Quick as a gunshot, Little Joe stick his hand behind his back. "I …just…uh…."

"Don't try to hide nothin from me, boy." Jolene put down her shotgun, pulled on Little Joe's arm, snatched the pineapple can. "Where you get this?"

"Fresh Farms." Little Joe's voice cracked.

The sack a bacon and flour slipped from his other hand when she come so close he musta seen her frickles disappear in her red face. "I tell you never talk to that no-tail-bear lady." She shake the can. "That woman nothin but trouble, you hear? Now get to work in them corn fields."

Little Joe take off, I followed. Didn't stop till we reached the springhouse.

"You see her wild eye?" I said. "She as grumpy as a bear with a corncob in his behind but I never think she get that mad. She bout to raise her fist to you."

"She never so much as take a switch to us."

Reckoned Little Joe right, Jolene ain't like that.

TEN

One night I sleep at the O'Hara's. Waked up when the front door scraped open. Find Jolene on the porch in britches, not overalls, and a white shirt, putting on shoes, a basket beside her.

"What'cha all dressed up fer?"

"Go back to bed."

"Sun gonna break in a minute. Want me make coffee?"

"Fix some for yourself. I got business to tend to." She picked up the basket. "I gotta figure out how to sell more shine. Goin someplace not right for a boy your size."

"Not like I sittin at my ma's knee." Not that I ever did cause Ma walked on a youngun what sat too close.

"If you must know, I goin to see my oldest and dearest friend."

"Like to meet a body that a good pal a yourn."

"Hmm." Jolene looked at me like she gonna sew me a shirt. "Topa your head only come up to my hat brim. But maybe I let you come. See if this visit make you grow some."

The house bigger than most churches I seen. The place got itself planted close to the river. Jolene pulled some tiny stones from her pocket, tossed them at a window on the top. Three pebbles in a row hit the mark spot on. A hand come out from under the curtain on that window, waved then disappeared.

Jolene go round back, sit on some steps with her back to a screen door, I plopped down next to her and that basket. We watched goats cross the yard. When the door creaked I jumped. Jolene stayed put.

Gal what open the screen wear a robe color a the inside a watermelon. But her shape nothing like a watermelon. She got curves on the top and the bottom with a small waist. She eyed me. "You bring me a new customer, Jole? We not open for business this early."

Didn't knowed what business she talking bout but feel what she mean. Wanna hide under the house.

"No, I bring you a sweet potato pie." Jolene didn't turn, she keep looking at me like she think I needed a new pair of overalls. That look make me not run.

The gal carried the basket inside. After the door flapped shut Jolene get up, go on in, me in tow. Jolene whipped off her straw hat, grinned wide as the pie the gal take outta the basket. "How you been, Ana Marie?"

"What else you got in here gonna make me feel pretty good."

"Sorry to say that likker's for sellin, not givin. Think your boss lady might be in the buyin way?"

"Nope." Ana Marie shake her head. "Miz Winter don't want nona that stuff in the house. That store in Pine Gap where your ma use to sell shut down long go. What bout the one in Cedar Springs?"

"Man's son take over and he don't touch moonshine cause the pa a drunk." Jolene take one of the jars from the basket, polished the glass with her shirt sleeve. "Fella that run the Mill Creek store a crook. We got two stills runnin and I gotta unload me some."

"Miz Winter in the parlor drinkin her tea." Ana Marie grabbed Jolene by the shoulders, turned her round, pointed her to the door. "If'n anybody talk her into servin whiskey here, that body be you, with that O'Hara charm of yorn." She give Jolene a tiny push. "I keep your little beau here company, fix him some pie."

"Boy's not my beau."

Ana Marie twisted and pinned up her long dark curls. "You think me pretty?"

"Sorry ma'am, don't mean to stare. You got you some right nice jewels there." Nodded at her wrist. "And you kinda look like somebody I seen sometime, don't remember them though."

"What bout that gal you got in there?" She jabbed a thumb to the parlor.

Studied on Ana Marie's face. "Law. Reckon you do favor Jolene a bit."

"You ain't the first." Ana Marie busied herself getting plates. "Me and Jolene ain't kin in no way but she don't got no sisters and I ain't got none no more neither so we the closest we got."

"You hate Harveys?"

"Don't gotta. Nona them got enough money to come round here. They do, I gonna shoo them way." She played with a locket round her neck. "My ma always say them Confederates a mean lot."

"Harveys fight on the Confederate side? Reckon plenty of folks round these parts did." Never knowed what side my people fight on cause nona them that go off to war ever come back.

"You ain't from round here," Ana Marie said. "Story go like this. Before the war tweenx the states the Harveys and the O'Haras good friends. Then Loucius Harvey get some medal in the rebel army and some say Will O'Hara, Jolene's great-grand pappy, hide union soldiers on O'Hara land." Ana Marie take a pitcher a cream from the icebox. "Same day Loucius get home after the war Will's prize-winnin layin hen go missin. Will hear it Loucius what do the snatchin. Will say he gonna get even. Zeek Harvey, Loucius' brother, go to talk sense to Will. Next mornin some farmer seen Zeek shot dead on the road next to O'Hara land."

Ana Marie's words tumbled round in my head. Tried to make them come together, mean something. Nothing right come to my mind to say. How come Will O'Hara shoot Zeek Harvey like that?

"Gotta watch out for them O'Haras and Harveys both." Ana Marie sliced the pie.

Followed Ana Marie to the parlor. She bring pie slices on a tray. Jolene and Miz Winter sat in padded chairs with wood rims carved like flowers.

"Take a taste, see what you think." Jolene poured a splash from a jar in a teacup.

Miz Winter sipped.

"The quality of the liquor is not the question. I do not want my patrons to get rowdy and out of control."

"Us girls can see to it the fellas don't drink too much," Ana Marie said.

"She right," Jolene said. "Water down the likker, ask a big price, the gents don't get too outta hand."

"Ana Marie, dear." Miz Winter grabbed hold Ana Marie's hand. "You know you are my favorite. But surely you know how hard it is to keep those men in line."

"Like I say," Jolene said, "a handsome price not many wanna pay make all the difference. This Prohibition bring you them fellas what got the means to dole out for whiskey and the girls."

"Well." Miz Winter take one more pull on her teacup. "The money part does sound good. But the risk is still too high."

Wanted to help. Gathered what fly in and outta my good sense. "Take some O'Hara shine, don't pay. If'n things work out with Ana Marie and tuther gals keepin fellas on good behavior, you buy more, pay Jolene's price."

"Oh!" Miz Winter looked like something good happened inside her. "I am happy to accept free libations to sell to my clients to see how the spirits will effect them."

Jolene glared at me like she gonna do to me what she did to them chicks what start to crow.

ELEVEN

By the time fall bring in the chill the Winter House selling plenty of O'Hara shine at a good price. Jolene said as how she glad she get the idea to give way the first batch for free. Didn't mind her taking my idea for her own long as I welcome on her farms.

Shivered under a blanket, watched over the still for a few nights. Big Jack give me a coat with holes in the pockets he wear for years. He and Jolene got clothes outta trunks at the Grady place. Little Joe wear what he got from the last year.

Got me some shoes from the poor box at the church in town. The shoes big for me and soft from use. Better than hand-me-downs back home.

Jolene worked us hard with whiskey making on top a harvesting the corn, picking apples, some other farm jobs. Said she tell the others what good work I do. Feel proud like I got me a new suit of clothes.

She gave us a day off for what she called Thanksgiving dinner.

Clyde said, "I don't give a flying rat's ass for that kinda shit."

Walked down to the O'Hara place by my lonesome. On the path behind Fresh Farms damp leaves covered the ground like burlap.

The house warm with cooking going on. A turkey Jolene shoot roasted on a spit in the fireplace in the front room. Big Jack sit on the hearth, brushed some juice on the bird.

Followed a trail a steam to the kitchen where more vittles gave off a welcome. Jolene's face glowed from the cooking heat. She wear the fancy duds like when she visited Ann Marie. "Take that corn bread out."

Little Joe stopped stirring mash tatters to do like she said.

"Get to them dishes in the sink while the water still warm," Jolene tell me. "Supper done directly." She hollered out at Big Jack. "Get that bird off the fire, set it aside to rest."

Got the last pot scrubbed.

Jolene spread a cloth on the table to put full bowls of green beans, all sorta breads and tatters, jellies and gravy. Enough to feed all of Cedar Springs. Them smells made me swallow before I get my hands on the food.

"Wash up, boys, grab a plate." Jolene disappeared, come back with a jug. "This a Holy Day, boys. Let's celebrate." Me and Big Jack poured some in cups. Little Joe pinched his nose, waved the corn squeezins way.

We eat by the fire. Little Joe tell me how they seen a picture in the newspaper last year a President Wilson eating a turkey. I never hear tell bout Thanksgiving. Little Joe said the newspaper say the day begin up north somewhere. "Abraham Lincoln invent this here day to make up for all the trouble the union did to the South." Abraham Lincoln to me nothing but a dead Yankee. Reckoned Little Joe knowed more than me.

"Injuns invent Thanksgiving, fool," Jolene said. "Rufus don't wanna hear bout that." She go on bout how she picked special herbs for the turkey cooking. Her pa learned her bout herbs. The fever claimed their pa when Little Joe such a youngun he in diapers, learning to use the outhouse.

"My pa got Cherokee blood in him," Jolene said. "He know bout such things as the Earth give. That's how I fix that turkey so right."

Turkey my favorite part, saved mine for last. The whiskey, food, and talking made me feel like staying put for days.

Big Jack gathered dirty dishes. Jolene poured more likker for us, tell legends passed down from their kin bout the power a living things. With every sip the shine made my mind conjure Injun spirits dancing in feather hats.

"My Pa always tell me I do anythin I want long's I believe in myself, " Jolene said.

"Pie got done." Big Jack stand by the door to the kitchen, sway a bit. "Y'all want some?"

Jolene stared at the fire, rubbed her fingers on her whiskey cup. "My supper got good flavor. But that turkey dry."

"Turkey not dry." Big Jack leaned on the wall. "Taste real good."

"I know how it shoulda taste." She swigged some shine. "I fix that turkey."

"Only the shootin'," Big Jack said.

On her feet, she stepped to him. "If I don't tell you how to cook that turkey, you woulda put it in a stew. You don't know how to use them herbs I pick."

Big Jack's nose raised when Jolene moved so close I seen how they looked like kin. "Good as Ma's," he said.

Jolene yanked him by his overall straps. "Don't go thinkin you cook good like Ma."

Law, if she didn't push him. He hit the wall like lightening strike a tree.

Tickle barked on the back porch. Little Joe moved the pillow he sitting on to the far corner. My eyes fall on the jug. Think bout taking nother pour. Stead I go helped Big Jack to his feet.

"You let him be." Jolene's fist hang over my head like a hammer ready to hit a nail. "You no O'Hara. You don't belong here. Git outta my house." Her eyes get real big. "Git. You hear? Don't show your ugly face round here gain."

Grabbed my coat, leave the cabin, get to the path before Jolene's words stopped ringing in my ears. Take a breath next to the dark Fresh Farms. Stared at the full moon what looked like a big custard pie. The trees look like old folk with the gray frost sticking to their branches. My head feel like a wad a cotton. I ain't no O'Hara. I nobody in Cedar Springs. I nobody nowhere.

Looked down the road, toward the Grady place. Go tuther way, outta Cedar Springs. Get loose of all them O'Haras.

CHAPTER TWELVE

When the words Jolene threw at me settled I feel cold like the wind that whipped round my head. Sneaked in barns, sleep in corncribs, henhouses. Before long find my sorry self in Dandelion Holler.

Ma looked up from the stove. "Fetch more kindlin."

Get some for her. No surprise she didn't say "Thank you" or "Where you get yourself off to?"

One big brothers got hisself hobbled with some gal, moved out, so my body in the bed made up for the loss a his. I sleep with my shoes on, my coat over me so nobody steal them.

Little sister called Sammy Jean the only onea my kin I cottoned to. Nobody but her asked bout my ventures. Tell her some O'Hara stories.

That winter I chopped firewood, patched buildings, hauled pig shit to the fields. I spread the stuff on the ground, getting the dirt ready for plowing in spring. Seen Pa coming. He slipped, his arms spinned, he fall on his backside.

Run, grabbed him. "Here…."

"Get off me. Get off me." He pulled his arm outta my hand. "Get back to work. This ain't nona your nevermind." He scraped pig droppings off his shoe with a rock. "Don't handle me again or I knock you into next week."

Pa stomped off, his voice ring in my ears like dynamite.

Funny thing, Pa didn't take to whiskey. Same as Little Joe, he hated the taste. Pa clumsy in his own right. Reckoned the reason cause he didn't see what right in front a his face.

Recollect bout a year before I leave, find Cedar Springs, I come running up to Pa waving a fish bigger than a boot. "Look what I catch."

Pa said, "Go help your cousin Rufus with them fence posts."

Ain't like he needed specs neither. When I whitewashing the house Pa quick to scream how I missed a spot.

One cloudy afternoon I come on Sammy Jean sitting in a field looking lonely, like a rag forgot on a clothesline.

"What you lookin at Sammy Jean?" Pushed the words out cause my windpipe itched me something fierce.

"Cut your eyes real hard at that dogwood. You see where the blooms gonna be."

Sat down, did like she said. Law, she right. The twigs on them there naked branches knowed how to stick out at the right places to give the tree a soul. "Gonna be a right nice..." A cough tied me in knots. Take a spell to catch my breath.

"Sound like you got the croup." She looked at me like a apple that got a worm. "Knowed somebody what heal that for you."

She tell me follow her to the back of Pa's farm, up steep rocks. Stopped to cough every few yards. We rested in a meadow where the grass growed thick like fur on some coon's back.

Sammy Jean said, "You ain't the only one what got somebody to learn you stuff."

"Nope, I ain't got nobody like that."

"That Jolene you tell me bout, she show you how to brew moonshine."

"Try to keep my mind way from her."

"You ain't gonna tell nobody bout where we goin? Promise?"

Swallowed hard. "If'n I do, may I get et by a bear." Nobody to tell.

Near the mountaintop, higher than I ever think to go, we come on a cabin built in the peak. In the front yard set a big brick oven. A woman feed a furnace like the ones I fixed for Jolene's stills, but this one for the oven. Her hair red like a sunset, her eyes like two water buckets so blue they bout drowned me.

Dullsaine stand me under a sheet in my union suit over a pot a some kinda boiling leaves. Sammy Jean helped with other dried plants, put them in jars.

All that steam made me feel like a morning glory wilting from the weight a spring rain.

Dullsaine sat us down, Sammy Jean with goat's milk, me with hot tea. The cups clay like the jars, bowls, plates all piled round the room.

Feel Dullsaine see through my skin while I sipped.

"Ye be missed," she said.

Sammy Jean said, "Our ma must be wonderin after us."

Surprised me my sister still a kitten enough to believe Ma knowed who there, who ain't. Stared in my tea, wrassled with what the red-haired woman mean.

We bedded down on hides stretched cross wood frames. Dreamed I swimming in a deep pool, kicking hard, trying to reach the top. I wake, soaked in sweat, not pond water.

Dullsaine in a corner with a harp to her chest. She sing bout someone named Gentle Annie.

My lungs didn't rattle no more. I tell Dullsaine much obliged for the doctoring.

"Now before ye young ones go the path, I must teach ye the way of reciprocity."

Such a word set my head spinning.

"Tis simple. I give ye healing, now ye must give something to me."

Sounded fair to me.

"I had a vision of ye bringing me a quart of moonshine whiskey. May take as long as the fates deem. But must be."

Dullsaine wanted me to get her shine? Only one place I knowed to get me white lightening.

Back in the holler I tell Sammy Jean I gotta go. Swear I see her again, with the whiskey for Dullsaine.

THIRTEEN

On my way to Swift River I seen the big house Anna Marie lived in. Hide behind a bush. Didn't spy nothing cept goats in a pen. Look up at the window where Jolene throw them pebbles. Think bout finding me somma my own rocks.

Stepped way from the bush. Two more steps.

The door opened, Anna Marie come out. She wear a robe brighter than any morning glory I ever seen. She hang a towel on the porch rail. She fancy with her long dark curls. I only wear my wore out ole overalls.

Feel like coming up on a honey tree fulla bees. Get back to the road fast, like a swarm after me.

In the couple days it take me to get to town, I do chores for folks what gave me a penny. Outside the shop with the wooden Injun I stopped to count the coins in my hand.

Somebody run smack into me. The pennies scattered.

A tall, skinny, dark haired boy kicked a coin. "Watch where you goin." He smelt like a wet log on a hot fire.

Gathered the money, go in the shop.

"See what happen." Fella at the counter shake his head. "Bout what one expects from the likes a Snake Harvey."

My insides turned soft to think I come face to face with a Harvey.

Plunked down seven cents. Take the stogie the shop fella gave me.

Night hang deep by the time I howled my signal coming on the O'Hara house. Little Joe meet me on the porch like I coming home from war, reckon that ain't too far from the truth.

"Glad to see you, sure enough. We bout believed you never come back."

"Where Jolene at? And the rest?"

"Big Jack up checkin on the mash. This the first batch we get to mix up with the cold weather. Poor Tickle don't make it through the winter."

"Sorry, pal." Knowed Little Joe missed Tickle a whole bunch.

"Well, seein you brighten this day, sure enough." He go to the kitchen. "Help yourself to that there stew."

Dumped a couple scoops in a bowl.

"Reckon Jolene ain't to home."

"She up to the Grady place. Say she got stuff to do with Clyde."

"Clyde?"

Maybe Clyde tell Jolene bout living with apes or tell her some other tall tale.

"She talk bout me at all?"

Little Joe quiet for a bit. "Nary a word. Reckon she think bout you. Jole not sayin nothin don't mean she don't think it. Oh, listen to me tell bout this gal I got my eye on."

Sleeped at the O'Hara's, wake early with a heavy mind thinking on Jolene and Clyde. Set out in the dark.

Made it up the path from the O'Hara place to the road. Hear a voice.

"Done see yor face round here in a coon's age." Glory set on her porch in the lamplight.

"Got stuff to do somewhere else. Now I back."

"Well, good to sees you. Bet them O'Haras glad you back too."

"Little Joe happy. Don't knowed bout tuthers."

"Dat Little Joe bring eggs in the store. He a nice boy, almost a man."

Surprised like a cardinal what find a duck in his nest.

"O'Haras tradin eggs in your store? Jolene say she never let that happen."

"Seem she give in, make less work for them all. I writes Mr. Comier, he happy we sells O'Hara eggs. But Miz Jolene claim she never show her face in the store." Glory's teeth sparkled in the flicker from the lamp. "I bets my granny rocker Miz Jolene give in on dat too."

"She tough as leather on that."

Something thumped in the cabin. Glory picked up the lamp. "I best gets in. Sound like Jimbo up."

Seen Glory loved her man. They ain't like my folks. Don't knowed if I ever that happy in my lifetime.

Grady cabin stand quiet. Inched open the door to stop creaks. A jug set on the table. Snoring come from behind the gray curtain what closed off tuther room. Peeked tween the flaps. Seen Clyde's big feet sticking from under a blanket. He ain't snoring. Crossed the room, Jolene sleep in a smaller bed.

Set on the front steps, watched clouds over the mountains get brighter with morning floating in. Jolene come out with her overall straps hanging loose.

"There you be. Work round here pilin up to my ears. This Clyde fella don't know the first thing bout farm work. Take most my time learnin him to plow. Now you got the job. I fed up. Y'all gotta grow a proper corn crop, you hear?"

Clouds cracked to let in sunlight the color of egg yokes fried in bacon fat.

"Reckon you and Clyde gone to courtin."

Jolene waved way my words like steam on coffee.

"Nah. He say he kin. Two laws for courtin. You don't go with them what share blood." She put her head down, watched her toes curl and uncurl. "And you don't go with them what spoke for." She looked out passed the tree tops.

Take the cigar from my pocket, hold it out. Reckoned it cheer her a mite. She stand. Stogie slipped outta my fingers. Her hand never touched mine. She go on in the house.

FOURTEEN

"Your jabber much better'n Clyde's no-moving slack mouth," I said.

"Your company pretty durn good too." Light from burning hickory flickered over Little Joe. "Don't go roamin off gain like you done in the wintertime. When Jole get in onea her moods they don't last long."

"Gotta find me some way that Jolene gonna never want me to skedaddle."

A howl sounded over the mash gurgling in the still. Jolene come in the clearing, carried her shotgun, weared her straw hat. She plopped down next to a barrel.

"Gonna need more jugs on the next run, sure enough," Little Joe said.

"That barn loft gettin full." Jolene stick a piece a chicory in her mouth. "I gotta figure out new places to sell."

"You sellin plenty at that place Ana Marie's at," I said.

"Yep." Jolene spit. "But gotta move more."

Wished I knowed me where to unload more shine.

Brightness come on Little Joe's face. "Reckon I sell some over in Pine Gap."

"Too dangerous."

"Been there, Jole. Safe, sure enough."

Little Joe never tell me bout Pine Gap.

"Don't know when you might run cross a revenuer. Or worse, a Harvey."

"No Harvey go there, Jole."

Jolene chaw that wad a chicory, moved her jaw like the gears on a coffee grinder. "I gonna head to town tomorrow. Come long if you got a mind to."

Set my mind to go too. If a place come up to sell whiskey, I wanna help.

We used the side of the road where the sun beat down. This time I knowed the reason cause the O'Haras stick to that side, the Harveys stick tuther.

In town me and Little Joe got so busy smelling food cooking at the café, laughing at a fella in a bowler what stepped in some mule droppings, watching the barber put cream on some gent's face. We let Jolene get away.

She shouted from the mercantile doorstep, "Stay out here while I do some buyin."

We mashed noses to the window. She studied guns on a rack.

"Oh." Little Joe tugged on me. His mouth open. "That no shotgun she pointin at. That one honest to goodness rifle. Me and Big Jack seen em once."

Like she petting a cat Jolene run her hand over the coal-black barrel. She take her time, pondered over three before she handed over the money.

Little Joe hopped like corn in a hot skillet. "Reckon she gettin that for me?"

When Jolene come out she hold up that shotgun I so used to seeing her carry. The stock scarred worse than a body with a the pox. Then she hold up the brand new rifle, slick like a wet rock.

Little Joe licked his lips.

"Things gettin so you need to protect my business. So I gotta do it." She stick out the shotgun. "There you go, boy. Take the damn ole thang."

Little Joe take the wore-out shotgun, put his head down.

"Now stay outta trouble. I back directly."

Through his teeth Little Joe said, "Sometimes I wish she go to hell."

Reckoned Little Joe oughta be happy. Jolene didn't give me nothing.

We shuffled long with him saying things like, "Damn female don't know nothin," and "She ain't no sister of mine."

"Might be worse," I said. "What if she give you the one what don't work?" Tuther O'Hara shotgun didn't shoot on count of a rusty barrel. A automobile roared by. "Wonder what ridin onea them there fast things like."

Little Joe didn't take a gander. When he did lift his head, he yanked me in a alley quicker than a blink.

"What...?"

"Hush." His hand covered my mouth. "That Stub Harvey and Crow Tritt."

Peered round the brick wall, seen two men. One sitting on a bench got the dirtiest overalls I ever seen. He said, "So, Stub, you find Turner?"

Fella he called Stub got a red beard thick enough for him to hide his money in. "Ain't find him yet."

Stub put a shotgun the likes of the one Jolene give Little Joe on the wall then planted a bare foot, missing two toes, on the bench to scratch his leg.

"Seen that O'Haras gal round town today," Crow said. "Reckon she lookin for Turner herself."

Behind me Little Joe shake like the weather turned cold.

Stub stomped his foot down. "Ain't no womankind gonna show me up. I get holda that O'Hara heifer, they be usin her for chicken feed."

Little Joe bout knocked me down when he jumped out, shotgun cocked, the butt on his shoulder. "No you don't, Stub Harvey."

Stub looked at Little Joe then at his gun by the wall.

"Don't move, Harvey."

Tried to conjure a way I might hook that gun before Stub.

"Boy, think bout this. Kicka that gun knock you halfway to Mill Creek."

Sweat poured down Little Joe's neck. But he hold steady. "No man say that bout my sister. Specially no Harvey."

Longed for onea them guns for me, make the score two to one.

They stared at one nother like birddogs at a pheasant.

"Why hey, Sheriff Clayton," Crow said.

The sheriff with the big ears crossed the street.

Sheriff Clayton take the shotgun from the wall. "Get lost Stub."

"You gonna let that O'Hara runt keep his aim on me?"

"What boy? What shotgun? I don't see nonea that."

"Sheriff you gotta remember you kin."

"Kin? You tell me where your brother Rupert run off to with my sister then we talk bout kin."

"Been twenty years, Clayton." Crow snatched Stub's shotgun. "Nobody ever hear from them. Put your sister outta your mind." Crow dragged Stub down the street.

After a while Little Joe said, "Don't tell Jole what happen."

My ears puzzled over that. "But, you jim-dandy back there. Jolene kiss you if'n she knowed you put your life out for her."

"Nope. Don't say nothin." He looked up the sidewalk. "Leastwise, where that she-cat git to?"

"Bet you a pot a tatters I find her." Didn't get to stand up for Jolene to a Harvey but I knowed something bout her Little Joe didn't.

Like I reckoned Jolene got one hand spread on that smoke shop window, the plain ole wooden Injun near by. A body'd think that glass a ice block keeping her cool.

On our way outta town Jolene tell Little Joe, "Be careful with that there gun. Our great-granpappy Will O'Hara kilt Zeek Harvey with that weapon."

Little Joe's face got the same gleam as when he think he getting the new rifle.

FIFTEEN

Little Joe started selling to folks over in Pine Gap. Jolene keep up in Mill Creek. Big Jack take care a business round Chimney. Got me nowheres to sell for myself. Then the idea hit me, the perfect place sat spitting distance from the O'Hara farm. Jolene bust my hide clean open if she find out I asked Glory to sell her whiskey. Hoped nobody twist her ear bout my deal.

One morning when the heat stick to me worse than thistles I put a few jars from the O'Hara barn in a basket, headed to Fresh Farms. A blue jay in a tree cussed me from yesterday to tomorrow. "Stop your fussin Mr. Jay. This ain't your path much as you think." A twig snapped. Reckoned the ruckus startled some critter. A tingle in my bones tell me somebody watching.

Glory moved boxes round, dusted a shelf.

"Got a offer for ya." I said.

"While you tells me, you drink dat lemonade. Nobody touch it." She drink from her glass. Store got ice, she put shavings in, a special treat.

"Mm mum. That good and sweet." Smacked my lips.

"I makes dat for Miz Jolene but she leave. I figure if a body need extra sugar dat be her."

I bout dropped my drink. "Jolene come in here?"

"Uh huh. You help with dat shine done you? Well, she asks me to keep some in the store, under the counter, for folks what mights wanna buy some."

Surprised me like a squirrel gnawing a shotgun shell.

Supper at the O'Hara place set my hunger to hopping. Stewed chicken in gravy with applesauce. Jolene finished the cooking bout the time Little Joe come in from his trip over to Pine Gap. She meet him, hand out. "Let's see the money." She grinned like a fox with the key to the springhouse when he dropped the cash in her hand. "Done good, boy."

We pulled up to the table. Little Joe said, "What we gonna do with all them there greenbacks you collectin, Jole?"

"I take care you all this time? Done my best by you?"

"Yep, sure enough."

"Then don't worry. I tell y'all soon as I get ready to."

We eat fast like newborn pigs sucking on their ma. Before I finished I set my eyes real close on Jolene. "Glory's doin a fine business with the eggs. Reckon she might sell the whiskey good."

Little Joe's fork stopped on the way to his mouth. He looked from me to Jolene. She picked at her chicken. "Not gonna do no more with that store than we gotta."

"But..."

Her eyes meet mine. "That the end. You Hear?" She leave the table. Stopped at the door. Without turning round she said, "Pie's coolin on the back porch if you want some."

She go in her room. Little Joe put water on the stove to boil for dishes. "She in there countin that money, sure enough." His face gleamed like creek water in mid-day. "Well, I don't care. I got me something better."

SIXTEEN

Helped Little Joe pick apples in the O'Haras' orchard. Every one a them long, sweaty days we worked from sunup to sundown with some sorta chore or nother. Till I find me a place to sell whiskey, leastways I pull my weight on the farms, and then some.

That day Little Joe said we gonna take a break, get us a dip in the swimming hole.

When I get deep in the orchard I seen Little Joe's bushel baskets, he nowhere round. Run to the swimming hole. No Little Joe yet. Stripped off my overalls, dived in.

Splashed my way from one end of the swimming hole to tuther and back. Little Joe oughta showed by that time. Stayed put in one place to scout out for him. Something nipped at my feet. Reckoned I didn't scare way all the fish with my splashing, moved a few feet way. That fish followed me, grabbed at my leg like the thing got fingers. Hightailed it outta the water. Plopped down on the bank, tried to catch my breath.

"What…" Where he come from?

Little Joe climbed outta the water, gasped and laughed.

"Oh, I get you, sure enough," Little Joe said tween chuckles.

"How the hell you do that? Never seen you get in that damn water."

"Course you don't. I here for nigh on a half hour. When I seen you comin I go hide."

"Hide in the water? With no air?"

"We got a cave down there. Big Jack pull that trick on me not long after he learn me swimmin. Them the days back then. Not so many chores. Granny get after Jole and Big Jack to get their work done but she let me play."

"Chores don't bother me none. Keep me busy. Say, I don't seen your clothes neither, nother reason I don't think you here." With the Indian summer heat h.e stripped down to what he born with, I keep my union suit on.

"Hide them under a bush yonder. Your face quite a sight when I come outta that there swimmin hole, sure enough."

"We a bit ole now for playin games and that sorta shit. Reckon you ain't gonna scare me no more after this."

"I like bein growed. Like doin what a man do."

"Big Jack take you to that jenny barn in Chimney? He take me."

"Yep, that dark haired gal a sweety, sure enough. Give some good lovin too."

"Oh, yeah, she nice." Glad she didn't care bout no romance shit or if I keep on my union suit. She let me stay in the room for a bit after I done that first time so nobody knowed I so quick.

"Nice, but she not the kind you court. Not like this gal I got in Pine Gap." Little Joe got a spark in his eye. "Courtin nothing like I think when I young'un, sure enough. Back then I play tricks on gals. Go up to the Cedar Springs store, wait till they come long with their mas. One time I get this fancy box, say I wanna show em somethin purdy. When I open the box a big ole bullfrog jump out. I use to love to hear them gals scream. You ever play tricks like that when you a boy?"

That question hit me like a cold wind on that hot day. "You make that up. Nobody recollect that far back."

"Somethin wrong with you if scarin little gals don't sound fun."

"Ain't bout fun. Folks don't recollect life as a young'un."

"What'cha talkin bout? I don't remember my pa but I remember Tickle when he only a pup, plenty other stuff too. Like falling outta the hay loft when I four."

"That ain't right. One's mind don't go back to four, maybe ten, that all."

"Jole say she recall learnin herself to walk."

"You one lyin sonabitch." Snatched up my overalls, stomped off, keep going all the way to the Grady place.

SEVENTEEN

Next day I picked apples from the few scrawny trees in the yard at the Grady place. Little Joe showed. "Wanna come to Pine Gap with me when I do my sellin?"

Reckoned that his way a saying he sorry for what he said. Maybe going selling with him help me think on places for me to sell whiskey.

I hitched up Ole Abe cause Little Joe didn't like that chore, we get us on our way. "What make you so dang happy these days, that in Pine Gap?" I said.

"Try to make time with all the gals in Cedar Springs, sure enough. Ones in Mill Creek too, them what don't got Harvey blood. Started before Big Jack get winda womenfolk wiles. Nonea em got nothin on this jewel I got me up here. Her name Lulahbelle."

Over the pass in Pine Gap now and again a shack stick out, most got trash lying round. The long cabin where Little Joe stopped got a tiny front porch on one end. Reckoned this a nice family cause the yard tidy with flower bushes and everything. My ma keep a clean house but she didn't pretty up the place like this one.

Little Joe hollered a greeting. While we waited he give me a small jar a likker he called a sample. "Keep Lulahbelle's brothers busy. I wanna be sure to get lone time with her."

Lulahbelle stand nose to nose with Little Joe. Blue eyes and copper-colored hair.

"How do?" I onea them snapdragons by the porch for all they knowed.

Set off for the cornfield to find her brothers. Reach the hilltop. A rock missed my head by a inch. Duck behind a tree, hold out the jar like a white flag.

"You ain't the shine fella," a boy, not quite a man, with a slingshot said.

"I helpin Little Joe today."

"Well, stop pissin yourself, come out from there. I be Johnny Gibbs."

Johnny whistled and three younger boys come running. "Y'all sit on the ground. Everybody get a swig." They passed the jar.

The runt of the four said, "Stinks. Don't wanna."

"That there good medicine," Johnny said. "You take a nice big gulp or I hold you down and pour the whole jar down your gullet."

Runt pulled a face. Johnny snapped his fingers, waved at the boy next to the runt. That boy pushed the jar to the runt's mouth, hold back his head till he swallowed.

Didn't wanna see no more. Make a move to get up.

"You ain't leavin now," Johnny said, "We gonna play the shoot off game, it lotta fun. First one to get off a shot win."

"We ain't got no guns," I said.

"Ha. Sure we do." Johnny pointed at the runt. "Cause your gun ain't big nuff yet you come help me play." Johnny undo the middle button on his overalls, stick his hand inside, go for his tallywacker.

Feel like I spinning round real fast. Scrambled to my feet, make for the woods. Run with branches hitting me upside the head. Fall to my knees. Heave up everything I et for days. Fog filled my head, weighed me down like a boulder. Squeezed my eyes shut. In that fog I seen a face. My gut try to twist more mess out but nothing come. Sit there, breath heavy, dripped sweat.

EIGHTEEN

"You think I doin the right thing?" Little Joe looked like he gonna jump off a cliff.

"If my sister Sammy Jean live in a house like the one Lulahbelle do, I get her outta there faster than a frog catchin a fly." Didn't knowed if Little Joe seen the kinda things I seen there. Ain't gonna talk bout that with nobody.

Lulahbelle's pa got two laying hens, five jars a strawberry preserves Big Jack put up, and a jug fulla shine when Little Joe fetched her over to Cedar Springs.

"Stay here," Jolene tell Lulahbelle. "You boys come with me." In the yard Jolene said, "What's got into you, boy? Bringin nother mouth to feed to this house."

Like pleading for his life, Little Joe said, "But Jole, she..." He take a breath. "She won't be no trouble. She pull her weight. I promise, Jole."

"Your voice still squeaking now and again." Jolene shake her head. "Why you wanna get yourself snared so young? You don't see Rufus here wantin to get stuck with a wife. And he older than you."

What she talking bout me for?

Little Joe looked to Lulahbelle on the porch. "Hear tell Ma and Pa only fourteen when they marry. And Lulahbelle's worth shuckin all them girls round here, sure enough."

"I see a big risk in somebody round here that might flap their mouth to the wrong folks."

"But Jole, she smart. Don't say nothin bout nothin she not posta."

"Nope." Jolene shake her head again.

"Then I take her and we live somewhere else. Some place far. You never hear from us again, like how Rupert Harvey run way with Sheriff Clayton's sister. Take Rufus with me too. Then you down two men to do the work."

Hoped to heaven he didn't mean them words.

Jolene crossed her arms. "Why her?"

Little Joe waved at Lulahbelle. Then he looked Jolene square in the face "I like talkin to her. Makin her laugh feel better than doin a whole day's work. When I sit close to her I feel like a thunderstorm gonna come. Jole, I love her."

A slow grin spread on Jolene's face. Then she turned stone-like gain. "She works hard like the resta us. You hear?"

Little Joe run to Lulahbelle like a thirsty man going for the creek.

Jolene watched him. "Nothin get in the way a good sense like love."

NINETEEN

The church in Swift River hold near on a hundred folks. A tower with a bell set on the roof. I knocked but reckoned no one to home. Cross the way spied a bearded fella pacing. Didn't place his bird's nest face at first. Then recollected him. A Harvey. I jumped over the rail, dropped behind the steps outta sight.

Stared hard at that Harvey.

"That's Stub," a deep voice behind me hissed.

Bout dirtied my overalls.

"Shhh. This way." He tugged on my union-suit. To get way from Stub I followed this other fella round the church, over a hill to the riverbank.

He skipped stones while I watched him in his white shirt and suspenders. He looked silly playing a young'un's game. "I'm Cob Turner. Guessing by the way you hid from Stub Harvey, you're an O'Hara."

"Not by birthright."

Cob shrugged, tossed nother stone. "My mistake. Hear the O'Haras are moonshiners. Now I look at you, you're too scrawny for a moonshiner. Gotta be strong to lug those heavy bags of flour up to their stills."

"You mean sugar."

His eyes sparkled. My breath catched in my windpipe. Wished I got me a shotgun. He trapped me easy as a sleeping kitten. Might be onea them revenue fellas Jolene warned bout.

"Don't worry, Bucko," he said. "I'm the one Stub's waiting for back there. He wants to get paid for his whiskey. But if he don't follow my instructions, send the right person, that's not gonna happen."

Looked at Cob like he a watermelon growing on a tomato vine. He dropped his rocks, stepped closer. "I'm a bootlegger. A moonshiner's best friend. You make the stuff, I distribute it. Far and wide these days with Prohibition. I've wanted to deal with the O'Haras for a while now. Word is they put a nice squeeze on their corn."

"You wanna buy shine from me?"

"From the O'Haras. Not sure you're the one I oughta deal with. What about this Little Joe I've heard of?"

Little Joe got hisself a place to sell. I need one for me. Jolene happy to get shut of more likker. "Little Joe too busy gettin hitched."

Cob cut his eyes at me. "Married? How old is he?"

"Fourteen."

"Oh." He picked onea them rocks back up. "How old are you?"

"Don't knowed. My folks never keep track like the O'Haras. Fifteen I reckon."

He pulled a face, studied on me. "Yeah, you look around fifteen. Any other little O'Haras I should know about before I agree to buy your product?"

"Jolene the oldest, she make us all behave. That why our likker the best in these here parts. Lots better'n the Harveys."

"Bet you never tasted Harvey whiskey. Bet you never seen a Harvey except ole Stub." He tossed a rock at a squirrel, scared the critter back in his hole.

"Get in a run in with Stub's boy Snake."

"You should meet Snake's younger brothers. Those boys are something." A smile crawled up Cob's face like a spider on a outhouse wall.

"If'n you dealin with the Harveys, I best not sell to ya. Jolene whip me good for gettin hobbled with somebody that do business with them Harveys."

"Hold on, Bucko." Cob put his hands on my arms. "My customers and my suppliers alike are top secret. She'll never know. You bring me your goods and my association with the Harveys remains our little secret."

He rubbed my arms before he take his hands off me.

"Reckon no harm with Jolene in the dark bout that part." My hankering to sell whiskey on my own clouded my good sense.

Cob waved me to trail him to a dead tree up the bank. He pushed on the bark. Law, if a door didn't pop outta that tree, the thing hinged so a body never knowed. Inside, room to stack twenty jugs. Cob said for me to fill the tree every other Tuesday at midnight then come back at dawn. Look under a rock where he dig a tin cup in the ground. That where I find the money.

TWENTY

"Got good news."

Jolene set some sacks on the O'Hara porch, looked at me like I some egg she waiting to hatch. "Well, get on with it."

"I go to town to get a preacher for Little Joe and Lulahbelle."

"Fool. There a church right over in Mill Creek."

"Little Joe don't tell me that. Find out in town. But put a ear to this...."

"He must forget cause the church in Harvey territory. Preacher come to us, you hear?"

"Yes'm. He here Sunday afternoon. But that ain't my news." Want her to hear good. "I meet a bootlegger."

"Boy, you don't know no bootlegger if one sit on your head."

Tell Jolene bout Cob Turner, leave out the part bout Stub Harvey.

"Don't know." Jolene spit some chicory she chewed on. "A bootlegger in these here parts buy from the Harveys too. Don't like that."

"Cob look me square in the eye, tell me he refuse to deal with Stub Harvey." Don't say the reason cause he get the shine and give the money to Stub's boy.

"You don't tell a lie worth a lick. I reckon you speak the truth. I don't know bout that bootleg man." Jolene looked like she eat something what give her gut pain.

"You say we gotta unload more whiskey. Cob pay a good price."

"I give him a try, I reckon." Jolene didn't seem happy like I hoped.

She waved a hand at the sacks. "Get Ole Abe, get this stuff up to the Grady place. First you help Little Joe with the chores. He got his head somewhere else with that gal he got."

Jolene pointed a finger at me.

"Don't go shootin your mouth off."

Do like she said, do the hoeing with Little Joe, don't tell him bout Cob. Take Jolene's load up to the Grady place by suppertime. Smelled something good cooking. Jolene on the front porch with Clyde. I tie Ole Abe to a post.

"Sit on down." She said. "I bring supper out directly. We celebratin with a drink first. I get you one."

Jolene turned up nother cup, poured me some from the jug, mixed in cool creek water. After a while she fetched plates with biscuits, chicken gravy and mashed taters.

Think I knowed what the celebration for. "This some good cookin."

"I showin you how proud you make me. Cause you do such a good job findin a bootleg man to buy our shine, I gonna put you in charge a sellin O'Hara whiskey in Glad Town."

Feel like I done floated right off that porch, hang over the house like a cloud. "Where Glad Town at?"

"Down the road from Chimney, by them springs. Some fella got a huntin and fishin camp down there. He got a Cherokee show too what bring in plenty a folks, Sherrif Clayton onea em."

Clyde put down his vittles, he ain't touched them. "You tell me the boy too scrawny to do that."

"You say you not goin to Glad Town. I got no choice but to send somebody else. I got too many other things to do myself." She take his plate with her empty one and mine so clean it might not need washing. "Rufus show he a good seller now."

With Jolene inside Clyde pour hisself more corn squeezings. Face looked sour like he drinking dog piss.

Jolene come out get the sacks off the mule.

Clyde jumped to his feet in fronta me, his big ears red. "You think you something."

Get up from the stool. Didn't help cause he got a couple years and more than a couple inches on me. Ain't in the mood to get my guts knocked out.

"Last week Jolene tell me you ain't man enough to sell in Glad Town."

Clyde's whiskey breath hit my face. Jolene come up the steps, didn't say nothing.

"She tell me you don't want the job. Too much law skulkin round Glad Town. Reckon you ain't good at duckin em."

"You don't know shit about me and the law. Don't want to but I sell down there. Not you." His hand thumped my chest.

I stepped back. Looked at Jolene by the door.

"Reckon I slice the pie now," she said.

Clyde stomped on by her, go in the house.

"You lettin that big galoot sell in Glad Town?"

"If he willin to do it, I think he the better man for the job."

"Why you let him get way with hittin me like that?"

"I didn't see no hittin. Clyde bother you? Wait couple years, you grow. I bet you turn out handsomer'n Clyde ever dream to get." She winked at me.

Go down the steps. Hoped she didn't see the warm glow what sparked up in me.

"Get them other sacks for me. I stayin here with you boys. I give my room to Little Joe and his girl."

TWENTY-ONE

Sunday Lulahbelle's folks come, her four brothers in tow. Her ma bring a cake with white frosting. Lulahbelle fried a whole messa chicken. Big Jack cut a big watermelon he traded some eggs for.

Waiting for the preacher to come I wanna tell Little Joe how I mad as a snared rabbit at Jolene for how she get Clyde to do what she wanted while she tossed me to the dogs. Little Joe ain't in a listening mood. He wringed his hands, moved round a lot. He wear a good shirt used to belong to Big Jack, sleeves too long for Little Joe.

"You scairt?" I scairt if I in his shoes. Maybe he back out, not let that gal take up all his time. "You ain't gotta get hitched."

He looked like I got me a shotgun on him. "I wanna do this. Gettin the deed done what the hard part."

"This here shine help." Put my cup out for him. "Give some a try. You see. This stuff make you loose." Stuff make my head light like a feather in the wind.

Little Joe waved my cup way, pulled a face. "Smell a that coffin varnish make my gut turn, sure enough. Worse'n them Gibbs on our land."

"Jolene like them folk fine. She say they gonna start up a church in Pine Gap. She gush over the quilt what Miz Gibbs bring. Then she show off the O'Hara farm, chicken coups and all, to Mr. Gibbs."

"That Jole for ya. Y'all only see what they want you to see, sure enough. Not what Lulahbelle tell me what worry me. What she hide what worry me."

Preacher ride in on a white mule. He get off, smoothed down the ten hairs on his head, said he gonna do the marrying in the yard in front a the steps. Miz Gibbs go inside to fetch Lulahbelle.

Little Joe stand with Big Jack beside him. Think Little Joe might ask me to stand by him. I the one go find a preacher. Reckoned Big Jack right fella for the job, them kin and all. We set on the porch, Mr. Gibbs with his boys on one side, me and Jolene on tuther.

"You tell Clyde to come down today?"

"Course I tell Clyde." Jolene wear a blue shirt I never seen her put on before, britches not overalls. "I want Clyde here. But gettin him off the Grady place like pullin rotten teeth."

"That why I the one oughta sell whiskey in Glad Town. Clyde too busy hidin out." Wished I got good clothes like hers to wear.

"I tell you I make up my mind and I stickin to what I choose."

Lulahbelle come outta the house. She got on a stiff white dress with shiny buttons, carried pink daisies in a bunch. Her ma got her by the arm. They go down the steps to where Little Joe waited for them with his grin so big all his teeth showed.

"Ain't the pa posta walk the gal to her husband?" I whispered to Jolene.

Jolene shrugged. "That woman do what she want."

Preacher tell a story bout the war tween the states. Didn't knowed what that gotta do with folks making their bed together. Dark patches on the preacher's jacket grow under his arms. Think bout Jolene favoring Clyde, Little Joe giving up his freedom for a gal, make my blood boil like a pot fulla dirty shirts.

After Little Joe give Lulahbelle a ring he whittled outta hickory, he kissed her. Miz Gibbs grabbed Lulahbelle, pulled her close. "My little girl. My special girl."

Lulahbelle looked like she smelled pig shit till her ma let her go then Lulahbelle show a happy face for us folks watching her.

Mr. Gibbs wiped sweat from his head, pumped Little Joe's arm. "You gettin you one good woman."

We get to eating. Johnny Gibbs showed a plate a cake to the runt, snatched the plate way when the runt grabbed him some. He hold the plate high, the runt jumped, tried to get at the cake.

Miz Gibbs bring a big hunk to the brother a bit taller than the runt. Mr. Gibbs looked at his wife like she stepped on his foot. He dragged the boy way by the union suit before the boy take the cake. "Got somethin better for you sonny. You old enough now to give some a this here a try." He poured shine in a jelly jar. Think Miz Gibbs gonna throw the cake at Mr. Gibbs. Them Gibbs folk got them some peculiar ways. See why Lulahbelle wanna come live at the O'Hara place. Wished I get to stay at the O'Hara place more'n the Grady place.

Preacher ride off on his white mule with some canned preserves as his pay.

Sit by my lonesome, eat me more cake, drink nother splash a white lighting. Big Jack clapped time, hummed, while Little Joe swing Lulahbelle round in a dance. Wondered where Jolene get off to.

Seen her come from behind the house, cross to the barn. Everybody else in the yard cept Johnny and that there runt. Go to the barn to try getting lone time with Jolene. Opened the big square door. Hear Ole Abe braying. Reckoned Jolene put him in the barn when she ride down before day break.

Johnny hold tight to a rope he got on Ole Abe. Jolene got her rifle to her shoulder.

"This here beastie might like it," Johnny said.

The runt on his knees under old Abe's belly, got his hands where the mule's tallywacker come out.

"Get away from there." Jolene gonna cock her rifle.

Barn turned, flipped, clouded-over. Words ring far off, deep in my head. "You gotta do it cause I say so." My legs give out.

Come to. Seen Ole Abe chomping some hay. How he get here? What I doing in the barn?

Find Little Joe picking plates and cups off the porch. "Where you git off to? You miss Jole shooin the Gibbs off our land."

"Reckon I drink too much shine, take me a nap." Recollected only a couple drinks, a bushel fulla vittles. Didn't make no sense. "Why she do that? She like em."

"Jole don't say why she do it. She wave that gun round like she after a pack a chicken hawks."

"We lucky we got Jolene round with her rifle." Feel safer with Jolene than I do in my whole life.

TWENTY-TWO

At first Cob Turner leave the money in the can under the rock like he said. One time I didn't find so much as a dime. Tracked him to the boarding house in Swift River.

His room, up three floors, sit right next to the stairs to the roof.

"What brings you here, Bucko?"

"My money what bring me."

"Thought I left the jack in the cup. Guess I forgot." He slapped the two-day-old whiskers on his face. "I have to go get the dough from my hiding place. Before I do, come upstairs, take a look at the sights."

Law, if on the roof I didn't see the river twisting through the valley like a big blue-green snake. Cob said the taller the buildings the better the view. He said tall buildings also good for pissing off.

Back in the room he tell me sit tight.

"I come back later."

"Won't take me long. I'll bring back a couple blue plate specials from the diner. I bet you'll like their meatloaf. Help yourself to the whiskey while I'm gone."

Gotta get that money outta him, good grub didn't sound bad neither. Didn't touch the bottle he said got likker. Pass the time with the pencil and paper on his table. Scratched out what I recall Little Bear Lake looked like from the Grady place backdoor.

When Cob got back he set down two covered plates, take off his jacket, his suspenders, his shirt. Don't think nothing. Then he peeled off his britches, his undershirt.

"Clothes make me sweat no matter how cool the weather. Don't bother you, do it, Bucko?"

"Nope." Keep my eyes on the meatloaf, a special treat, shoveled the stuff in my mouth.

"I wouldn't call you a man but you're not a baby," Cob said. "And you're not a pansy."

His feet clomp like fish flopping on dry rocks when he take off his undershorts.

"Back in Dandelion Holler some fella don't wear britches cause he say he don't wanna spill food on em cause he ain't got money to buy new ones."

"Smart man."

Reckoned I think fast, make up a good story, cause I didn't recollect much bout home. Feel like I stepped on some anthill, ants crawling on me, make my eating slow down.

Cob swallowed half his meat, didn't bother to chew much. "Be my guest if you want to strip down yourself."

"Not like you. I get cold easy." Didn't so much as take off my union suit to take a bath. Reckoned washing the suit when I wash me make sense.

Cob pushed way his empty plate, poured dark whiskey from a bottle. Poured one for me. Never seen likker didn't come outta a jug or jar.

"So, Bucko, you got any people other than the O'Haras?"

"Them's the lot, cept my sister, Sammy Jean. Ain't seen her in many a season. I like stayin with the O'Haras." Take a swallow from my cup. Stuff didn't got that sharp taste like O'Hara shine. "Little Joe the best buddy I ever got."

"You looked sad when you said that."

Cobb see right through my clothes, through my skin? Feel more ants crawl on me.

"We usesta fish, sit out watch the sky. He whittlin, me scratchin pictures in the dirt. Now he got hisself a wife. Don't got no time now."

"You draw this?" He pulled over the paper. "Not bad. You're a smart kid. If you worked for me, I'd teach you a lot."

"I knowed plenty. Jolene got me to learn Clyde some farmin."

Slide the picture over, slipped the paper in my overalls.

"Clyde's an O'Hara but he doesn't know about farming?"

Cob take the pencil, stick it behind his ear.

"Say some apes bring him up."

Seen a spark in Cob's eye. "What does Jolene say about that?"

"Say I done good learnin him to plow and plant. Say I do good work. She gonna let me mix my own batch a shine soon."

Eat the bit a bread I use to sop up the gravy, put the fork on the clean plate. "Thanks for the vittles. Take my money now."

Cob poured the last a the whiskey in both cups.

"Help me kill this bottle. Give me an excuse to get another."

"Best be goin. Jolene gonna start to wonder where I at."

"She your boss or she your girl?"

Searched my mind for the right answer. Tell my body not to squirm.

"Jolene a lotta things to a lotta people."

"You ever kiss her?"

Take a long swig a dark likker. Hold the warm drink in my mouth.

"You ever kiss any girl?" Cob squinted at me. "Maybe you're more wet behind the ears than I thought."

"I go to the jenny barn in Chimney on a Saturday night."

"You like that?" Cob winked like he giving a secret cookie to a young'un, a cookie what got ants crawling on it.

"Yep, like them gals fine. But if'n I got more jack I go to a better one." Put the empty cup down. "Speakin a money, I need what you owe?"

"Oh, yeah, of course." He grabbed his pants from the corner, pulled out a wad of bills. "You know, you ever heard of the Winter House?"

Spot a chance to act like a man. "Got me a friend what work there."

Cob chuckled. "I know you mountain boys tell some tall tales, but that's a good one."

"Ain't no yarn. True." Swear to never to let on she ain't my friend, she Jolene's. "Ana Marie a fancy gal. She cost lots."

"So you know Ana Marie."

Cob looked at me like I a duck what fly in his window, sit on his table.

"I'm upping my order to fifteen jugs a week. That's more than I buy from the Harveys." He peeled some jack off that wad, give me my money. "And if you keep doing a good job delivering, maybe I'll give you a bonus. A whole hour of time to do whatever you want with our friend Ana Marie."

Deep down I knowed Cob never leave the money in the cup again.

TWENTY-THREE

From them years I recollect how hard we worked. Running whiskey in the cold months go slower cause the mash didn't turn quick so we setup more barrels, keep the stills perking through the winter. We make so much white lightening, it likely fill the river.

In the spring we cleared more land, planted more corn than the year before. Do everything the way Jolene tell us.

Funny thing, Jolene said she stayed at the Grady place with me and Clyde cause she didn't wanna stay near that store Glory got. Then she tell Lulahbelle to help Little Joe with the chickens, but Jolene go down from the Grady place two days a week to take the egg delivery to Fresh Farms, said only her allowed to deliver eggs.

Jolene buy a new mule and cart to haul the whiskey. Tell Little Joe and Big Jack to get rid of the old mule cart. Big Jack looked at Little Joe, said, "Make good firewood." They take a ax and crowbar, busted that cart in teency pieces. They get more joy outta that chore than a hot meal on a cold day.

Me and Little Joe scratched our heads over what Jolene do with all tuther jack we hand over from selling the likker. She only give us a little money of our own. Got me a ten-gauge shotgun. Little Joe got clothes for the baby coming. Clyde got hisself a banjo.

Hear him in the cabin making them banjo strings ping like pebbles falling in a tin bucket. The ruckus put more knots in my gut when I loaded up my weekly drop for Cob.

Never did cottoned to going to Cob's room. He bring in good food from the diner, poured me dark city likker, but when I climbed them stairs I feel like I going to a hanging. If not for getting the money that make Jolene so happy, I soon as forget all bout Cob Turner.

"You might get your wish," Cob said one night.

"Get what?"

"Yours and that O'Hara girl's."

Reckoned he wanted me to jump like a fish after a worm.

He make me wait a whole half a minute before he said, "I might have to stop buying Harvey whiskey."

"That good news."

"You know how I only do business with Stub's little boy B. J.?" Cob scratched a patch a hair sprouting outta his flabby chest.

"Ain't nonea my dealin's, them yourn." Keep my eyes on his face, not his bare hide.

"Paid old Stub a visit the other day. And I'm gonna show you why."

Cob take two little plates, pulled up two jars. Splashed some whiskey from one jar in a plate. "Now watch carefully, Bucko." He lighted a match, set the likker to flaming. "This O'Hara whiskey, the last batch you drop. See the blue glow?"

Never seen a flame flicker blue as back feathers on a jay.

"Now watch this." Cob slopped shine from tuther jar in tuther plate, lighted nother fire. "What color you see there?"

"That there one red as a cardinal flyin in a snowstorm." How he do that?

"Good boy." Cob grinned at me like I a pup what rolled over for him. "That's from the last load of Harvey moonshine. The red flame means it's not pure alcohol. Somebody used something to make the mash turn quicker. My guess is Potash. People use that for fertilizer."

"The blue flame make the O'Hara shine better." If I showed Jolene that trick reckoned she find the magic right nice.

"Mmmm, the red flame make the Harvey liquor undrinkable. If I take those goods to the warehouse, I'll get my head cut off. That's why I called on Stub this week. I told him I won't buy Harvey whiskey if he tries that shit again. He claims he didn't know a thing about it."

"Reckon Stub a liar." Wanna give the right answer so Cob give me the money, let me go on my way.

"Suspect Snake got something to do with the situation. Now B. J. a good boy." Cob poured me more city likker that he learned me got a dark color cause folks age the stuff in oak barrels. "Drink up, Bucko. You a growing boy. Those new overalls? Not tight like the ones last week. Don't show as much."

If I knocked him silly, take the jack, he never buy our product again so I sit tight.

"Reckon Snake that smart?"

"Got my sources. Make it my job to find out people's secrets." He gave me that fishing look again. "You work for me, you know those secrets too."

"Got me plenty work on the O'Hara farms" Gotta get outta that room.

"But I taught you so much."

True, he done learned me lots with telling bout how to shake a jar of shine to see how strong the alkeehol, all his yarns bout the Great War.

"And I got more to teach you. More than you ever get from that O'Hara girl." Cob pulled a face when he said 'O'Hara girl' like Jolene do when she said 'Harvey'. "Bet some of her secrets turn your head."

Knowed he ain't so much as meet Jolene in person. Reckoned he wanna make me squirm. Drink my whiskey, turned the talk to the price a corn.

TWENTY-FOUR

Sleep in the cart them nights Cob keep me late. The sky bright by the time my eyes cracked open, bare tree branches spread out like cracks in broken glass. Dragged my behind outta the back, got the mule moving, this one they call Wilson. My mouth dry like the hay I bedded down in. Reckoned vittles and coffee help.

A new café in Mill Creek sat just off the road on the O'Hara side. Red towel on the porch rail mean law round. I safe cause the cart ain't got no more likker jugs. Cob warned me that if I ever run into to Sheriff Clayton to act specially nice to him.

Frying sausage smelled like the maple wood they smoke the meat with. Sheriff Clayton got his hat off what make his big ears stand out more. He at the counter talking to the fella what give out the food.

"What I say? Them negres ought not be trusted," Sheriff said.

My ears perked. Glory and her man the only colored folk I knowed. Keep my head down over the biscuits baked crisp on the outside, soft underneath, like a pasture on that icy morning.

"Clean run off, leave the damn woman to run that there French lawyer's store by herself." Some mill-workers roared in so I only catch a few more of the sheriff's words. "A white woman no less. Figured her for the old maid type. And her poor family. I know what it like cause my sister run off with that Rupert Harvey weasel and all."

Hightailed myself to the O'Hara place. Little Joe and Jolene quick to tell what they read in the newspaper. This my chance to spill chinwag first.

Nobody to home cept Lulahbelle mending clothes.

"Little Joe and Big Jack ain't round since yesterday. Sure hope they get home soon." She patted her swelled up belly.

Fetched some firewood from out back for her, spied the shaving mirror. Some time back Big Jack learned me and Little Joe to use their pa's razor. By the look of me, reckoned I needed a shave. If Jolene showed, she liked to say I got peach fuzz.

On the steps I pulled out a smoke to take the chill from my bones. We all take up the habit when Glory gave them way free at the store. When we wanted them bad, she said the company started charging so she charged too.

Something pricked at my insides. Glory must feel worse than a blind man at a gal's swimming hole. Here I excited bout sharing news when Glory done lost her fella. Run over in my head what Sheriff Clayton said. Jimbo take off with a white woman, old maid type. Jolene near on twenty. She didn't go in for courting.

Grinded the butt in the dirt with my shoe, kicked at the orange sparks. Somewhere in my dizziness I hear a howl, then nother, and a nother.

Go round tuther side of the house, send out my own "Ooouuu". Like a pack of wild dogs three howls answered.

"I got that fella confused like a dog chasing his tail." Jolene talked so much she didn't touch the vittles Lulahbelle set out. Chicken stew and cornbread with honey.

"I go off tracking turkeys with Thanksgiving on my mind," Jolene said. "Dadgum, if I didn't scent me a revenue man. After prowling behind him, sneaky like a Injun, I come get Little Joe and Big Jack. They help me with my bumper crop plan. Together we tote the still long way round to a spot the lawman scout before. We wait till he check the first place before we move the whole mess back."

Reckoned that trick throw me off if I a revenue fella. But seemed too easy in some way. He might look round some more. Didn't say what I think cause that get Jolene mad. Lay out the news bout Jimbo taking his leave.

"The Stewart girl, sure enough." Little Joe said. "Seen em together, feel somethin not right."

"Poor Glory all by her lonesome now." Wanna help Glory somehow.

Jolene watched us. A second later she go for the door.

"Where you off to, Jole?"

Little Joe hold the chair for Lulahbelle to sit down with her supper.

"Gettin a jug from the loft. Gotta celebrate." Jolene stick her head back inside. "Not everyday we outsmart a revenuer."

"None for me," Little Joe shouted after her.

Hoped they seen the last a that revenue fella.

TWENTY-FIVE

Me and Jolene hunkered down round the fire with cups fulla shine. Little Joe sipped water. Much as he tried he never cottoned to the likker taste.

For me, after a few swigs I feel loose, at home, not like drinking with dirty ole Cob. Downing a few with the O'Haras come easy as tipping back the jug. Cepting when Jolene in a mood like a cornered skunk. She happy that night cause we finished a run of shine.

Jolene tell me and Little Joe load a box with jars of whiskey "for a special customer."

"These for selling outta the back a Fresh Farms, sure enough," Little Joe whispered. "Jole think I too dumb to know."

One jar didn't fit so I carried that one while Little Joe bring the box. We gonna put the whisky in the wheelbarrow what got a heavy log tied to its handles, that log drag behind, wiped out footsteps and the wheel track. We never get to the wheelbarrow.

The bushes rustled. "Hold on there." We stopped real quick like. Some fella stepped in the firelight. Orange glow twinkled off a pistol in his shaky hand.

Our shotguns behind the barrels. Jolene's rifle leaned on a tree outta reach. "Nice setup." He weared a stiff shirt buttoned to his windpipe, a suit jacket. His hair combed like he come from the barber. Handgun looked new, shiny like a fish in a clear pool.

"Back away from those containers."

Jolene did like he said. Wondered if he needed new spectacles cause that get her closer to her rifle. With the hand the pistol ain't in he whipped a hanky outta his pocket, picked a lid off a barrel. "Ah ha. Fermenting corn. A federal offence. I'll have to take you in."

"You sure you a revenuer?" Jolene said. "Don't look no older'n these here boys."

"You two gentlemen come here."

"Reckon he talkin to us," I said to Little Joe.

"You can put down that box. Looks heavy," the revenue fella said.

Little Joe let go. The box dropped. Glass jars clattered, revenuer jumped like a rabbit in a doghouse. Jolene snatched her rifle, ducked behind a tree.

The revenue fella looked round, get his back to her hideout. "Where'd the other..." He jerked when Jolene poked her rifle out. Stick him right in his behind.

Little Joe run behind the barrels.

Jolene take her rifle out from twinxed this fella's balls, come round to face him. "Get your hands up."

He put his weapon down on a barrel lid, get his arms in the air. "They're going to love this back at headquarters. Probably taking bets on how long I'll last out here."

"Work too much for ya, huh?" Jolene chuckled, grabbed the pistol, put down her rifle.

Look like that revenue fella gonna cry for his ma. "Don't know what I did for them to send me to this wilderness." His hands come down a bit. "Haven't brought in any moonshiners."

"How you find my setup?" Jolene asked.

"Some farmer invited me to his house to assist me by mapping out possible still locations."

Jolene got closer to him. "What farmer?"

"A real proponent of Prohibition." Revenuer mopped his forehead with his hanky. "A Mr. Harvey."

Jolene jabbed the handgun in his belly. "You working for the Harveys? Say your prayers cause you good as dead."

My mind glued itself to that pistol pressed in the revenuer's shirt. Jolene's finger tight on the trigger.

"But Jole." Little Joe popped up from behind them barrels. "He...he not no Harvey. You ought not shoot him."

Jolene give a grizzly growl. "That's right." She backed off, eased down the trigger. "But this pistol look like a keeper."

"Jole," Little Joe piped in again. "You always say not to steal."

She looked like she wanna whip Little Joe. "Only seein if you payin attention."

She come over to me. Rolled open the pistol, slide out the bullets. "We gonna tie him good'n tight, stick him in that cart bed. Blindfold him. Then you gonna carry him far off, somewhere he get so lost take him a year to find his way back. Before you leave him, loose them ropes so he work free in bout a hour. Set this twenty yards way." She put the pistol in my hand.

Where to drop this fella so we all feel safe? Looked down at the shine jar in my tuther hand. Recollected I posta bring that corn squeezins to somebody.

TWENTY-SIX

Josephine Belle O'Hara got herself borned on December 19, 1924. When Lulahbelle started screaming Jolene get a Cedar Springs lady to help with the birthing.

"Why bring her?" Big Jack said.

"I not gonna be in that room with a sticky bloody baby comin out," Jolene said. "She offer."

Good thing O'Haras raised chickens that come out in eggs, not cows or pigs.

"Glory offer too."

"That Fresh Farms woman never gonna come in this house."

"She know birthin. She wanna help."

Jolene crossed her arms. "Get more water on to boil."

The baby a girl. Little Joe danced round like Clyde when he drink too much whiskey. But Little Joe ain't no drinker. For the celebration I bring out the stogies I stashed after I dumped that revenue fella off.

On the ride to Juniper County the revenue fella tell me his name Mason. Said he glad he going to a place where nobody find him. Turned out he a real nice fella. Wanted to learn carving, his pa didn't let him. His family didn't mean nothing to him no more.

"Knowed the feelin. My little sister the only kin I take to."

Mason get to meet Sammy Jean sooner than I think. She leave our ma and pa, lived on the mountaintop. Tell Sammy Jean how I getting long with the O'Haras while Dullsaine plucked her harp. By the time I skedaddled them three act like they ole friends.

Dullsaine gave me cigars made from tobacco she growed and rolled herself to pass out when Lulahbelle's baby get here.

"Yep." Jolene hold the hand rolled stogie high. "Y'all be ready to take a ride nice'n early Christmas morning. I got a surprise."

She slipped the stogie in her pocket, lighted a cigarette, leave the house.

My innards glowed brighter than the tips on them there smokes cause I got something I fixing to surprise *her* with.

Christmas Eve rain made the road muddy, the creek top its banks. That morning cold settled in.

Stopped to say 'Hey' to Glory, Clyde go on ahead.

"How that chitlen be?" Glory said.

Tell her Big Jack's words, "Not too healthy." Poor Jo Belle the smallest baby I ever seen. Didn't take easy to sucking on her ma neither.

Glory pulled a face, send me off with Christmas presents for the O'Haras.

Lulahbelle sit home to keep the baby warm, tried to get her to eat some. Me, Little Joe and Big Jack wear the scarfs Glory knitted us. Jolene's stayed wrapped in red paper.

I gave everybody drawings I do on good paper from the mercantile. Big Jack said, "Thank you, Rufus." Little Joe and Lulahbelle gushed over them. Clyde, that don't give nobody nothing I knowed bout, put his shine cup down on his drawing. Jolene don't so much as take the ribbon off hers.

Big Jack drive the mules with Clyde beside him. Not three words passed between them two. In back talk fly like a flock of ducks after a gunshot.

Little Joe said how Jo Belle cooed when he tickled her under the chin. Didn't tell him I worried bout that baby girl.

Jolene jabbered on how the Harveys'd never make as much moonshine as us cause they only run one still.

"Way I got it planned," Jolene said. Her breath come out like she smoking when she ain't. "So much O'Hara likker gonna flow in this county, Harveys be drownin in our shine."

Little Joe looked at her. "Jo Belle favor me, sure enough. Ya think?"

Where we going? What Jolene got for a surprise? How she gonna like what I got for her?

The mules trotted easier on the streets in town with not so much mud. Folks scarce with the stores closed up. A family honked at us when they rolled by in their new automobile showing off their Christmas plenty. Cob talked lots bout them cars, called them tin lizzies. Said he might get one someday soon.

Jolene tell Big Jack hold up. We followed her down the sidewalk to that smoke shop with a wood Injun. She pulled a key outta her overalls bib pocket.

"Boys, welcome to the new O'Hara family business."

Her grin spread like a scoop of butter melting over a stack of flap jacks.

"What bout the whiskey?" I said. "Our business runnin the stills."

"Y'all handle that now. I gotta tend the store."

We stepped inside where the wind didn't bite our noses.

"This how you spend them bills you squirrel away?" Little Joe looked like somebody eat his turkey dinner when he ain't watching. "Reckon you buy stuff to build bigger stills, sure enough. Then we run more shine."

"You make do with the stills we got." She patted Little Joe on the back. "Smart folks know to buy whiskey here. Think bout the money I make then."

"What bout Sheriff Clayton?" I said. Cob said Clayton one tricky fella.

Clyde said "Humph." Stick his nose up at the stogies, lighted a cigarette, stare out the front window like he in the place by hisself. This the first time he seen Swift River from what I knowed.

"Don't worry bout the sheriff. I charm him easy." Jolene winked at me.

Breathed in the heavy tobacco smell. Looked over the shelves fulla boxes. Pictures showed different kinda stogies: a man with a long mustache in a red frame, a woman with a pink feather in her hat, a fluffy white cat. With so much to take in I almost forget what weighed down my pocket.

Jolene said we gotta get back to the house, put vittles on to cook. The O'Hara's headed for the door. I stayed by the counter, called Jolene back. "This bein Christmas I got somethin special for you."

"Don't go spendin money on such foolishness." She looked up at me, cut her eyes. Reckoned she finally notice I taller than her now.

"Didn't cost no money." I opened my coat, take out Mason's pistol.

She looked surprised like baby Jesus getting licked by a donkey. Then fire come in her eyes. "I tell you give that back. And you go'n steal it. You sure soft-headed."

Her sharp words stabbed at my giving spirit. "No stealin. He give me the pistol. Say he ain't cut out for bustin stills. He quit the job, don't need no weapon. Gonna make clay pots and grow herbs with my sister and that Dullsaine woman. Honest, Jolene."

"That different." She plucked the gun outta my hand. "I best take this then. Too dangerous for a young'un like you. What I gonna do with a pistol, I don't know."

She called me a young'un when I probably older than Little Joe what already a poppa. I dreamed her tickled to get that shiny handgun. Wished I never think to give her the thing.

"Reckon I keep it under the counter." She wiped the pistol with her coat sleeve. "I might need a weapon hid way if a Harvey try to come in this here smoke shop."

TWENTY-SEVEN

Piles of new years snow melted in puddles under a clear sky. People come out like ants scouting crumbs. Me, Little Joe, and Jolene sleep in the back of the smoke shop that night. Next morning we get up, helped Jolene scrub that store top to bottom. Clean enough to eat a church supper off the floor.

After we painted the front Little Joe washed the big window. I set my mind on the Injun. Got bits a paint in different colors. Mixed them together with dabs a white to make bright shades. Lines in the wood tell my brush where the paint wanna go.

"Find me the right log I carve a Injun like that, sure enough."

"This one here, so I gonna keep paintin him."

Peeked to the next corner every so often cause from the smoke shop I see the rooming house where Cob Turner holed up. Hoped Cob didn't catch sight of me, come over. Spied somebody else duck behind a post. Ain't Cob, it Snake Harvey.

Jolene walked up wearing shiny new shoes, packages under her arm. "Well, lookie him." She grinned at the Injun like he her first customer. "He so lifelike he bout ready for a pow wow. He gonna need him a good red-man's name."

Her favoring my work make me feel like a war hero.

"How bout Sitting Bull?" Little Joe said.

"Naw, somebody already got that one." Rubbed the stubble on my chin, checked the post outta the corner of my eye. Snake still there. Jolene and Little Joe must not seen him. Then the name snapped in my head like a slingshot. "Stands Like Wood."

Jolene showed the Injun her open hand. "Why, how, Stands Like Wood." She chuckled. "Stay out here. I out directly." She in such good spirits I suspected when she get back to Cedar Springs, she make a right nice pie from last spring's canned berries. Her moods lasted longer than most folks.

Fixed up bare spots on Stands Like Wood while Little Joe finished painting words on the front window. When Jolene come out she wear a wool suit, black, with britches, a new white shirt. She stick a gray felt hat on her head. Turned to the wet paint on the window. "Jolene O'Hara, Proprietor." She looked proud a them words like Little Joe proud a tiny Jo Belle.

Jolene stepped back inside. I checked the post, Snake gone.

Breathed easy with Snake gone bout two seconds.

"What'cha doing in town today, Bucko?" Cob looked at Little Joe. "Who's your pal?"

Swallowed a lump in my windpipe. "This, uh…."

Cob pointed to the window. "Well, well, well. That your Jolene that got her name on this window, Bucko?" He gave me a grin like he catched me with my hand where it didn't belong.

"Reckon so." Feel like a rabbit in a snare.

"Must be her inside. I'll go in, introduce myself. Don't seem like you're going to do the introductions."

Little Joe eyed me like I got a sickness. "Who that fella?"

Shrugged, followed Cob in the shop. Little Joe stayed outside.

Jolene stand up straight, like when she wanted something.

"Welcome to my first day a business. How may I help you?"

"I enjoy puffing on a pipe."

"Let me show you some Velvet, that my most popular brand. I give you a sample, if you like." Never reckoned Jolene act nice to a stranger. Knowed she didn't show her real self.

"No. I'll take a pouch of Three Nuns and one of King's Head." Cob put a finger to his mouth as if he thinking what the tobacco taste like in his pipe. "Sometimes I'm in the mood for a small flavor, sometimes I'm in the mood for a big one."

"Now there's a smart man." Jolene searched up and down the shelves, picked up then put down a couple boxes before she find the ones she wanted.

"Guess you're a little disorganized, this your first day and all."

Jolene painted on nother clown face grin. Didn't think she knowed I in the shop. "Next time you come in, this store gonna be so tidy them boxes'll come when I call em."

"Maybe I'll have you order some special blends for me." Cob pulled out a thick wallet, handed over a greenback. "By the way, name's Cob Turner. I'm sure you heard of me."

"Yes, sir. Nice to meet'cha." She stick out her hand, shake his like they making a deal.

"I've heard plenty about you Miss O'Hara, from our boy here. He's a smart one, he is."

Jolene's eyes flicked on me, back to Cob. "He know farmin fine enough, not much bout other things."

Why didn't she hush up after 'He know farmin'? Get my hackles in a bunch.

"Pleasure doing business with you." Cob leave.

"What I gonna do with you?" Jolene shake her head at me. "That fella nothin like you say."

"Didn't tell you a thin bout him. You never ask."

"Way you talk he some ole man. He not more'n ten years older than us." Jolene make her eyes big. "You see that suit? He throw down some bills on that. Best material they got."

Reckoned she knowed cause she buy a new suit that morning. I didn't see him in clothes cept on occasion.

Go outside to find Little Joe. Didn't see him, seen Cob heading back to the shop.

He stopped part way, called out, "Hey, Bucko. Forgot to tell you, looking forward to our next visit. I got a surprise for you."

TWENTY-EIGHT

Cob talked, I keep my glass close to my nose. The powerful smell from the city likker helped hide the stink a piss and sweat. A indoor toilet down the hall, Cob used a bucket in his room so he didn't gotta dress.

"You should see the sights down in Winston-Salem," he said. "Cars, all kinds, everywhere."

Snuffed out my cigarette, scooted up on the chair. "Best be goin. Gotta get Jolene at the smoke shop."

"That's right, I forgot, you're at that woman's beck and call. What does she want now?"

Said the wrong thing. Didn't want Cob to knowed the smoke shop closed Wednesdays cause he sometimes talked to Stub Harvey.

"Well?"

Reckoned he gonna see for hisself the store closed.

"She goin to Cedar Springs for the day."

"Oh, going to see the family." Cob blow a couple smoke rings off his pipe. "You took a while to answer that question. You must not like why she's going to Cedar Springs."

"Nobody to watch the shop what ain't to my likin." Maybe Cob help, if I asked nice. "Seen Snake Harvey scoutin round. He knowed Jolene got the place."

"You think Snake's smart enough to do something to the shop?"

"If'n you talk to Sheriff Clayton he might keep a special close eye out."

"I'm not familiar with how these feud things work." More smoke rings floated round Cob's head. "Now the Harveys don't like Jolene and she don't like them, then there's other people Jolene don't like. Didn't you say she's got a beef with a Gloria?"

"Glory. Reckon Glory ain't Jolene's favorite." slided my empty glass way from me.

Cob leaned over, take my glass then the whiskey bottle, screwed off he cap.

"No more for me. I gotta go."

"You can stay for one more little one." He put the drink by me. "Now I don't blame Jolene on that one cause didn't you say the woman's a negro?"

"Glory a good woman, I trust her." Take a sip cause the likker there. "Now Snake Harvey, Stub too, them trouble."

"But you have to admit those negros can be tricky." He cut his eyes at me. "Oh, sorry." He put his hand on mine, feel like a nesta fire ants. "Think I remember you say you feel sorry for the ni...negro woman."

Breathed easy when he take his hand way.

"Her man run off. Glory need better."

Cob's words didn't surprise me, lotta folks said bad stuff bout negres. "You gonna talk to the sheriff bout keepin his eye on the smoke shop?"

"Why not. Hear Clayton don't like the Harveys anymore than Jolene does." Cob grinned like he gonna tell me to pull his finger. "Why haven't you said anything about my surprise?"

"Reckon I forget with fixin up the smoke shop and all."

From his coat what hang on the chair back Cob pulled a key. "I bought a truck."

"Good for you." Why he think I cared? "How bout givin me my money?"

"Will do, Bucko." He dig a stash a bills from the same pocket the key come outta. "Thinking I'd teach you to drive my new truck. But sounds like you're not interested."

In my head I hear how them automobiles roar when they started. Think on how with one push on a pedal they raced like a chased rabbit.

Slide back in that chair. "I interested."

On Sunday I go down to the O'Hara place to get way from Clyde killing them banjo strings. Planned to crow bout learning to drive a truck. Big Jack gone somewhere. Jolene and Little Joe set with Glory by the fireplace. Reckoned Little Joe seen my face cause he shrugged.

My head spin trying to reckon how Glory get in good graces with Jolene after all the bad words Jolene said bout her. Keep my mouth shut. Never complained when folks' spirits run to happy.

Coffee in Little Joe's cup. Jolene filled the other two from a jug. She get a cup for me then get back to telling her tales.

"Fella come in, say he need a new brand. His wife claim his old one stink like he breakin wind. I say, 'don't change your tobacco, let your dog sleep in doors.'"

Jolene's eyes sparkled when Glory laughed, slapped her knee.

Lulahbelle come outta the sleeping room looking like a rabbit after a near escape from a hound dog. Her hair stick out in all directions. "Jo Belle doin bad. Fever ain't broke yet."

"You say she gettin better, sure enough." Little Joe thumped down his coffee.

"She were. Now she ain't." Lulahbelle sounded like a mouse in a trap.

Glory pulled a face. "Give her spoonful dis whiskey."

Spark go outta Jolene's eyes. "You know what you doin. Get in there."

Her arm round Lulahbelle, Glory go in the room. Jolene get things Glory asked for from the kitchen.

Me and Little Joe stayed by the hearth. Wanna give a hand somehow. Keep Little Joe's head off what going on only way I think to help. Tell him all bout Cob's truck. How Cob said it a Model TT cause the frame longer and heavier. How the gears did better in the hills. How Cob gotta figure out getting more speed outta the motor. When no more talk come to mind the quiet hang round us like the smell a Clyde's feet on a hot day.

Sometime later Jolene come outta the sleeping room. She stared in the fire, not at us. "Glory done everythin she know. Wait all we got left to do."

From the room we hear Lulahbelle cry out long, loud, like a wolf at the moon.

Little Joe's eyes get big.

Jolene stick her head in the room, come back. She poured whiskey in a cup, put it by Little Joe. "When Big Jack come home we take her up to the burrin yard."

Wished I ain't there. Nothing to do to help.

Little Joe pushed way that cup, stand. Swayed like he drink the likker he passed up. At the front door his hand squeezed the knob so hard his knuckles go white. He leave the door open, ambled out into the dark.

TWENTY-NINE

"Don't bother sitting down, Bucko."

Law, if Cob didn't got money on the table ready for me when I walked in his door.

"Not expecting that, huh, Bucko?" Cob take a deep drag on his pipe. "I got another one for you. See that package there?"

Box size of a brick wrapped in paper sit on the table by the bills.

"Need you to deliver that for me."

"Tell you I get Jolene, take her back to Cedar Springs after I do my drop for you."

"Won't take long." Cob opened his hand, showed the key. "You need more practice driving."

"You ain't goin?"

"Not this time." He pushed his hand at me. "Take it. Or maybe you prefer sitting around here."

Shoved my money in a pocket, snatched the box, slipped the key from Cob's paw quicker than a fly hopping from one mule dropping to nother. Wanna feel them wheels rolling under me faster than a rockslide.

"Guess you forget all about Jolene when you can get your hands on my truck."

"Where I gotta take this?"

"I wondered when you'd ask." A cloud a smoke weaved round Cob's head.

"You know the Tiffany House? That goes to our friend Ana Marie. Get there in time to be her last customer of the evening."

Reckoned she knowed me. She said 'hey' couple times I seen her in town. One time Jolene bring her to Sunday dinner at the O'Hara place.

"Customer?"

Cob waved his pipe. "You'll find an extra ten dollars in that cash. Pay for her services with that. A little bonus. You earned it."

Ana Marie cost ten dollars. Me and a gal that cost ten dollars, didn't add up.

In the truck I tried to recollect what Cob said to pull, push, shove to make the thing go. Did pretty good. Didn't grind gears no more. Happy stinky Cob ain't beside me.

On the front steps remembered the first time I come with Jolene, now I wanna run like a scared pup. Feeling come back. Didn't get what Cob called the heebie-jeebies at the jenny barn in Chimney.

A gal opened the door to let out a fella, showed me in. Find Ana Marie cranking one a them machines what play music outta a big horn. She wear a slick black dress with plenty a frills, no sleeves, cut down real low in front. Dark curls loose round her white shoulders.

"Why, hey." Ana Marie tickled my nose with a feather scarf. "Fancy meetin you here."

"Bring you somethin from…a friend."

Ana Marie eyed the box, the couple gals in the sitting room talking to fellas. "Me and you goin to my room." She slipped her arm through mine.

Her hands on me gave me tingles, not where they posta.

"Reckon that box ain't from Jolene. You doin somebody new's dirty work." She clicked shut the door. The room only got one chair. Didn't wanna sit on the bed.

"Mr. Turner sent me. Do his chore this one time." On a table she got all sorta little bottles.

"Turner?" She shake the box next to her ear. "Reckon Mr. Franklin forget his own name."

Wondered why Cob gave her a different name.

"You mighty curious bout my powders and such."

"Lotta colors."

"Wanna try some? Bitta peach right here." Ana Marie put her finger on my cheek.

More tingles, down my back, nowhere else.

"No. Not on my face. You got some paper, like to try some on that."

Ana Marie take the wrapping off, put the box in a bottom drawer.

"Use any of them there bottles you want on that wrappin, cept this one." She picked up a small bottle, unscrewed the cap, stick in her pinky, put it to her nose, take a big sniff.

Paper brown, not white way I liked. Dab on some red and orange. Use a dark brown pencil to draw a mountain in front, sunup in back.

Ana Marie sit on the bed, read onea them books Jolene called a magazine.

Few minutes later Ana Marie come look over my shoulder. She smelled real good, better than any living thing I knowed.

"Keep that paper with you. You ever wanna bring me some a them bottles, it tell you what colors I like."

"That where you get em all? Customers?"

"Some. Some I trade with girls in the house. Think Jolene bring me one or two. She so good to me."

"I lucky if'n she give me greenbacks for the work I do."

"Really?" Ana Marie go back to the bed, sat, put her legs up. Them legs smooth like the fine china they sell at the mercantile. "Reckon she treat you nice, you onea the strangers and all."

"Stranger? I ain't no stranger to Jolene."

Ana Marie laughed like I some young'un with a dirty face.

"She never tell you bout the three strangers? Long time ago some fortuneteller say Jolene gonna meet three strangers in one day right in her hometown."

"Three strangers in Cedar Springs? Never." Reckoned Ana Marie make that up, try to act like she knowed Jolene better'n me.

"Jolene say hooey too. Then she meet Glory, Clyde, and you all in one day in Cedar Springs." Ana Marie rubbed her hands long her dress like the cloth feel good to her.

Sunup picture on the brown paper didn't look right.

"How come you knowed all bout that?"

"I there Jolene's big day, long before y'all show up, when the fortuneteller say Jolene gonna be a legend. Onea them strangers posta help her get fame."

Jolene a legend make sense. Knowed I do a better job than Clyde or Glory.

"Reckon I help by makin sure no Harvey do nothing to that there smoke shop." Crumpled the paper. Picture no good. "Seen Snake pokin round."

Ana Marie get up, opened the door.

"You one a them strangers but me and Jole like sisters. So she do somethin great, I right by her side."

Gave Ana Marie the ten dollars, leave. Too spooked to get the job done anyhow.

THIRTY

Go to the O'Hara place for Sunday dinner. Glory sat at the table with the others, a red scarf round her head, go nice with her brown face.

Jolene wear onea them white shirts like she did in town with crisp new overalls. She gave me a lemon sucking face.

"Don't remember invitin you."

What got me on her bad side? "You try stayin in that cabin with Clyde after eatin collard greens all week."

Good to see Little Joe enjoyed the fried chicken and mash tatters with gravy. Last few weeks after Jo Belle passed he spend lotta time by hisself, didn't eat much. He drink apple cider not turned hard.

Lulahbelle take a splash or two from the jug cause she didn't hate the taste like Little Joe. We all tell her how life ain't fair, how she get in the family way again soon.

We eat biscuits with strawberry preserves Lulahbelle's kin bring when they come pay respects.

"Glad her folks don't stay long, sure enough."

"Me too." Lulahbelle show Little Joe her sweet girl face.

"Some folks don't know when they not welcome," Jolene said.

Get a feeling Jolene's words mean me.

"Now for my surprise." Jolene nodded at Big Jack. "Get that cigar box from the sleeping room. Don't open it." After he put the yellow box with a orange rim in fronta her she looked round the table at us like she gonna do a magic trick. She opened the lid. Inside a flat bottle fit snug. "This how I gonna sell my shine at the smoke shop."

"Right good idea," Big Jack said.

Glory crossed her arms. "I find dem bottles."

"I make the whiskey. I wanna sell the stuff in my shop. So I say the idea mine."

Glory waved a hand at Jolene.

"Funny thing you show up." Jolene eyed me. "Got a job for you. Come on."

Followed Jolene to the barn. Couple boxes of bottles next to some jugs.

"I need you to fill them flat bottles with shine. You spill one drop, see what trouble the mess get you."

She sat on a hay bale, I sat on the ground, uncorked a jug. White lightning smell covered the stink of mule and chicken shit. Poured real careful like. Tried not to look at Jolene's hawk stare, tell my hand not to shake.

"Somethin you wanna tell me?"

"Yes'm." Capped the first bottle. "A cone up at the still. Make this here job easier."

"Don't got time to go tote that down."

Why didn't she help or tell Little Joe help?

After I filled five bottles she said, "I ride with you all the way to Cedar Springs from Swift River Tuesday night. Why you don't tell me you seen Ana Marie? Got somethin to hide?"

Freeze still holding up jug and bottle. "Didn't knowed you care much."

"She say you play with her face paint, that all."

Poured some more. Drip rolled off the bottle, down my hand. Set down the whiskey.

"Try drawin a picture. Never put nonea that goop on my face."

"You didn't pitch no woo with her. She say you not no real man."

Wished Jolene kicked me, not said them words.

"She a good pal a yourn. Doin them things with her didn't seem right."

Jolene leaned close to me. "Then why you go there?"

No come back jump to my head.

"I gonna tell you this one time." She stand, looked down on me. "You work for me. Not that bootlegger."

"You say Cob a nice fella."

"Don't matter." She pointed her finger at me. "You might like his war yarns and his fine café food, but no more. Pick me up on time."

Didn't knowed how I gonna get loose a Cob. Gotta sell to him or the O'Hara likker business go down to a trickle. Gotta stay with him to get my money but Jolene kick me out if I do.

When the bottles full I sipped at what left in onea them jugs.

THIRTY-ONE

"Back in the Great War we used to say there's more than one way to kill the Hun." Cob looked at me like he a hound, me a possum he got up a tree. "Maybe you make your delivery earlier then you'll have plenty of time to get that tomato."

"Not safe unloadin in daylight." Reckoned he testing me.

"Well, Bucko, maybe you come into town, get my truck, drive to Cedar Springs, pack up, come back here. Save me time loading the goods from the hollow tree."

"If'n Jolene get wind she ain't gonna like it."

"Who's to say she'll find out. She still don't know I buy from the Harveys."

Driving funner than chasing a greased pig, truck run like a greased pig too. Reckoned no way Jolene gonna sniff out them there secrets. Little Joe ain't gonna tell but I gotta take care not to let on to Clyde.

The next week I get the truck bout noon, headed outta town. Right before the Mill Creek turn off I spotted a colored fella. He shine his white teeth at me, waved friendly like. Reckoned no whiskey in the back so it fine to offer him a ride.

"Where you headed?"

He jumped in. "Place they call Glad Town." His skin darker than Glory. Said his name John Henry.

"This here's the road, all right. They put on a Cherokee show down there. You parta that?"

"Yes, sir."

Smelled likker on him, he didn't act fried.

"Gonna play pie-anna for em," he said. "Surprise me you stop."

"That knapsack a yourn look right heavy. Ain't the kind thing to let a man walk when you can let him ride. Only take you far as Cedar Springs. Ain't a bad walk to Glad Town from there."

"Done see much chance makin pals round here."

'Glad Town got some right nice colored folk."

"They got pretty girls? I's shore wants to find me a nice lady friend."

Idea popped in my head. "Well, I let you off at Fresh Farms Country Market. Make sure you go in, say a howdy-do to my friend Glory."

Liked doing more than one good deed in a day.

THIRTY-TWO

Didn't knowed why Cob so good bout giving me plenty time to pick Jolene up for a couple weeks. Welcomed my good luck, hightailed it to the smoke shop.

"You stayin here."

"In town?"

"In here. I reckon I make more money with the store open Wednesdays. But I gotta check on things at home, deliver the eggs too. So you sleepin in the back, run the store tomorrow."

"Me? Run the shop?" Reckoned she gonna crack a smile, laugh soon.

"Why not. You know bout makin change, don't you?" Jolene grabbed my arm, dragged me to the cash register. She opened the drawer, take out three greenbacks. "Say some fella come in wanna buy a box a cigars with these here bills and they cost two dollars, seventy-five cents. What you give him back?"

My counting good. Put my hand in the drawer, pulled out a coin. "Two bits."

Jolene gave me a look what said I earned her trust. Still worry bout my lack a reading. Reckon when a customer name a tobacco I find the kind by the picture on the box. Gonna make that gal proud.

When she gone the store feel awful empty. Never stayed there at night cept that one time when me, Jolene, Little Joe fixed up the place. Use to tobacco smells, they get stronger when the doors locked.

Go in back. Table, chairs, cot, small coal stove all nice and tidy way Jolene keep them. Opened and shut drawers, tried to learn more bout Jolene, didn't touch nothing.

How I gonna sleep on the cot, not mess stuff up like Jolene tell me? Turned the key on the electric light to off. Keep my overalls on, lay down on the cot. Pillow smelled like Jolene, give me tingles.

Sleep played hard to get like a hanky a big wind blow off a clothesline. That shop quieter than the woods with no owls or fires crackling. Didn't sip much city likker with Cob. Knowed Jolene got whiskey in them flat bottles, a drink might help.

A rattle from somewhere make me sit up. Nother rattle. Reckoned Sheriff Clayton make sure all doors locked. Next sound ain't no rattle. Somebody break the front door.

My shotgun in the far corner. Fumbled in the dark. Bumped a broom. Catch the handle before it fall. Something else clattered.

Slipped in the front room ready to swing that broomstick. Only shadows round the window and open door. A match strike. Behind the flame lighting a candle shined Snake Harvey's face.

Run at him with the broom. He stepped sideways, dropped the candle, flame go out. Snake latched on the stick, twist. I hold tight. Snake drive forward. Backed me into a shelf, pinned my windpipe with the broomstick.

Snake smelled like pig slop. Outta the corner of my eye a shadow moved by the door. Pushed back. Take in air.

He stumbled. I go down on toppa him, didn't wanna let go my weapon what landed over his head. He twisted his hips, throwed me off. My grip on the broomstick come loose.

We both scrambled to our feet. My hands out, ready. Tried to guess where he at in the dark. He rushed me. I throwed a fist he catch. Snake trapped me with his chest on the wall fulla stogies again. Before I blink a cold sharp blade on my face.

A click sounded like a gun getting cocked.

"Stay right there." Jolene's voice.

Light go on. Snake's wild eyes inches from mine.

"Let him go or I shoot."

Snake stepped back. Jolene got her pistol on him. Gun I gave her from Mason the revenue fella. She pointed it straight at Snake's heart.

"Drop the knife."

He did like she said.

"She tell me you ain't here tonight," Snake said.

"Bet you eat dog shit if a pretty girl say to." Jolene hold the pistol steady.

"You get that harlot to lie. You don't dare shoot me after you pull that trick."

Jolene eyed me. "Get that rope under the counter, tie this here rapscallion's hands nice and tight."

Followed when Jolene marched Snake down the street to the courthouse. She pounded till the door opened. Sheriff Clayton yawned, twisted a finger in onea them ears as big as Clyde's. The Sheriff shoved Snake in a cell.

"Ou! You don't gotta get so rough." Snake hold his shoulder what hit the wall.

"I stop gettin rough when you tell your Uncle Rupert to fetch back my sister." Sheriff Clayton pulled a fart sniffing face. "Oh, that's right. You don't know where they get themselves off to."

"I gonna git you O'Hara sons-a-bitches," Snake yelled through the bars.

Back at the smoke shop I feel like Jolene pulled a chair out from under me.

"You knowed Snake gonna break in tonight."

"He didn't know Ana Marie my friend. She tell Snake she her new fella if he get back at the gal what steal her last beau. He happy to oblige cause I a O'Hara."

"How come you don't tell me the plan?"

Jolene looked at me like I some half-drowned pup. "How come you didn't tell me you seen Snake watchin the shop?"

"Didn't want you worryin." If I run into Ana Marie again gotta remember to stop my jaw from wagging. Still feel Snake's knife on my skin, my windpipe still sore. Lighted a smoke to get my mind off the fight. "What you do if'n I get hurt or kilt?"

"Seen you in action." Jolene squeezed my arm. "Reckon a big strong man like you take care a hisself.'

Leastwise she said I a man.

THIRTY-THREE

After spring planting Jolene didn't come to Cedar Springs no more, at all. Me and Little Joe wondered why.

"Reckon the shop make money on Wednesday," I said. "But her stayin in town on Sunday when the shop closed make no sense."

"I ask Jole who gonna deliver the eggs, she walk outta the room. Glory on her bad side gain, that worry me, sure enough."

We take to making trips to Swift River on Saturdays to pay Jolene a call. Little Joe liked getting off the farm when he get the chance. He happy that day cause he put nother bun in Lulahbelle's oven.

Heat so thick flies buzzed real slow. We walked down Main Street jawing bout all the people, automobiles and such till we come cross Crow Tritt flapping his chops with Sheriff Clayton.

"If I weren't married, she be the one I court," Sheriff Clayton said. "The woman sure a peach."

"You ain't the only man I hear them words from," Crow said.

When Crow leave Little Joe said, "Hey Sheriff. New gal in town?"

"Nope." Sheriff looked him in the eye. "We talkin bout that sister a yourn."

Little Joe looked surprised as a bitch getting humped by a billy goat. "Jole pullin in the fellas seem odd, sure enough."

Sheriff tipped his hat to Little Joe. "Give your big sis a howdy-do from me."

We watched the sheriff go. Little Joe looked up at me. "I hope that if Jole marry somebody she choose you."

Me? Getting hitched never come to mind, leastwise not yet. What I got to offer? Reckoned now I gotta go up gainst a bunch of other fellas. Pulled out my hanky, wiped sweat from my neck.

We stopped at the café. Get lucky cause they got some sodypop in. We take one over to Jolene. She poured her pop in a jar with some shine. Me and Little Joe drink from the bottles.

"Hear you got plenty a gentlemen callers, sure enough."

She waved a hand at Little Joe. "Oh, they only like me cause I give em free whiskey samples. Nothin to it. Who you hear that from?"

"Crow Tritt."

Jolene cut her eyes at him. "You ought not talk to him."

"He only a Harvey by marryin." Little Joe stand taller. "You talk to him too. Seen him in this here smoke shop."

"That different." Jolene smashed out a cigarette in a ashtray. "I nice as pie to him. Never know when I might need him to put in a good word to his brother the judge."

Didn't knowed them things, they come together in my head. "That why Snake get off so easy when he break in this here shop."

"You just now figurin that one out?" Jolene looked at me like I burped onions in her face.

"You keep sayin you gonna get back at them there Harveys for what Snake done." Tried giving Jolene a hard stare back. "You ain't done nothin so far."

"I been busy. But I workin on a plan of late." Jolene stirred nother splash a white lightning in with the pop in her jar. "Stub put on a poker game up to the Harvey place Saturday nights."

"Oh, yeah." Little Joe turned to me with a twinkle in his eye. "Harveys love them some poker. That how Rupert Harvey lose the land his pa gonna give him, then Rupert run way, steal his pa's pocket watch, never come back." That Little Joe's favorite yarn.

"I talkin." Jolene give Little Joe a look like he a young'un clinging to her leg. "I order some foldin chairs from the mercantile. Reckon I run my own poker game outta my store's back room. Folks come to mine cause it right here in town. I sell more whiskey, Harveys sell less."

Idea sounded like one that work. Wanted the Harveys to take a dip in their likker business. Only problem, the poker game mean more fellas in the shop, more fellas what might wanna court Jolene.

Next Saturday I go to town by my lonesome cause Lulahbelle didn't feel so good and Little Joe didn't wanna leave.

"Hey, Jolene," I said. "They outta cold pop at the café."

"You come visit me with empty hands?" She wear a clean white shirt with black britches, no suit coat with the heat hotter than a coffee pot at day break. "Hear they got strawberry ice cream today. Get me somma that."

She didn't gotta be so mean. Think maybe I get ice cream for me, not her.

"Why, hey." John Henry the colored fella what I gave a ride to that time run up to me right outside the shop. "Glad I bumps into you."

He got whiskey smell on him.

"Ain't seen you since I drop you over to Fresh Farms."

"Work on the Cherokee show shore keep me busy. I stays outta town. Folks done seem too fonda me."

A gal in a hat like a upside down basket come our way. John Henry stepped off the sidewalk so I did too, till the gal passed us.

"Oh looky there." John Henry pointed to Stands Like Wood. "You like them there colors on him? I do that paintin."

"Must say he one handsome wooden Injun. And I shore wanna thank you."

John Henry stick out a hand, I shaked it.

"Thank me?"

"Yessir. Done believe I runs into Glory for a long time, if it ain't for you. I owes you my happiness. Gonna ask her be my wife."

His face made me feel like one them rockets from the newspaper Little Joe keep blowing bout. Bring back my giving spirit. Go on over to the café for ice creams for me and for Jolene. They served the stuff in cookies shaped like cones. Best idea I seen in long time.

Smoke shop closed when I get back. Reckoned Jolene wilted in the heat, decided to try on a nap. Did her a favor by eating both strawberry ice creams. Headed on home to Cedar Springs.

Tuesday afternoon I find Cob coming out his boarding house with a chubby boy. "Whatcha know, Bucko?"

"Think you knowed what I knowed," Didn't want the boy figuring nothing out.

"Oh, Tuesday so soon? I clean forgot." He slapped his pants pocket. "Left my key upstairs. Hold your horses kiddos, be right back."

Cob go in. Me and the boy set on the steps not saying nothing. Bout fifteen minutes before Cob come out. Wondered what take him so long. He dropped his truck key in my hand, give me a dime too. "Get yourself a snack, Bucko." He go off with the boy.

Think on how I gonna use the money to get ice cream for Jolene cause I eat what I get her last Saturday.

Before I take two steps in the smoke shop Jolene come at me pointing a finger.

"You." Her face red like a boiling copper pot.

"Wha..."

"I seen you with that Harvey boy. Big buddies, huh?"

"What Har..."

"Don't tell me you don't know." Her whiskey breath blasted in my face. "On that porch where that bootlegger live."

"He didn't..."

"You lyin dog. Turner buy shine from the Harveys. You know and don't tell me."

Throw one a them ice cream cones, it knocked a box fulla stogies off a shelf.

"Cob pay us a lotta money. You keep most. Don't share with us like you ought."

"Get outta here. Never come back." Spit from her words hit my face.

"Don't wanna come back."

"And don't show your face on neither my farms. Gonna tell the boys you not allowed no more."

"Glad to get shut a that chicken shit."

Throw tuther ice cream. Some tobaccy pipes clattered off where they hang.

Slammed the front door so hard I lucky the glass didn't break.

THIRTY-FOUR

Moped round town, cooled off some. Didn't wanna lose the O'Haras. Didn't wanna lose Jolene. Gotta find a way to make her see reason. First gotta deal with Cob.

Slipped in the rooming house, sneaked upstairs. Didn't wanna set on the porch, Jolene see from the smoke shop. In Cob's room I sat backward on my usual chair so I faced the door. Stayed clear not to touch Cob's chair.

When Cob opened the door he looked at me like he coming in for breakfast expecting grits, find biscuits and sausage gravy. "You bring in your load already?"

"How come you put me out in the open with a Harvey?"

"What? You mean B. J.? You have a problem with him?" Cob yanked loose his tie.

"You knowed the O'Haras and Harveys in a feud and I on the O'Hara side."

He slapped a hand on his stubbled chin. "I forgot. These silly feud things don't mean a thing to me."

Stand, meet his eyes.

"How you forget somethin like that? Jolene ain't gonna sell shine to you no more now she knowed you deal with the Harveys."

Cob brushed by me, plopped in his chair. "Situation isn't that bad."

"Why you make me stay on that there porch with that Harvey pig for so long?"

"Had a bit of stomach trouble." Cob grabbed his gut, shoot me a prune face.

Stared down at him. He what come out when folks get belly pains.

"Now I got more trouble than I knowed what to do with. Jolene seen me from her shop. She madder than a bobcat with a knot in his tail. Tell me git."

Take his truck key outta my overalls, flipped it on the table.

"Hold on, Bucko." Cob put up a big paw. "I'll go over and talk to her. She likes me. I'll tell her the mistake my fault. Relax."

Sat, take out a smoke to puff on. "How I posta relax? I lose my best pals, my job, my place to bed down."

Cob slide his key my way. "Go pick up your delivery for me like nothing happened."

"Jolene tell me don't step foot on her land."

"They got telephones in Cedar Springs?"

"Nope."

"Then unless she's got a carrier pigeon, her brothers won't know she banned you. Meanwhile, I'll smooth things over. Everything fine by the time you get back."

Drive to the O'Hara place. Didn't wanna put all my eggs in Cob's basket. Reckoned I gotta get Little Joe to tell Jolene how I didn't knowed that boy B. J. Harvey.

Truck chugged to a halt in the O'Hara front yard. Little Joe set on the front porch, his hands on his face like his cheeks gonna fly off if he let go. Big Jack come over from the barn. I meet them two on the porch.

"Lulahbelle restin now?" Big Jack looked like he gonna get a tooth pulled.

"She fine, sure nuff. Gonna take some time to get over."

"This might help." Big Jack screwed the top off a jar. Smell a likker burned my nose. He set the jar on the side table.

Little Joe put a hand on the jar, moved the whiskey way. He stand real slow, go down the steps, crossed the yard to the creek.

Reckoned Lulahbelle lose her baby. Said nothing bout my problems when Big Jack helped me load the shine.

Go back to Swift River. One lucky thing, Cob still dressed when I get to his room but his shirt ain't buttoned.

"Got good news," he said.

"Jolene ain't mad no more?" Take in air, hold it in my chest.

"She's going to keep selling me her shine," Cob said. "Told her B. J. give me a fake name, that he tried to get me to buy whiskey from his daddy because the bootlegger they sell to don't pay as much as I do. She snapped up the lie like that." He snapped his fat fingers.

Let out the air, sit down. "So I still workin for her? Stay in Cedar Springs?"

"Well, that's the bad news." He shrugged outta his shirt, lay it over his lap. "For some reason that hardheaded woman's staying real angry at you. I couldn't convince her otherwise, no matter what I said. Don't know why."

Feel like a empty sack after all the taters dropped out.

"But I got a plan, Bucko." Cob slapped some jack down on the table. "Money for the load you bring in. How much of this does Jolene usually give you?"

"A whole ten dollars. Gonna miss that good wage."

"You work for me, I pay you twice that a week."

"Nope. That don't help me win back trust from Jolene."

"You save up enough money, you can buy her something nice. Then not only will she like you again, she might love you."

"If'n I stay in Swift River Jolene right under my nose. That make me sick when she don't care bout me."

Idea a working for Cob made me more sick, like a bad hangover.

"Where you going, Bucko? Work for five dollars a week shoveling horse shit? Nobody's going to pay you what I will. With your skills? Don't think you can even read."

"You learn me to drive. I do that."

"True. You'll do lots of driving for me. I'll ride along, show you where to go. You won't have to read directions."

"Think I learn me a new trade."

"You want somebody to teach you new things, I'm the man for the job." Cob jabbed a thumb at that hair on his chest.

Ain't gonna get no schooling from Cob, if it the last thing I do. Gotta figure out where I gonna go.

THIRTY-FIVE

Never wanted to learn me clay pot making but painting them pots sounded real good. Take the ten dollars for delivering my last load of O'Hara whiskey, headed out to Juniper County. Climbed that mountain to the cabin where I last seen my sister Sammy Jean and the redhead woman. Ain't neither a them in sight when I come up the path.

Mason, the revenue fella, walked a goat crossed the yard. He pushed up his spectacles with one finger. "Wondered if we'd ever see you again."

"Surprise me you still here."

"Nowhere else I'd rather be."

Sammy Jean run up from behind the big oven where they cooked the clay pots, hugged me, bout knocked me over. "So nice you visitin us."

Didn't say how I planned on staying more'n a spell.

We go in the cabin where they tell me Dullsain got bad headaches, she take some strong potions she mixed up to heal them, then passed on one night in her sleep. Reckoned doing for herself without the redhead woman what make Sammy Jean look so growed up.

For supper Sammy Jean put out greens mixed with nuts, covered with a sauce made with goat cream and herbs they growed in the garden.

"I snare a rabbit for us tomorrow. Maybe shoot a deer, keep us in meat for some time," I said.

Sammy Jean looked at Mason, he pulled a face. "Eatin meat not somethin we do much," she said.

"We can do some fishing." Mason wiped his mouth with a cloth. "Killing fish for food doesn't seem as cruel as killing other animals."

No meat? Mason ain't from them parts, got hisself some peculiar ideas. A picture a Lulahbelle's fried chicken come in my head.

Give the small cabin a once over. Food in my belly soured. Cut my eyes at Mason. "Where you sleep?"

"In the shed I fixed up on the other side of the yard."

Hoped my little sister ain't got herself defiled.

"I help wash up the kitchen."

"No need." Mason take my plate. "Sammy Jean and I have the clean up under control. We've got it running like Henry Ford's assembly line."

Watched them at the sink, arms close to touching. My hackles go up. Reckoned some defiling might happen soon.

When they get done Mason said to me. "Let's take a walk."

Good idea. Aimed on telling him what I do if he messed with my sister.

We stopped under a tree. I tapped out a smoke, seen only two more left in the pack. Didn't knowed where to buy smokes on that mountain. No Fresh Farms down the road like in Cedar Springs.

Mason set his spectacles straight, cleared a frog outta his windpipe. "I would like your permission to ask your sister for her hand in marriage."

"You wanna marry Sammy Jean? She too young."

"She thinks she's sixteen."

Reckoned that bout right. "Why you want my say so?"

"Sammy Jean went down to your folks' house to tell them she met somebody special. Your Pa didn't remember her name. When she told that to your ma, she got mad and told Sammy Jean to do some chores. Sammy Jean says she's never going back."

Knowed the feeling. Didn't wanna go back to the folks, Cedar Springs neither. "Reckon me and Sammy Jean the only blood kin we got for each other." Take a drag on my cigarette. "What you gotta offer my sister? You goin back to huntin stills to support y'all?"

"Never." Mason shake his head like a dog climbing outta a swimming hole. "Left the ATF far behind. I feel so at home here, like I'm meant for this place. We do well enough. Sell our pots and some rolled tobacco outside the trading post on Saturdays. We've got the goat and I find eggs from chickens that live in the woods."

"Lot easier gettin them there eggs if'n you keep them chickens in a coop."

"Oh, I couldn't do that to those poor little things."

Reckoned nothing wrong with that if he liked hunting for eggs and the chickens happier. Grind out my smoke. "Let me sleep on givin you my go-ahead to marry Sammy Jean."

In the cabin Sammy Jean got a book in her hands. Picture on the cover got onea them highfaluting ladies with a gent in a bowtie peeking over the gal's shoulder. "You readin that?"

"Yep." Sammy Jean   grinned like she got a secret. "Mason teach me. He get me this here *Jane Eyre* too."

She lucky she got somebody to learn her things like reading. "You like that fella?"

"I love Mason somethin fierce."

Reckoned in the morning I gotta tell Mason he get to marry my sister. Recollected how Little Joe said he like the idea of me marrying his sister. Feel sad, like a mule left out in the rain.

Sammy Jean sleep in Dullsain's bed, I sleep on my sister's old cot. Hard to drift off in a place so strange to me. Wished for white lightning but no place round there to get me nonea that.

Waked in the wee hours, music playing somewhere. Wondered why Sammy Jean playing the harp in the dark. Fumbled for a match, striked it on the box. Music stopped. The harp leaned on the wall, nobody touched it. Sammy Jean in the bed, eyes shut, mouth open.

Rest of the night sleep played harder to catch than a fly on a plowed field fulla chicken shit.

For breakfast Sammy Jean set out strong tea. No coffee. Apple sauce with honey. Studied the small jug the honey in. "If'n you make some bigger, they be perfect shine jugs."

"You gonna miss mixin up that there moonshine, ain't you?" Sammy Jean put her hand on mine.

"I only tired." Tried to perk up. "You hear that music last night?"

"Oh, that's Dullsain. Her spirit stay round, keep her eye on us."

Sipped the hot tea to warm the chill Sammy Jean's words send down my back.

"She still talk to me." Sammy Jean looked over my head like the redheaded woman stand behind me. "I got the special sight like her. Last night I dream she tell me you wanna stay here but you gotta go be a stranger." She moved her stare, looked me in the eye. "A stranger with folks you already meet."

That didn't make sense. What bout that tale Ana Marie spin for me bout Jolene and the fortuneteller? I onea them three strangers Jolene meet in one day in Cedar Springs. Spilled out the story to Sammy Jean, finished by telling her bout Jolene getting mad at me for no good reason.

"Oh." Sammy Jean made her eyes big. "I gettin this feelin. You the one gonna help Jolene become a legend. Somehow you gotta win her trust back."

All that talk bout special sight and fortunetellers set my mind buzzing like a beehive. Wished me a smoke, some grits and bacon, cup a coffee with a splash a corn squeezings.

Us three hiked into Juniper. Used the last five dollars from the ten I come with to pay for their matree-mony license. For a wedding present I gave Sammy Jean and Mason ten dollars I got saved in my shoe.

"Thank you." Mason pump my hand. "Now that I'm moving to the cabin you can stay in the shed. I've got it pretty comfortable."

"Much obliged but think I best take my leave." Idea of living near a cabin that got a haint round feel like my bare feet in creek water in January.

Take one thing with me from their place. Onea them hand-rolled stogies.

THIRTY-SIX

"Told you, Bucko." Cob pulled a scolding face. "You don't give a cigar to somebody that own their own smoke shop."

No way to put in words why I liked to give Jolene stogies. "Where's that there cigar if'n she didn't take it?" Hold out my hand. "What she say?"

Cob patted his chest pocket. "Must've left the thing on the counter. Only hand-rolled rabbit tobacco. Not worth a whole penny." He shrugged off his coat, unbutton his shirt. "She still real mad at you. Used some nasty words."

Take a pull on the city likker. My hope splintered like a pinecone from a tall tree falling on a hard rock.

"Cheer up, Bucko. Now that you work for me you'll make enough money to impress that hardheaded woman the way a gentleman should."

Put my mind on what I gonna do with the jack Cob said I gonna get working for him, how to use that money so Jolene think me somebody she needed to take up with. Buy land? No, O'Haras got plenty of land. Maybe a truck like Cob's. Gotta think more on that problem.

Parked the truck down by the river in a place right handy for picking up that night's load a shine. Walked the long way into town cause the shorter way take me by the smoke shop. Wanna steer clear of Jolene. Ain't gonna think bout her till she forgive me.

Rounded the church, crossed to tuther side of the street. Law, there be Ana Marie looking in some store window. She wear a flat hat, her hair in a braid down her back. Her blood red dress got no sleeves, showed off her milky white arms, black gloves halfway up. Black stockings and tall shoes make me wanna stare at them long legs for a spell.

If there one person what talk Jolene into liking me again, Ana Marie the one. Get myself ready to do some fast jawing. She strolled my way, a few shops down. Outta a doorway stepped Snake Harvey, stopped Ana Marie in her tracks.

"You trick me harlot."

Ana Marie peered at Snake like he a beetle crawling on her kitchen table. "Excuse me? We meet before?"

"Stop your actin. You and your tricks land me in jail two damn days. Gotta pay for a door you tell me break."

"You must think me nother girl."

"You the one tell me break in that there smoke shop, I your fella then. You lie. Cost me plenty. Now you gotta pay. Give me somma your sweet ass for free."

Ain't gonna let Snake get way with talking to nobody like that, leastwise a fancy gal like Ana Marie.

Get up close behind the bastard. "Leave this here lady be."

Snake turned on me. "You. You give me problems too. But I takin care this one here now. So you git. Let me to my business or I take your head off."

He grabbed onea Ana Marie's gloved hands, she tried to pull her arm free.

"Get your stinkin paws off her, you rat." Reckoned I take Snake in daylight. He skinny like the slithery critter he named for.

"Now boys," Ana Marie said. "Fightin so ugly."

"Ugly. This varmint's face gonna get more that way when I done." Snake let go Ana Marie. "I gonna knock him so silly he be pissin in his shoes."

Blocked a punch from Snake, throw my own. He get me in the jaw, I sluggged him in his. He staggered back, I closed in on him, aimed nother blow. Get him in the nose. Snake backed right into Ana Marie's stuck out leg. He tumbled in the street right on his backside. Blood drip down over his lips. Shake my sore hand.

A automobile come so close to hitting Snake his hat fly off. Lotta folks ain't got automobiles, ride mules to town. Snake land on a big pile a mule shit.

Crow Tritt crossed the street. Yanked Snake to his feet. "You givin me a job keepin you outta jail." Crow dragged Snake toward tuther side a town. "Gonna tell your pa to keep you on the farm."

"I bout to learn that son-a-bitch a lesson," Snake said to Crow.

"Like how I take care ole Snake for you, ma'am?" Hoped to see Ana Marie show her pearly whites.

She didn't. "I the one what trip him."

"I stand up for you, make sure you safe. That gotta count for somethin."

Ana Marie eyed me like a hat she might wear for a party. "Maybe."

"You the only one in the world I knowed to help me." Go with her to the Cardinal's Nest Café. Hold the door for her. "Let me buy you some vittles. Ice cream sundae with a nice juicy cherry to go with your pretty pink cheeks."

"I ain't goin in there with you. You on Jolene's bad side. That one place I ain't goin."

"If'n you talk to her she sure to see reason, forgive me. How she gonna look in your fine green eyes and say no?"

"Nope." Ana Marie closed the café door, us still outside. "Makin Jolene listen a job for a hundred fellas with a hundred mules."

Rub my aching jaw. "I save you from stupid Snake Harvey."

Ana Marie turned up her apple red lips. "You do good back there."

"So you talk to Jolene for me? I knowed you get to her. You got you a special way bout you."

"Nope." She flipped her braid over her shoulder, petted the end. "But you come by the Tiffany house some time. I show you some fun, no charge."

Idea a fun with Ana Marie sounded like going over a high waterfall and down a fast creek with no log to grab hold. She walked off in her tall shoes what make her behind look like it kneading bread dough.

THIRTY-SEVEN

Cob showed me where to pick up and deliver the shine. Seen lots of new places, bigger towns than Swift River. He tell the fellas over at the warehouses I his 'associate'. Reckoned that mean I worked for him like a mule.

After he learned me them places Cob said, "Now you get to do the job all by yourself. I've got my full trust in you."

Packed lotta hay round the whiskey barrels, slide a tarp over the truck bed. Drive to a warehouse near Keelville. Cut the headlights when I get close. Fella with a handlebar mustache stopped me. "Mincemeat," I said. He rolled open the door, let me in.

Only couple lamps lighted the place, bigger'n any barn I ever seen. I wrestled the barrels outta the hay, set them on the end of the truck. "Where you want em?" I asked nother fella. Recollected Cob said his name Daniels.

Daniels studied my whiskey like I got rat piss in them barrels. "Where's Turner? I don't trust no hooch from some hick."

Them fellas wear suit coats and ties. Daniels got a black tie with a red shirt. Overalls and union suit all I wear. "Turner tell you last time I do his deliverin."

"Nah, that guy look much smarter'n you."

"This the same one," mustache fella said. He watched from over by the rolling door.

Jolene used the words 'no-tail-bear'. This white fella, Daniels, looked more like a bear than any negre I ever seen. His face like the back end a onea them bears.

"I gonna have to tap every one you bring. Don't wanna get swindled by no rube." Daniels go get something outta some box.

"You knowed Turner ain't gonna pass off no bad goods." Picked up my shotgun from beside the truck. Bad idea.

Daniels slide the strap off his shoulder, get his gun in the bend of his arm. He got him onea them guns what named Tommy. "I gonna sample every barrel. Gonna start with that one." Rat-tat-tat. Rat-tat-tat. Rat-tat-tat.

Jumped like lightning come at me. Barrel on the end got holes in it like a wasp nest. Shine spilled everywhere.

Stepped back. Daniels tried all the whiskey from the other barrels. My shotgun longer but them Tommy guns got more power. Maybe I save up, get me onea them guns. Maybe two, give one to Jolene. That might make her like me gain. She sure liked the pistol I gave her.

"Name's Ace." Fella with the mustache stick out his hand to me. He smelt a bit like he get friendly with a skunk, but then he lighted a smoke. Stink come from his cigarettes, not no critter. "Daniels ain't always such a palooka. Sometimes he one sharp cat."

"Fella like him oughta get a job as a seat in a shithouse."

"Nifty truck you got. How fast that machine go?"

"Depends if'n I drivin in the hills or smooth roads like y'all got down here."

"You got dough, I can put swell speed on for you."

Studied Ace. "Why you do that?"

"Can use more green. Warehouse owner don't pay much. More work come long I snap the job up." He snapped with both hands. "I don't saw many logs anyway."

"Sorry, pal," I said. "Truck ain't mine. Belong to Turner. I work for him."

"Talk to your big cheese bout me and that engine. I talk to Daniels bout his bein a drag. We all get long fine."

Tell Ace I think on his deal. Go get the jack for the load from Daniels.

Counted the greenbacks. "This short."

"I ain't gonna pay for the barrel you let get shot up."

"Still ain't enough." Reckoned Daniels think my counting ain't so good.

"Your boss complain, give him this." Daniels handed me a package, something soft wrapped in paper.

"What's in here?"

"You best hope your boss think this little surprise worth the dough I keep."

Wear holes in my socks pacing out back of the boardinghouse. What I gonna tell Cob bout the missing money? Gotta get the telling over with.

Something come to me on my way upstairs. What I fret for? Things worked out for the best. Cob ain't the sort to kill me over a few dollars. Gotta tell him I careless with that there barrel. Likely he tell me git, then I free. Didn't knowed where I find me nother job, worry over that later.

"Oh good," Cob said when I come in his room. "You bring the package." He snatched the bundle outta my hand, tossed it on his bed.

"What's in there?"

"That's my business." He poked his finger at his hairy chest peeking through his open shirt, then stick the finger at me. "Not yours."

Gave Cob greenbacks I collected. He cut his eyes at me. "This all? You already take your pay?"

"Nope. I drop onea them barrels. It break in pieces. Reckon I ain't workin for you no more."

"Hold on, Bucko. You going to let that happen again?"

"No sir." Why I go and say that? Something inside me want this job? Weight like a soaked-through blanket dropped on me.

"I said I have my full trust in you and I stand by that. Accidents happen. Now run along, play in the river, do what you do." He waved his meaty paw at me.

"I wanna tell you what some fella say bout your truck."

"Not today, Bucko. Got a new supplier to entertain. One day you'll understand."

Cob didn't make me sit and drink with him no more. On one hand I welcomed my good luck, on tuther I missed him learning me bout different kinda likker, his stories bout the Great War.

"Only take a minute. You gonna wanna hear this. Pour me somma that dark whiskey."

He gave me the half-full bottle, shooed me on my way.

Passed a young'un on the porch, he ain't more'n two and half feet tall. Cob tell his moonshiners to send their boys to make the drop-offs, tell me the law didn't suspect the half growed one so much.

Nona the boys I seen bringing the goods looked old enough to knowed a whisker from a sprig a grass, cept maybe B. J. Harvey.

THIRTY-EIGHT

That winter frost hunkered down like a handfed house cat. Cob talked his boardinghouse lady into letting me sleep in the cellar for chopping firewood and shoveling coal. Lots of times after deliveries I bedded-down in the back of the truck.

One Saturday in January Cob tell me to haul him to Glad Town. Go in to get me a drink while Cob get done what he go there to do. Hoped to watch John Henry on the piano. Clyde sat on a stool, ain't seen him in a coon's age.

"Reckon you get you a lotta corn butterin time at the Grady place with me gone."

Clyde looked like he trying to do arithmetic with letters. He ain't got the brains God gave a rutabaga so I pumped my open fist.

"Disgusting." He acted like he talking to the jar he drink from. "I told not to talk to you."

"Jolene say that? You see her much?"

"She check on the place a whole lot, every week."

"What she say bout me?"

"Nothing. I take care of the place so good she don't notice you gone."

"Your farmin get that much better so fast? Where'd you get them blisters?"

"Lost my gloves, that's all."

"Real men don't need no gloves. Jolene got her some good calluses."

"I know more about her hands than you ever will."

"Then why ain't you onea them fellas at her poker game right now? Why don't you march right down to Swift River and sweep her off her feet?"

Clyde's face glowed red. He stand. Ain't much taller'n me.

"Why don't you?"

He shoved me. His skinny arms didn't budge me much.

"Cause I got me a plan."

Shoved Clyde back. He stumbled, balled his fist, cocked his arm.

Ain't scared of his punch. Gonna clobber him good.

A hand catched Clyde's wrist.

"Hold it there," Cob said. "I'm not going to let anybody hit my friend here."

I headed the truck back to Swift River.

"How come you tell Clyde you borrow my money?"

"So that's Clyde. Makes sense. Figured if you fighting with another gent it be over that Jolene bearcat."

"You the one what loan me dough, if'n I ask, which I ain't."

"No need to ask. I'm giving you a raise. You now make $25 a week."

"What? How come? What I gotta do for that?"

"You deserve it. You load this truck up with product faster than I think possible."

"Ain't hard work. Only liftin and shovin."

"You're smart too. Great idea you presented me with to increase the horsepower in this truck."

"That my pal Ace."

"So you'll see why I told, what's his name, Clyde, you loaned me money. We have to spread the word that you're a man of means. Follow my lead and you'll impress that woman in no time."

"But I don't care none bout what Clyde thinks. He never go to Swift River to visit with Jolene. Ask me, I say he fraida Sheriff Clayton."

"No, no. I believe I saw that Clyde in the smoke shop with Sheriff Clayton too."

"When that?"

"Doesn't matter, Bucko. You should just sit back and let me handle your reputation. Of course we won't let on what business we do, but I'll let people know you're my best associate. We'll get you a new suit of clothes too."

Cob stand up for me to Clyde, said I do a good job selling the shine, he wanted folks to take notice of me. Maybe I wrong bout Cob, maybe he ain't so bad after all.

THIRTY-NINE

Work go long like a stick caught in a creek after a rainstorm. Before I knowed winter turned to spring, spring to summer.

Little Joe the only O'Hara I got to see. When he bring in a load we sat down by the river. I sampled the shine, he drink water.

"You got the life, sure enough."

"Me?" I said. "Got you for a pal. But I ain't got your kin."

"I never been outta these here parts cept a couple trips to the county fair. You get to go places. Excitin places."

"Excitin ain't always so good." Think bout them warehouse fellas, like Daniels, what Cob called goons.

"You know that tale bout Rupert Harvey. I like that yarn cause Rupert take his wife, Sherrif Clayton's sister, leave these here parts for good. Rupert go find him some adventure. Gotta get me somma that. You gotta need help doin what you do."

"Got a bad feelin bout this. What Lulahbelle do if'n somethin happen to you?"

"Nothin gonna happen. You good at what you do, sure enough."

That what Cob said that winter. He leave me to my lonesome that year, let me do the work, only seen him to hand off the greenbacks, get orders. Only job I liked better, the one on the O'Hara farms.

Little Joe musta seen in my head cause he said, "You let me go long sometime, I talk to Jole bout her forgivin you."

"Cob get awful mad if'n I go behind his back."

"What'd you care? You never like that bastard, sure enough."

"Make lotta money. Don't wanna mess that up."

"He not gonna find out nothing. I gotta get me some adventure."

"Gonna pick up some new barrels in a couple days. You help with that, all go well, we talk bout somethin more." Reckoned that job safe enough. Hoped Cob didn't get wind of this.

FORTY

Little Joe showed early. His overalls bib hang loose on one side cause he said the end come off, he didn't take time to find some wire. He seemed happy like a worm in wet dirt.

Loading barrels go fast with his help. Not big barrels like we mixed mash in or folks keep pickles in. Them ones bout the size a washtub.

Ride back to town go quick too with Little Joe's gabbing. He praised my driving, asked me to learn him.

We stick some barrels in the hollow tree for Cob's suppliers to get when they delivered the full ones. Others I planned to stash in the bushes. Wanted to get the chore done quick like, get Little Joe outta there.

Parted branches, come on the business enda a handgun. Sweat poured down my back. Knowed something bad gonna happen.

"Hold it right there, Bucko." Cob break through. Dusted off his shirt with the hand not holding the pistol. "I don't remember enlisting two guys for this job."

"Sorry Cob. Reckon no harm this one time."

"You ever think to ask first, Bucko? I need to know everything that goes on in this operation. Get it? You don't know when someone can't be trusted."

"But this here's my best buddy," I said.

He gonna tell me git? Didn't wanna lose that job.

"Not Rufus' fault, Mr. Turner. I beg him to let me. And I aim to do more work for you, sure enough. Help Rufus deliver to the city, if you want."

"I'll think the proposal over. You a friend of Bucko here, you must be a good egg." Cob stick his handgun in his belt. "Right now let's take care of the rest of these containers. Long as I'm here I'll lend a hand."

Cob didn't carry on like a wet rooster like I reckoned. Happy that he trusted me to bring on a helper.

Little Joe take the last one off the truck but the button on his loose overalls bib catch on the barrel ring. "Dadgum thing not gettin loose." He jerked one way then tuther.

Tried to take the barrel but he shake me off. "I get it."

I stepped back.

Cob come over. "Stop twisting, kid." He hold Little Joe's shoulder, get the button out with one tug.

A shotgun get cocked. Where? Behind me. B. J. Harvey hold the stock. A Harvey got a gun on a O'Hara. I shoved Little Joe. The shotgun go off.

Cob hit the ground. Hole in his chest.

FORTY-ONE

Stub Harvey stomped into the clearing. "Wonder where my shotgun get off to. Trail you all the way from the house. Whatcha go'n shoot the bootlegger fer?"

"He shootin at Little Joe and miss." The barrel Little Joe tussled with lay under the truck, he nowhere in sight. Glad he got way from them Harveys. Wanted to run too but I gotta help Cob.

"You shoot at a O'Hara?" Stub take the weapon from his son, neared poor Cob on the ground. Stub crouched, hold a hand over Cob's mouth.

"We gotta get him up," I said.

"Barely breathin. The way he bleedin, ain't gonna last but a few minutes."

Blood pooled under Cob's arm. Doctoring ain't gonna fix him now.

Stub pulled out the empty shell.

"I ain't no O'Hara."

"A body dead or good as. I ain't worryin bout no feud, I worryin bout my boy. Sheriff Clayton, my good ole brother-in-law, gonna hang him if he get wind of this. We gotta get ridda the body."

Didn't wanna lay no hands on no dead fella. Gotta find some place to hide.

"Don't go thinkin you gettin outta this." Stub stepped close to me. "If you try'n run, I tell the Sheriff you shoot the bootlegger."

Stub tell me and B. J. bury Cob on Harvey land where no law gonna find him, ask questions. B. J. go fetched shovels. I paced round.

What I gonna do with no more Cob? I lost somebody what learned me so much, I lost my job.

B. J. dig like he throwed Cob's soul outta the hole with every shovel full. When it deep enough we dragged Cob over, rolled him in. He landed face up, eyes open. Something slithered round in my innards. Seen dead eyes like that before, don't recollect where.

"Ain't done it cause of what he did to me," B. J. said.

Wanna up-chuck. Tell my head go someplace else. Piled dirt on Cob's face.

"That Turner bastard say I too old now. Gotta send my little brother Toot."

Knowed then B. J. ain't shooting at Little Joe. His aim spot on.

Cob ain't got no kin I knowed bout. If he did they probably reckoned he get hisself kilt by a goon over some bad goods. Nobody gonna miss him.

That truck belong to me now. Cob getting the evil fate what coming to him don't mean I lose my job. It mean I the boss now.

FORTY-TWO

Find Little Joe on the porch at the O'Hara place. "Hey, Rufus. Glad you scape too." He take a sip from a tin cup. "Pretty slick how I get way, huh? I run...almost...the whole way home. I drink bunch a water. Then I start shakin. Get in a bitta this here corn squeezins." He raised his cup to me, take nother gulp.

Scratched my head in wonderment at Little Joe drinking whiskey. He never touched more'n a sip before.

"He save my life," Little Joe said to Jolene when she come up the porch steps.

"Hey, Jolene," I said. "What bring you to these parts? Hear you ain't come round in some time."

She stared at Little Joe, pay me no mind. "Stub Harvey braggin all over town his boy shoot at a O'Hara."

"He done." Little Joe hiccupped. "But Rufus here shove me out the way. He a reeeaaal pal." Nother hiccup.

"What's got into you?" She picked up his cup, smelt the white lightening. "You in the bag, how bout some for me?" She fetched a cup.

"When I push Little Joe the shot hit Cob Turner. He get hisself kilt."

"Now Cob gone you help round the farms gain, sure enough." Little Joe's glassy eyes peered at Jolene.

"Nope. Folks need somebody to sell their whiskey to them warehouses," I said.

"They make do," Jolene said like she never yelled at me months back. "We manage with the stuff I sell in them false cigar boxes at the store."

Little Joe hiccupped gain. "And I do well sellin some out the backroom at Fref...Fresh Farms."

"See," Jolene said. "You back to helpin Clyde up to the Grady place."

"But y'all got two stills runnin most all the time," I said. "You gonna supply me with plenty."

"You get caught totin shine, you go to prison," Jolene said like she worry after ne.

"But, Jolene, this my business now. You got the smoke shop and I got this work, and I good at it."

"Suit yourself."

She gave in quick-like. Maybe she ain't forgive me after all.

"You gonna see, Jolene. I gonna haul in bushels fulla greenbacks, pay top dollar for O'Hara likker."

"You do what you gotta do. But tomorrow I need you to drive me to the city."

FORTY-THREE

Get to the O'Hara place nice and early like Jolene tell me. Wondering why she wanted me to take her to the city got my gut popping like dry pine on a hot fire.

Lulahbelle said Jolene gone to take eggs to Fresh Farms, back directly. "She mighty excited bout goin to the city. She iron her shirt." Lulahbelle moved the iron off the stove, get the broom. "She musta trim her hair. Leave all this for me to sweep up. Little Joe still snorin like a bear in winter or he wanna go too."

Knowed Little Joe ain't going nowhere with the drinking he done. He more like a bear that get his head hit by a rock and gasoline poured down his gullet.

When Jolene showed she got her sleeves and collar done up, a black vest with white stripes buttoned over her white shirt, black trousers.

Take us as long to drive to where Jolene wanted to go, than it take to walk from Cedar Springs to Swift River.

The fella Jolene talked to said, "You gettin a good deal here. These cars ain't made no more, ya know." He called that Model T a runabout. Looked like my truck cept smaller, and stead a the pickup part on the back it got a extra seat what pulled out.

Kicked at one wheel, shake my head

"Them some right sturdy tires," car selling fella said.

"Not for them dirt roads we got in Cedar Springs," I said.

"How much for good heavy tires?" Jolene said to the fella.

He talked to me like I the one what asked. "Thirty dollars."

"I give you twenty," Jolene said. "Cause I gonna tell all them folks that complement my new runabout where I get this here beauty."

Feel like a king cause she take my side bout the tires. Gotta keep in mind what I learned from her bout talking down a price.

We gotta wait for the car fellas to change the tires so we go see one a them moving picture shows. Law, them photographs moved round on a wall like them folks right in the room with us. One we seen got sound. Jolene tell me she read all bout how they gonna make more a them "talkies" out in someplace called California.

Coming outta the playhouse like coming back from a whole nother world. "Why they paint that fella up that way? If'n they want a no-tail-bear, they..."

Jolene grabbed my overalls bib, shoved me into a wall. "Where you hear them words?"

"Why, from you."

"I never use such language. I ever catch you usin them words again you gonna eat em. Ya hear?"

"Yes'm," That Jolene for you. Glad she didn't tell me 'git' again. Glad cause I get to spend all that time in the city with her.

Hoped she never find out I tell B. J. Harvey make his shine drop like before.

FORTY-FOUR

Dealing with the Harveys made me feel like a man stepping out on his wife. Counted out greenbacks for B. J., stick them in the tin can dug into the ground.

One arm grabbed my middle, nother come round my shoulder. Seen a knife close to my face.

"Where that Turner pig at?"

Knowed that mouth and that knife.

"He get here soon." Wanna keep Snake Harvey guessing. Wished I a turtle with a shell to pull up in.

"You in with the O'Haras. Not right you touchin Harvey shine."

"Ain't set foot on O'Hara land nigh on a year." Truth when I said the words to Stub, a lie now I said them to Snake.

"You tell Turner Harveys ain't gonna deal with nobody what deal with O'Haras."

"Your pa happy with the price we pay."

Snake slide his knife closer to my windpipe. "Ole Stub plain lazy. Now I take my turn at sellin Harvey shine to somebody what ain't in with O'Haras."

Somewhere I hear a crack, then nother crack. A branch fall from heaven, crashed at my feet. Snake loosed his grip, pointed his knife into the dark.

I grabbed his arm with both my hands. Pulled him off his feet. He landed next to the branch.

A coon scrambled outta the branch, jumped on Snake's belly, scampered way.

Run to my truck. Wanna grab my shotgun from the bed. Stead I find mongst Harvey shine the shovel I used to bury Cob.

Snake on his feet. Come at me. The knife blade cut my arm before I knocked Snake in the head with the shovel.

The sonabitch rolled on the ground. Reached in the truck nother time, find my shotgun. Circled round, aimed at dirty ole Snake. Kicked the rock off the tin can.

"Take that there jack for this load. Never shuck off Harvey whiskey on me gain."

Snake gathered the bills, crammed them in his pocket. "Been one killin on the O'Hara side, one on the Harvey side. In my mind that leave the Harveys with some one-uppin to do." He slithered off, leave me with blood dripping down one arm.

FORTY-FIVE

With the runabout Jolene come to Cedar Springs two times a week like before. She helped with the stills and chores round the farms. Then she back at the smoke shop a hour after she delivered eggs to Fresh Farms.

Did my share round the O'Hara place, helped Clyde some at the Grady place too. But my business keep me busy. Find two suppliers tuther side the river that make up for the lost Harvey goods with some to spare. Goons at the warehouses gave me top dollar for every drop. Long as I did my pickups and deliveries I come off free and clear with plenty of dough. What to do with all the extra cash made my head spin so I buried some here, some there.

Jolene pulled in quite a haul at the smoke shop. "All my money I put in the Swift River Commerce Bank. Frank Peuddy what run it say he investin heavy in the stock market. I gonna tell him buy me some them stocks. You should do that."

If Jolene got a hand in the plan I reckoned it the smart thing to do. Something tell me to keep my jack buried, not follow Jolene this time, no matter how much I wanna. "Puttin money in somethin I ain't gonna feel or see seem wrong to me."

She looked at me like I a stump what needed pulling outta a field. "President Coolidge, up in Washington D. C., believe in the bull market, so so do I."

O'Haras made good use outta some cow, but I got no need for bulls or stock.

Little Joe acted happier since he take to the whiskey. He no longer pestered me bout going long on my bootlegging duty.

With the booming businesses and a good mix a sun and rain to make the crops grow, the summer of 1928 seemed like 'the cat's meow' for everybody. Well, almost everybody.

FORTY-SIX

Ain't gone to Glad Town in a while but get my hands on somma that dark city whiskey. Knowed the fella what owned Glad Town wanna buy some. When the deal done I sat a spell and sucked on a drink, celebrated that Clyde ain't there.

Watched the negre fellas play music and dance round in Injun clothes. John Henry did pretty good on piano. Sometimes he too drunk, messed up. Word from Little Joe and Lulahbelle that Glory mad bout how much John Henry drink, but she liked how he always happy.

Show ended. John Henry come over, his teeth gleamed like the ones on his piano. "How bouts you buys a po' boy a drink?"

Obliged him.

"Seen you shake hands wid my boss. You here steada Turner?"

How John Henry knowed Cob? Franklin what most folks in Glad Town called Cob. Gotta think quick. Tell the lie I used if somebody asked. "He move to Juniper."

"That why I ain't sees him in so long. You knows where bouts?"

"He owe you some clams?"

John Henry laughed, slapped his knee. "Nah. We's pals."

Surprised me like watching a rabbit pop outta a chicken egg.

He clamped a hand over his mouth. "Turner done like folks knowin we's friends. Like to play de massa."

"Yep." Ask me, Cob hated negres something fierce.

"But reckons you knows by now. He say's you one good kid."

Talk of Cob made my gut go sour. Seen some fella, looked like Cob, think it him. When the fella turned round I feel like a fool. Hoped recollecting Cob ain't gonna follow me like a haint.

"Turner use to come in de juke joint I plays at outside Charlotte, say's can he try my pie-anna." John Henry did a little jig. "Dat cat makes dem eighty-eights cook."

Cob talked bout piano playing a time or two. Reckoned John Henry knowed Cob pretty good.

"He ain't in Juniper." Covered one lie with nother. "He get kilt over owin some dough."

"No." John Henry looked like a baby what lose his rattle. "Onea his suppliers I bets." He tossed back what left in his jar.

Get him nother drink. "Sorry I the one what tell you." Why Cob never talked bout him?

"Turner pull my behind outta de fire when he gets me dis job up here." John Henry wiped his wet cheek with his sleeve. "He tells me bouts Glory, say's I gonna fall hard for her and he right."

Scratched my ear. Did I hear him right? "Cob never meet Glory that I knowed. I the one what get you to stop in at Fresh Farms."

"He so kind…were so kind." John Henry take nother long pull on his jar fulla shine. "He wanna build your faith in you self. He yap at me bout Glory fore I comes here. He gets him a plan, tell me when to walk dat road, hope you picks me up. Then he tell me to helps you look good to some gal you likes, make shore she see me thanks you for makin my life better."

He downed rest of the shine, go back to his piano. His story get my mind to spinning like a water wheel, make my neck get tight. Why Cob think John Henry help me with Jolene? Recollected how Jolene shut the smoke shop down for the day right after John Henry thank me. My head filled with questions I gotta ask John Henry.

Stayed late in Glad Town, get in a poker game. Wanna practice cause I get to go to the game Jolene run in her shop on Saturday nights now.

Win me some to begin with. What John Henry said keep coming back, my mind slipped off the game. Drink more white lightning to push Cob's face outta my head. Lose what I win and a little more. Smashed out my smoke, leave the card table. Reckoned I best take a piss, crawl in the back of my truck, catch some shuteye.

Outside night air still thick with the heat from the day. Some music fellas and them what do Cherokee show sat on a roof not far way. They hooted and hollered over a harmonica whine. Knowed John Henry by his shape when he stand.

John Henry slipped, fall on one knee, get up. Others cackled. He get to the flat part of the roof over the porch, moved his feet fast, make the tin rattle like he beating a drum. Other fellas clapped, whistled, called. He danced to the harmonica from one end of the roof to tuther.

Get closer to see the fun. John Henry all over that roof, jumping and spinning like a top. Harmonica player ended one song. John Henry take a pull on a jug, danced to the next song. Him moving like that up so high didn't seem like a good idea

He get near the edge plenty times. Then he missed the end. His foot hit air, not tin. He fall to the ground head first.

Harmonica stopped. Folks screamed. The negres climbed off the roof. Me and couple other fellas run to where John Henry landed. Face in the dirt, legs up on a hitching post, neck bent like the end of a hoe.

Some fellas pulled his legs so he on his back.

"Get Jesse." Somebody called. Jesse the head negre.

Closest doctor I knowed in Swift River. Take a hour to get there with my truck in the dark. What the chance that doc willing to treat a negre?

Jesse brushed past me and the others, get on his knees by John Henry. "He ain't breathin."

John Henry liked folks to laugh. He playing a trick. Harmonica fella blow his nose on a hanky. John Henry get him good with his game.

Jesse raised his head from John Henry's chest. "Somebody gotta tell his wife."

FORTY-SEVEN

Sun shoot needles through the trees, waked me up. Climbed outta the bed of my truck, stumbled down to the springs to wash my face and neck. Mad now cause John Henry gone, never gonna tell me why Cob didn't tell me they knowed one nother. By the time I drive to Cedar Springs, parked by Fresh Farms, I reckoned I oughta not buyed John Henry them drinks. He might be live now if I didn't.

Get to Glory's house a few yards behind the store. How I gonna tell her? Reckoned she gonna cry. Hoped she didn't wail, hang on me. Some women folk run to falling to pieces. Ain't pretty.

"Why, hey. Come on in. I gots plentya coffee?"

Didn't knowed what worse, the sun like to blind me outside, or walls closing in on me on the inside.

Glory set a cup by me. "You looks like somebody say awful mean words to you."

"Nope. That ain't my problem."

"How you gets dat scar on yore arm?" She touched near where Snake knifed me.

Nobody asked before. Gotta dream up a quick lie. "Broke tree branch cut me."

Take a breath. Smelled coffee, fresh-baked biscuits. My belly did a inside-out flip.

"Glory, sit down." Commenced to tell her what happened to John Henry.

Glory blinked bunch a times. "Thinks he leave me one day. Don't thinks he leave like dis." She looked at me. "How you wants yore eggs?" She didn't wait for me to say no thank you.

Let her keep busy. Shoved down vittles what like to make me sick.

Take her to Glad Town. On the way I said how I sorry I didn't tell him take care on that roof.

"Not yore fault. He drinks, do stupid stuff. Some folk knows how ta handle whiskey, some folk done. John Henry likes to stand out in a crowd, I likes dat bout him."

"A mighty shame," I said. "Folks sure like John Henry."

"I knows more'n one dat don't like him." Her face hard like a oak tree. "He get what he deserve."

"John Henry never say a mean word bout nobody."

Her face now soft like a willow. "Dat true. Some folk nice sometimes, mean others. John Henry always nice. I likes dat. I de one rush in not knows him well as I oughta."

Dropped Glory in Glad Town. Wanna get more sleep. Gotta go back to Cedar Springs to tell the O'Haras. Air so hot and heavy, cigarette smoke like to stand still. My arms and legs like rocks. Never so tired in my life.

Come on Little Joe by the chicken coops. "You look bad as I feel, sure enough." Reckoned he did a mite of drinking hisself the night before. "What eatin you?"

"Gotta wait for Jolene to get here to tell y'all."

The runabout chugged in from the road, I pepped up at seeing Jolene.

We meet her at the porch. She looked like she doing a puzzle in her head.

"Somethin diggin in your craw too, sure enough."

She pulled a face at Little Joe like he spit on her shoe. "Mind your own pints and quarters."

Lulahbelle fried up a messa fish Big Jack catch in the stretch a Mill Creek that run by the O'Hara front yard. We sit down to Sunday dinner. Nobody said nothing much till we bout finished. Then I tell what I seen in Glad Town.

Tears showed on Lulahbelle's cheeks, she get up, go to the sink.

"Sad to hear, sure enough."

"Glory know yet?"

"I tell her," I said to Big Jack.

"Where Glory at now?"

How Jolene knowed Glory ain't to her house? "I take her to Glad Town."

Jolene leave the table, go to the sleeping rooms. She come back in overalls steada her stiff black britches and white shirt.

"Tell you what we gonna do," Jolene said. "Little Joe you go'n kill a nice fat fryer. Big Jack you get somma our best can goods outta the cellar. Lulahbelle, you go over tidy Fresh Farms, clean that store like the place never been clean before." Jolene throw her arm out in the direction a Fresh Farms like she sending Lulahbelle off to war.

Lulahbelle wiped her face with a dish cloth. "But the store got a lock. How'm I posta get in?"

"Key hid under the second rock."

"You know that, sure enough. How come, Jole?"

"Never you mind," Jolene waved her hand at Little Joe. She pointed at me. "Rufus, you get a jug from the barn, meet me over to Glory's house."

Jolene blowed outta the kitchen like she on fire.

Dragged my behind to Glory's, Jolene already on her knees scrubbing the floor. "Bout time. You slow as honey runnin uphill. I need your help."

"Don't knowed how to clean floors."

"Course not. You wouldn't know a clean floor if one bite you on the behind. This here a bucket, this here soap. Now move them chairs and that there table."

If Jolene ain't the one learning me, I throw down the pail, leave. Wanna do good cause of her.

"You mess up them floors." She go over a spot I reckoned I missed. "Go chop some kindling. When you done pull them weeds in Glory's garden."

Think the floor not so bad. "I tired, Jolene. Loose some sleep last night."

"Quit your whinin. Plenty time for sleep when you meet your maker. This place gotta knock Glory off her feet when she seen what I done." Jolene snapped a wet rag like she cracking a whip. "After the weeds, go find me some late summer berries in the strawberry field."

"Jolene, I gotta get goin. Got a load a shine to pick up tonight."

"I gotta bake a strawberry rhubarb pie. Which onea them things gonna make Glory happy? Folks live if you don't deliver shine."

"Reckon Glory ain't comin back for a couple days."

"Well, when she do get here, I gonna be ready. Not that you help much."

Reckoned I sleep after I deliver that load to the warehouse tomorrow.

FORTY-EIGHT

Saturday night, more than a week later, take me a bath, put on a new shirt under my overalls, hoped Jolene see I get slicked up for my first go at her poker game. In the shop a couple farmers sat round puffing stogies, drinking whiskey.

Jolene wear a string tie she keep playing with. She got the pistol I gave her in a leather holster she get for it. Grip of that gun oiled up nice'n shiny. She pay no mind to me standing in plain sight.

One fella peered at Jolene like she a three-layer cake with white frosting. He keep turning his head, reckoned so Jolene see his gold tooth. "First you close for two weeks, then most the day yesterday."

"Gotta death in the family. Yesterday I drive to the city to find some new tobacco." She peered at him like he the rabbit and she the snare. "I might pop open a can a that Red Feather, if you good," Jolene said.

Gold Tooth lean on the counter a mite too near her hip. "Oh, I as good as you look runnin round in that automobile of yorn."

"A fella in the city say my runabout onea the best Ford ever crank off his line."

"Yep, much fancier'n that pickup Snake Harvey storm round in." Gold Tooth moved closer to Jolene. Wanna go shove him. Knowed Jolene yell at me if I did.

"Hear he miss a pony cart by a inch the other day." Jolene patted Gold Tooth's arm, slipped way from him. She never put a hand on my arm. She got a jug fulla shine from a bottom shelf. "Draggin out my good stock to celebrate me spectin a nephew in a few months."

"Lulahbelle's with child gain?" How come they leave me outta family news. Eyed the jug. "How come you knowed the baby a boy?"

"I feel it. Glory say she think so too." Jolene poured me a drink. I take a pull on the shine, tried to believe I belonged in that place.

Jolene sit at the head of the table like a king with a new throne. She lighted her stogie, not with a match, but with a contraption she clicked with her thumb. Poker playing commenced. After a few hands fellas packed the shop. Jolene filled her pockets with jack what with selling shine and smokes. Every now and again she gave out a free sample, pulled a you gonna want more face. Customers beamed like they think they special cause of the way she treated them. She didn't treat me like that.

Gray haze of smoke settled over the room. Farmers whooped, hollered, laughed their way to forgetting the price a corn and the new shoes their young'uns needed.

On this one card hand Crow Tritt bet heavy then passed on new cards. I take one new card cause I got a two, three, four, six a spades. Lucky thing I draw a five cause on second look one a them spades a club. The likker musta disguised that there card. Crow raised, Jolene folded, the other fellas at the table called. I raised Crow, making the others fold. Crow showed two twos, a five, a nine and a queen. I win fifteen dollars.

"You done good, boy," Jolene said.

"The one what bluff the most, the one with the worst hand." I didn't tell Jolene Little Joe learned me that.

Next hand I lose ten dollars, stepped out, let nother fella sit in. Crow lose too, get up, bumped me. "Careful now," I said to him. He tapped his jelly jar to mine, stumbled off. Jolene ought not allow Crow at her game cause his sister married a Harvey but Crow's brother a judge what help if Jolene get in trouble with Sheriff Clayton.

Jolene shuffled. The stogie in the ashtray next to her ain't but half smoked. She pour water in her jar, not whiskey. Not like when she home cooking supper, getting deep in the jug. Get me nother drink.

Two farmers talked bout the jenny barn in Chimney said how the redhead the best. "I like the dark-hair gal myself," I said. We jawed a bit. I bout promised to give the redhead a try.

Jolene didn't allow spitting inside. Gold Tooth come in from having hisself a chaw outside. Crow bumped him going out. Gold Tooth pushed Crow, Crow push back.

Gold Tooth crash into me. Make me drop my shine. Punched him before I think. He fall on the table. Cards fly. Everybody jumped up, yelled.

Gold Tooth get up, clobbered me in the gut. I sidestepped his next blow, slipped in the likker from the jar I let go, landed flat on my back. Gold Tooth's shoe come at my face.

A shot exploded. Shoe smacked the floor, not my head.

Everybody got quiet. Seen where the bullet made a hole in the wall a inch below the ceiling. Jolene hold her pistol. If Jolene didn't knowed how to handle that pack of rowdy farmers, my nose mighta looked like a tater.

FORTY-NINE

I become a regular at the poker game. Plenty of drinking go on at them games. Most times I stumbled out after, sleep in my truck. When morning come the runabout all the time gone. I headed to the O'Hara place for Sunday dinner. Jolene never there early, she parked at Fresh Farms, visit with Glory at her house for a spell before they come down.

Meet Glory in the yard. "You look a mite glum. Where Jolene at?"

"She come later. She be mysterious."

Reckoned that big word a good one for Jolene.

The runabout chugged into the yard. Jolene ain't the only one in the car. Ana Marie ride next to her, Clyde sit in the rumble seat.

Ain't enough chairs round the table so I eat my dinner on the porch. Law, Lulahbelle knowed how to put some crisp on some chicken. Clyde gotta eat outside too. Reckoned I peck at him a bit. "How come you ride with Ana Marie and Jolene?"

"Jolene get me up early. Make me go to the O'Brien house."

"You mean the Tiffany house."

"Sign say O'Brien house. Jolene say Miz Tiffany pass away."

Miz Tiffany said Ana Marie her favorite, mean Ana Marie now in charge of the gals. "You got eyes for Ana Marie?"

"No. I don't go for no highfalutin girls. My eyes wander out to the goat pen."

"So you got you a eye for the nannies?"

"No, stupid. I like the girl that feed the goats. Sadie." Way Clyde said that gal's name sounded like he gonna drop plenty a greenbacks visiting her.

Growed tired a Clyde. Ambled down near the creek, kick at dead leaves spread over the yard, sit on a log, lighted a smoke. Think bout the happy voices in the house at dinner. I oughta stayed in with the folks, eat standing up.

Leaves crunched behind me. Ana Marie stepped careful with her tall shoes. Her dress short, come up almost to her knees. She wear a fuzzy hat color a morning glories down to her eyebrows.

"Jolene say some nice stuff bout you," Ana Marie said, sat next to me on the log.

"Jolene? Me? Nice stuff?"

"You funny." She chuckled, showed lotta teeth.

Her sitting near me feel like driving on a slick road in a rainstorm.

"She say you take over Mr. Franklin, or Turner, or what's his name's business."

"Yep. Cob move, try somethin new."

"Uh huh. Like Miz Tiffany move on. Let's hope you do what's his name's business good like I do Miz Tiffany's."

"Reckon I knowed a mite bout sellin shine. But you get your likker direct from Jolene. You ain't got no need for me."

"Ain't likker I need." She lay a hand on my leg.

World stopped spinning, time stand still.

"What I got you want?"

"You drop some off to me that one time, remember?" She rubbed my leg.

Take in air, let it out slow. Heart beat hard. My innards all befuddled. "Uh, nope. That box? What in there?"

"Hm." Ana Marie take her hand back, played with the beads what hang down to her middle. "Well, get a looksee." She take a small tin box outta her handbag.

"Snuff? Jolene sell that at the smoke shop."

"Nah, this ain't no tobaccy." She opened the lid. What inside white and powdery like fine sugar. "This here special stuff. Fella gotta find the right place to do the gettin."

"I buy and sell me some whiskey. Don't knowed bout nothin else."

"Your dead friend bring me my medicine, reckon you gotta good idea where to get the stuff for me. You playin dumb?" Ana Marie flicked the tip of my nose with a black gloved finger. "I countin on you to come visit me soon and bring a nice ole present." She get up off the log, crunched more leaves with her tall shoes, stopped, turned back to me. "Course there more'n my sweet company in it for you, get you some green too."

FIFTY

Only one place I reckoned Cob get hisself that white powder. Them packages I delivered from Daniels at the warehouse in Keelville. Idea of dealing with Daniels sound to me like eating dog shit. How I gonna say no to Ana Marie? Got no choice but to talk to Daniels. Leastwise I didn't get to go to Keelville that week cause the moonshiners didn't bring in enough product. Cold weather the problem.

Snow come, throwed white bed-sheets over the ground. Too cold to sleep in my truck. Planned to get a bed in Glad Town till I lose all the jack I got on me in a poker game. Reckoned I go to the Grady place. Clyde's mash due to turn, take so long with all the ice round. Needed him to run off a load of shine soon.

Parked my truck at the bottom of the hill, make my way up the trail. In the snow covered yard I seen shoe prints. Too small for Clyde, too big for Little Joe. Reckoned Big Jack come up here to check on Clyde's mash too.

Give a "Ooooouuuuuu" to signal my coming. When I opened the door Clyde looked like I catch him buttering his corn. His hands on the table with two cups so reckoned he hiding something else.

"Where Big Jack at?"

Clyde blinked. "He just leave."

Reckoned Big Jack set a while cause Clyde talking with only three words like him.

Set on the hearth to warm my froze behind, throwed nother log on the fire. Next to me I find a pad of paper with writing on it and a drawing of a goat. Picked up the paper. I draw much better than Clyde. "You writin a love letter to a goat?"

Clyde charged over like he onea them mad billys, ripped that pad outta my hand. "Don't touch my stuff. You ever tell anybody what you seen on that tablet, I tear your guts out."

"So I right bout that there goat?"

He tilted his head, peered at me like I something he never seen before. "Your ass so sorry you can't read."

If he punched me that hurt less than them words he shoot at me. "I get by. Make me more green than some farm hand."

"Why you come here?"

"Sleep here often enough. Come to see if'n you got me some whiskey to sell."

"Don't want you around. You nothin but a noose around my neck." Clyde stomped to the next room, the curtain flying behind him.

Ain't gonna go in that sleeping room with that ornery bastard, ain't gonna sleep on no floor in the front room. Spied a jug in a corner. Ain't much shine left inside. Take a swallow then spit in the jug cause I reckoned Clyde use some extra flavor in his whiskey. Turned out the lamp on the table. Slammed the door on my way out.

Take me seven tries to crank up that truck engine in the cold. Drive down to the O'Hara place. House dark so I go in, stoked the fire, creep into the bed Little Joe used before Lulahbelle come long. Big Jack snoring. Reckoned he get down from the Grady place right quick like, go to sleep first off. Less maybe them ain't Big Jack's footprints I seen. Who else leave them prints in the snow?

In the morning Big Jack gone. Find Little Joe in the kitchen waiting on some bacon Lulahbelle got in a pan.

Lulahbelle paced the floor, her hand pressed to her back. "Oh, Lordy. This baby buckin like a angry mule."

"That what Jole say we gonna name the baby," Little Joe said to me. "Mule?"

"Nah, Buck." Little Joe said like I a naughty young'un. "Jole right bout this one a boy, sure enough."

"Give my right leg for onea them cans a pineapple." Lulahbelle flipped the bacon.

Little Joe gotta tend to the chickens so I said I go to Fresh Farms for a can of pineapple soon as Glory opened.

First I go to the barn to fetch a shovel cause I gotta dig up some greenbacks. Jolene keep telling me I oughta put my money in the Swift River Commerce Bank, I reckoned the jack safer in the ground.

When I come in the barn a body sitting on a hay bale, hat pulled down. He stand, staggered closer. Law, if he ain't B. J. Harvey. Feel like I slipping on ice. Slammed the barn door behind me. "What you doin on O'Hara land? You gonna get you shot."

"So what."

"They gonna kill you, dead."

"Fine. Wanna die." He swayed on wobbly legs. "Fixin to go in that house yonder, sass somebody. Hope they got some shotgun."

"You drunk." Searched B. J.'s brown eyes. "You get hold some bad shine what make your head go soft?"

"No!"

"Hush. Little Joe or Big Jack gonna hear you."

"Don't care!" B. J. shake me. "You good as a O'Hara. And you ain't my cousin or nothin. You shoot me."

Cousin? What he talking bout a cousin for? "My gun in the truck." Shoved B. J., get him way from me. "Boy, you gotta sober up."

"I kilt a man. You done that before?"

"I…." Cold wind hit my back. "Take what bother you, push it deep, deep down, get on with life."

"Killin Cob don't sweep way what he done to me."

"Forget all that. Somethin bad, no matter how bad, don't think bout it."

"What go on fill my head, don't let up. His face swim in my head."

Jerked B. J. by the arm, wrassled open the barn door, throwed B. J. facedown in the snow. "Don't say nothin bout that shit."

"Beat me up. Kill me." His lips blue.

Yanked B. J. to his feet. Dragged him in the direction of the road. "You gotta live. No matter what." Let go, pushed him. He take one step after nother till he off O'Hara land.

FIFTY-ONE

Feel like Benedict Arnold letting a Harvey get way from the O'Hara place with no harm. Reckoned, like I tell B. J., best way to get past something, go on like nothing happened.

Lucky I put a big rock over where I buried my jack cause more snow fall over night. Counted what I dug up, get what I needed, put the rest back in the ground. Got other money buried other places. Reckoned that dough added up to what Jolene got in that Swift River Commerce Bank and what she called the bull market. Maybe I oughta do like she said, buy me some a that stock. Gotta get more money than her so she think I worthy. That nother reason I gotta get that white powder from Daniels, mean more green in my pocket.

Soon as I get enough hooch from my suppliers I hightailed it to Keelville. Always keep a hawk-eye out in them parts. Steered clear a folks cause I didn't knowed who to trust.

Daniels doled out for the load I bring in. I scraped off the top what I recollected Cob pay for them soft packages. "I need onea them there special surprises."

His eyes run over my face. "Cost more'n that."

Peeled off nother double sawbuck.

"Don't got none of that around." Daniels tugged the money from my hand, shoved it in the pocket of his wrinkled jacket over that red shirt a his. "Come back tomorrow. Get what you want then." He slipped off to the dark part of the warehouse like a rat stealing cheese.

"Hey, cat." Ace, fella with the big mustache, stopped me. "How that engine run, run, running?"

Happy to answer him. "Goin right fast after the work you done."

"Why you want go-blow from Daniels for?"

"Like you say, need more cash."

Ace pinched out onea them hand rolled reefer smokes. "Ain't such a good idea."

"Reckon haulin whiskey ain't a good idea neither."

"No, no, no." He peered into the shadows behind me, speak in a whisper. "Lemme tell you. He ain't changed his clothes in days. Don't know why. Don't ask. But get the idea he don't go home. Act like he see a spook around every corner. You don't wanna be dealing with him, him, him."

Too late. Daniels take my money. Gotta go back the next night, get the package. Daniels still looked like he tying the rope at both ends but he didn't give me no trouble.

Ace trapped me again. "Hey, cat. Got a job for you." His mustache twitched. "A speakeasy I go, go, go to need more mountain dew. You up for it?"

"How I knowed the law ain't on to them?"

"You say you want more cash."

"I think on the offer." Didn't tell Ace I needed to find me more moonshiners so I get more whiskey to sell.

Did everything I think to put off delivering that there package of white powder to the O'Brien house. Turned out I didn't gotta go there to get the stuff to Ana Marie.

Stopped in at the smoke shop to say 'hey' to Jolene. Reckoned Ana Marie got the same idea cause she jawing with Jolene.

Bells on the front door ring, Jolene pay no mind. She keep her eyes on Ana Marie. "Course I make a better pie but Glory got me beat on every other dish. Glory the best cook in the world."

"Her fried chicken good as what Lulahbelle fix?" I said.

"You dare put Glory next to Lulahbelle." Jolene gave me a look like I a possum in a corn crib. "They as different as milk and cream. One floats to the top, other sinks to the bottom."

Wondered what one Jolene mean goes to the top. Lulahbelle her sister-in-law but I think she mean Glory.

"Been lookin forward to you payin me a visit," Ana Marie said to me, "brinin me a present."

"Got somethin out in the truck got your name on it."

My eyes stick on Ana Marie's pink lips turning up at the ends.

Jolene laughed. "You with anythin Ana Marie want enough to tickle my funny bone."

"Well." Ana Marie grabbed my arm. "Maybe I ought take a gander." She dragged me out the door before I seen how Jolene take to this.

Down the street, by my truck, gave her the package size a baby pillow.

"This ain't in teeny-tiny jars. How I gonna sell this to my customers?"

"You don't want it?" How I gonna tell her what I gotta do to get that?

Ana Marie opened her coat, slide her gloved hand down tween her two white loafs, pulled out a wada bills. "Why, sure I do. Reckon I gotta get them there little jars on my own."

That jack she gave me a good price.

She lay fingers on my face. "When you bring me nother batch, be sure to bring that to my house, so I can thank you right nice like."

I gotta bring her nother batch?

FIFTY-TWO

That winter I learned me how to sniff out roadhouses, get friendly with the fellas what run them. Same fellas buy whiskey from me and make my acquaintance to moonshiners what supplied me with more shine I sell to warehouses. Things looked up.

Pulled in at a roadhouse, spotted Jolene's runabout. A piano player tinkled out a zippy tune, made me miss John Henry. Laughing mixed up with talking sounded like wild dogs calling to one nother. Got a beer, lighted a Camel.

Jolene cozy-like with a buncha farmers, some from her poker game at the smoke shop. She looked my way but stayed put, she busy. She tugged a fella's hat down over his eyes. Lotta fellas wear overalls over union suits, like me. Some wear shirts with sleeves rolled up, collars open. Jolene got her white shirt buttoned nice and tidy under a pinstriped vest. She got that pistol I gave her on her belt in that leather holster. She didn't go nowhere without that handgun.

She come over, set her cup on the bar. "Send me home, sir." She swigged the whiskey he poured her. "Who makes this?" She said to me.

"They make this here beer out back, but the last batcha shine I sell them come from Clyde."

"Hmmm." Jolene pulled a face. "O'Hara whiskey gotta taste better'n this. Gonna tell Big Jack to give Clyde a talkin to."

"Why don't you go up to the Grady place and jaw at Clyde?"

"Got better things to do when I go to Cedar Springs." She winked at me, pulled a cigar outta her pocket. "That gentleman in the green shirt keep askin after this stogie, but I save it for you."

"Why, much obliged." She treating me like a prince.

A table fulla drinkers whooping at a fella dancing with the only other gal in the place. Her skirt fly round when he twirled her, she moved her feet quicker than hens pecking at corn. Green shirt fella come up, ask Jolene to give a dance a try. She said, "No, thank you. I got some business with Rufus here."

Green Shirt gave me a look like I throwed a rock in his fishing hole. Jolene slipped on her coat, signed me to follow her outside. A string of paper bags with candles in them lighted our way past a line of trucks to where she parked her runabout in near dark.

"When you takin the next load down the mountain?" She leaned on her fender, crossed her arms. Piano playing and laughing far way now.

"Pickin up some from Little Joe tomorrow, headin to the warehouse from there."

"Then I reckon I meet you at my house."

"You gonna be at the O'Hara place when I come get the shine?"

"Yep. Cause I goin with you."

Wished there enough light for me to see her face, see if she funning me.

"You got you a car, don't need a ride down the mountain."

"No, fool. I goin with you to that warehouse."

That come at me like getting hit in the face with a switch.

"I ain't bringin you to no warehouse."

Jolene moved to the driver door but didn't get in. "You will if I say you will."

"I don't work for you no more."

"You owe me. If not for me, you don't know the first thing bout whiskey."

Warehouse I delivering to next night the one in Keelville. No problem with Ace. Didn't wanna think what Daniels say when I showed with a female. Of late, Daniels acted jumpy as a baby chicken in a hawk's nest.

"No. Them fellas don't take kindly to strangers. They got them some nasty guns."

Jolene stepped up on the running board. She tugged on my coat so I get closer. With her up that high we bout nose to nose.

"You watch me handle myself."

Whiskey hang on her words, smoke in her hair. She right. Jolene hold her own at her poker games. She like a general in some army.

"Them warehouse goons ain't no Swift River farmers."

"Don't you think I know that. I smart enough to teach myself how to run my smoke shop. You, if that Turner fella don't learn you bootleggin, you be walkin behind a plow resta your life."

Her hurtfulness made me step back. She put a hand on my shoulder, pulled me back in.

"Don't you know I posta become a legend? I want you to help me."

I gotta take the bait cause it Jolene what do the fishing.

"How me bringin you with me on a delivery gonna help you be a legend?"

"I wanna learn everythin bout you. Everythin you do, everywhere you go." Her fingers slide from my shoulder to my elbow.

"But if'n somethin happen to you I feel awful bad."

"Nothin gonna happen to me." She got her mouth close to my ear. "Trust me." She set her other hand on my face. "You get a shave today?"

Get my mind ready to float up to the clouds. Then she jumped down, strolled back to the roadhouse. I gotta go sit in my truck for a bit.

FIFTY-THREE

"Lotta times Jole say she gonna do somethin and she never do, sure enough." Little Joe helped me pull the tarp over my truck, I hitched up the tailgate. "Fore you take off, let me and you get us a drink. Jole ain't here by that time, you go on."

Hoped he right. Jolene going long made me wanna hide somewhere. Never knowed what she gonna do. Gotta get me some a that white powder, ain't gonna tell Jolene it for Ana Marie.

We sit inside, listened to pine logs crackle in the fire.

"Your eyes out for more whiskey makers?" Little Joe patted the jug.

"Got a new supplier tuther side the river."

"Well, I been thinkin. We get nother still, maybe we build one, then we get Lulahbelle's brothers to run off some shine."

"Why them?" Knowed Little Joe ain't friendly with that bunch.

"Sometimes onea her brothers come round here. Not to see us, sure enough. He want free corn squeezins."

"Don't wanna deal with them peculiar boys."

"If we get them to run some shine we don't gotta run so much here. Hard keepin up the still and the farm, sure enough." Little Joe complained bout too much work of late.

"Tell Jolene I wait but now gotta go." I waved way the jug he tried to pass me. He take nother drink hisself.

Opened the door, my hope sink. Jolene come up the steps. "You think you gonna leave me behind?"

"Goin to look for you now. Don't hear your car. How you get here?"

"Park at the store, spend time with Glory." Jolene wear a black suit with that string tie. Felt hat snug on her head. "You got a problem with that?"

Little Joe come up beside me. "How bout I go too?"

Wanna clobber him for them words. One O'Hara on this trip worried me enough.

"Boy, you one sorry fool." Jolene shake her head at Little Joe. "You go with us, you mess up everthin."

"I never get to go to the city." Little Joe pulled him a whipped puppy face. "Reckon I get me nother drink, sure enough."

"When we get there, don't say nothin."

"You not somebody that tell me what to do." Jolene swigged from her silver flask.

Reckoned she gonna do what she gonna do. Now I ain't in for a drop-full, I in for a jarful. Maybe Daniels ain't there that night. Then how I gonna get me that stuff for Ana Marie?

Only couple them gas streetlights on this edge a Keelville and somebody break them with rocks. Flipped the headlights off when I find the alley. Go slow till I seen the warehouse with help from moonlight.

Cranked down the window when Ace come up. Crisp air hit my face. "How the rats in the cage tonight?"

Ace squinted, looked past me. "Who that guy?"

"Learnin somebody new for deliverin."

"Daniels a pussycat tonight compared to last couple days." Ace go slide the door open. Rolled my truck inside, parked sideways. Ace tugged the door shut.

Keep my head down, tried to pay no mind to what Jolene did. Prayed she sit tight in the truck. Tussled with a whiskey barrel. Ace moved my way. "Hey cat, that a girl?"

Peeked over to where Jolene stand. She got her suit coat and hat off. She run her hands through her short black, wavy hair. Lucky for her she got her pinstriped vest on cause that warehouse cold.

Daniels over by the lantern wearing his usual wrinkled red shirt. He pulled his tommy gun round to his front. His face blank like a field a fresh snow. He take a gander at the pistol on Jolene's hip, then her face.

"Nice place you got here. You sure well armed." She stepped closer to Daniels.

A spark come in his eyes. "You got a piece. Know how to use that?"

"I real good with a handgun." She take a couple more steps with a little sway in her hips. "Never seen a fancy gun like that one you got. You gonna teach me to shoot that?"

"Don't think your pretty little arms can handle this gun."

"How bout I show you with a bitta arm wrassling?"

Daniels looked ready to pounce. He sling his tommy gun back over his shoulder, dragged out some wood crates for them to sit on. They put their elbows on a taller box, Jolene grabbed his dirty paw. She gave the fight her all. Daniels better not hurt her cause then I gotta hurt him.

When I think Jolene bout to break, she put on a big grin. "Wanna shoot dice?"

Daniels dropped her hand, let out a belly laugh. Ace popped his eyes wide open. Reckoned like me he think Daniels never find nothing funny. Leave it to Jolene to tame the bear.

"How bout you show me round this place." Jolene smoothed some of the wrinkles on that red shirt Daniels wear. "Bet we see plenty stars from the roof."

Her touching him gave me a pain like eating bad meat.

Daniels take Jolene by lantern light to show her the view. Me and Ace unloaded shine barrels, stacked them on shelves what smelled like they damp for a long time. Then we sit on them wood crates by a candle in a empty bean can.

"I gonna skidoo from this job pretty soon, soon, soon." Ace church whispered.

"Where you goin?" Didn't want to deal with Daniels with no Ace round.

"Told you about that blind pig that need some of your whiskey. Gonna work there."

"You fix engines real good. When you learn you hair cuttin?"

"Guys that work at that barbershop don't need to know hair cutting."

Stand when I hear Jolene and Daniels snail back. She got holda his arm like they going to a Sunday afternoon picnic. If I go to that picnic I bring the ants.

"We best skedaddle," I said.

Daniels leave Jolene, he come close to me. Smelled onions from his supper. "Whatcha in such a hurry for?" He slipped out my greenbacks from his pocket, handed it over. "Sit on down. I think this lady got more tricks up her sleeve."

"I be back." Jolene gave Daniels a wink, go to my truck.

"Lemme roll, roll, roll the door open for you," Ace said.

Get in the truck real quick like, revved the engine, backed round so the nose pointed out. Daniels watched us from the shadows, tommy gun hang on one shoulder. Remembered bout the powder for Ana Marie. Set the brake, let the engine run. Said nothing to Jolene. Opened my door, take couple steps.

Three shots come from somewhere deep in the belly of the warehouse. Daniels fall on his face, his back wet with blood.

FIFTY-FOUR

"Go, go, go, cat. Go!" Ace shoved me hard.

Jumped in the truck, slammed off the handbrake, blasted outta that there warehouse like bullets from that gun. Chest hammer like I run ten miles uphill. Five minutes before I dared slow down, turn on headlights.

"What the hell happen?" Jolene take a pull from her flask.

Fumbled under my seat for a snake oil bottle fulla shine. "Daniels." Pushed what I seen outta my head. "Somebody get him."

"Get him? What'cha mean?"

"Gun him down."

"Them not no gunshots. More like sody pops openin." Jolene screwed the cap back on her flask. "I shoot my pistol, shots sound louder'n that."

"Come from somewhere way back inside the warehouse." Didn't say nothing bout the blood I seen. Take a swigga white lightening, welcomed the burn in my windpipe. Keep my bottle handy.

"Who wanna kill Daniels? He so nice. A upstandin business man, besides sellin likker. But he say they gonna overturn that Prohibition law. When they do he gonna keep his warehouse and sell whiskey legal like."

Hill got steeper, I shifted to low gear. "Why you call the place *his*?"

"You diliverin there for how long? And you don't know Daniels own the place?"

"Ain't what Ace say." Road leveled out, shifted back into high. Dig in the chest pocket of my overalls for a smoke to calm my nerves.

"Hmph. Daniels tell me that fella a rube."

"Give me a light."

"You don't know how to drive and light a match?" Easy for her to say, she got one a them contraptions she clicked with her thumb. Jolene snickered, lighted my cigarette. "Ace lie bout flyin aeroplanes. He only work on the engines." She waved at the smoke. "Open your window."

Puffed my Camel. Didn't matter none to me if Ace fly or not cause a fella what get close enough to put a hand on a aeroplane a hero to me. Pictured Daniels face down with his back all bloody. He ain't no nice fella. Warehouse too dark to see the shooter. Tossed the cigarette butt out, cranked up the window. Take nother sip from the bottle. My mind get cloudy.

"Wake up fool."

Mill Creek turnoff disappeared behind my truck. Never missed that before. Nother truck passed me. In the mirror I seen him make a wide turn, speed in my direction.

Jolene twisted to look back. "Snake Harvey."

Thumbed down the throttle. Truck gave me all she got. Why I gotta miss the turnoff?

"You goin fast." Jolene got her face to the back window. "But he gainin on us."

Ace did a good job putting juice in my engine. Snake's headlights come close. Reckoned somebody fixed up his engine too. Mountain road curved this way then that. Worked the brake, worked the throttle. Gotta outrun that dirty bastard.

Jolene aimed her pistol, fired out the window. Snake swerved. Put a piece of road tween us. Not for long. He got close again, fired his weapon. Jolene sit on her knees faced backward in the seat, take nother shot. Snake shoot off a blast what pinged off my roof. I pushed that throttle with a sweaty hand.

Jolene got her pistol to spit three quick shots. Gunpowder smell filled the cab. "Damn!" She throwed her gun on the floor. "Give me your pistol."

One hand on the wheel, rummaged under my seat. Grabbed a wrench, dropped it.

"Hurry!"

Headlights waved behind me. Swing round a bend in the road with no brake. Find my handgun what used to belonged to Cob. Jolene snatched it. Nother bullet fly past in a yellow streak. In the mirror Snake's truck swerve close to the shoulder. Jolene hang out the window, head and all. Pulled off a shot. Snake's truck slide sideways in a ditch fulla mud.

Turned up a mule path, chugged over the backcountry.

"I nail his front tire with a perfect shot."

Knowed Jolene gonna tell bout that for years to come. She shake her flask, empty. She tossed it on the seat, slipped nother flask from her pocket.

Got me enough gunfire that night to last me till I in my grave.

FIFTY-FIVE

Words spread cross the big city newspaper. Picture reminded me a what happened to Daniels. More'n one fella on the ground in that newspaper picture. Plopped down a penny for a copy, go on the errand I didn't wanna do.

Pulled in at the O'Brien House when the sun half way to his top spot. Ana Marie answered the backdoor in onea her shiny robes what made me wanna pet her arm like a cat.

"Look like you come with empty hands."

"Tell you bout that." Lay open the newspaper on the table. "First I need you read me what that say."

Ana Marie leaned over the paper. Wildflower smell tickle my nose. She shaded her eyes with a creamy white arm. "Eeeewww. Why you bring me that?"

Covered the picture with my hand. "Now, you read them words."

"What make you think I read?"

"Fancy lady like you must go to some good school."

She put her arm down, stared me square in the face. "I growed up in Pine Gap. Ain't no school there."

Pine Gap lot like Dandelion Holler where I from. Reckoned me and Ana Marie more alike than I think. Why didn't I see before she a simple gal under all them frills?

"Forget that evilness." She planted fists on her hips. "Where that there package I need?"

"Like in that newspaper picture, my supplier for the stuff get gunned down." Maybe I tell her gunfire happened in front a me, get her to think me brave.

"Well." She waved at me like she shooing me out. "Reckon I don't need you no more."

"I find nother supplier." Moved to where she stand by the counter. "Other times I deliver you some, I never take you up on spendin time with you."

"I run the house now. I ain't spendin time with no country boy."

"You say you a country gal."

"Ain't no more. But lookie you." She take a gander at me from hair to shoes. "You never wear nothin but them overalls what say rube louder'n a car horn."

Sparkly necklace pulled my mind to her neck.

"Ain't got no white powder, or nice clothes, but I got greenbacks." Leaned close. Wanna pull down the hair she got wrapped up under a scarf.

"Take it easy fella."

"Why you ain't gonna do good by me?"

Ana Marie looked way from me. "Jolene."

"You think Jolene my gal?"

Hear a knock.

"Jolene at the door."

Turned, seen Jolene outside the window with a big box. Ana Marie let her in. I folded the newspaper, stick it under my coat. Jolene tell me I made up what happened to Daniels. Didn't knowed what she say bout that story I needed somebody to read me. Maybe she say the newspaper lie like she think I lied.

"Leastwise you don't come with empty hands, Jole." Ana Marie lay hands on the box Jolene dropped on the table.

Jolene dressed for work in her smoke shop, Ana Marie looked like she needed coffee, but they looked like sisters.

"This fit me so I reckon this coat fit you." Jolene whipped off the box lid.

Ana Marie fingered the wool. "Mighty fine."

"Got nother one in the car." Jolene pointed outside like she telling somebody git. "Do me some fast talkin. Get me a special deal for two. Gonna bring Glory that one."

"There you go gain talkin bout Glory." Ana Marie fling the coat outta the box. "I sick a hearin bout Glory. But this here right nice."

"I gonna go." Gotta find somebody to read me that newspaper.

"Nobody invite you." Jolene looked at me like I a mouse poking my nose outta a hole in the wall. Wondered how she see me if I get me a nice suit like she got.

"You ain't got no bun in your oven yet?"

Sammy Jean poured boiling water in cups. "Someday."

Mason ain't to home. He take clay pots to sell in town. Sammy Jean read real good by then. Tell me they called what happened a 'Valentine's Day massacre'. Said six fellas shot in a warehouse in Chicago.

"Worry bout you somethin fierce," Sammy Jean said.

"North Carolina ain't no Chicagie." Drink tea Sammy Jean set down in front a me.

"Hurry and finish that."

Ain't bad stuff with honey mixed in. How some shine taste in this? When I emptied the cup Sammy Jean snatched it. She studied the picture the tea leaves made. Her face like she trying to add a bunch of big numbers in her head.

"You best watch yourself."

"That newspaper story get you to worry. Like I say, ain't nothn like that round here."

"Nope." Sammy Jean keep peering at them tea leaves. "I see three messy spots here on the side. That mean three folks close to you gonna get kilt. One spot real small, may be a young'un."

"That tell what happen before." Think a Cob, John Henry, Daniels. John Henry the only onea them three I get long with but they all close to me in some way or nother.

"No, no." Sammy Jean shake her head. "Tea leaves never tell your past. They only tell your future."

FIFTY-SIX

"Bet you like workin here more'n some warehouse where folks get kilt."

"Yep, this place great, great, great." Ace sweep the black and white checkered floor. He ain't sat down one time since I get there. "Men that come in this place, they got dough. I can get you a job if you want. Don't gotta know barbering."

"Deliverin whiskey my job." Leaned back in the barber chair, catch a whiff a witch hazel, peered out the window at the blue and red striped pole. "But if'n you hear bout other blind pigs what need shine, you tell me."

Ace clinked little bottles round on a shelf. Wished he stop moving for a second. "Guy that the boss of this speak easy got others. You should talk to him."

"Sound good. How I do that?"

"Guy's name Big Ben." Ace looked round. "Where my broom?"

"By the window. How I find that there Big Ben?"

"He going to this revival." Ace tapped a handbill somebody stick to the window.

"Revival and whiskey? Odd mix."

"Big Ben tell me that his plan." Ace rubbed spots off the window. "Happening in Glad Town. A great place. I go there all the time. Where my drink?"

Never seen Ace in Glad Town.

"Your drink over here. How I spot that there Big Ben?"

"First you find my pal Jesse." Glad when Ace sit down. "Jesse owns the camp in Glad Town. Good guy, use to be mayor of some town in Maryland. Jesse point out Big Ben to you." Ace lighted onea his hand rolled smokes what smelled like burned coffee and skunk.

Sounded like Ace didn't knowed Jesse a negre, head negre in Glad Town but ain't no owner. Wondered what true bout the tale Ace tell. Gotta grab the chance, go to the revival. If I can sell whiskey to a line of blind pigs, I didn't need to deliver to no warehouses where bullets fly.

Take me out a Camel, strike a match. Idea in my head flickered like that dancing flame.

"Hey, Ace. Where I buy me a nice suit round these parts?"

Showed up at the smoke shop in new clothes feeling like a big city fella. Get the wind knocked outta my mood when I seen the same handbill in the window like the one Ace tell me bout. If Jolene go to that revival she like a downed tree in the road to me finding Big Ben.

Bells on the door jangled, reckoned Jolene didn't hear cause she keep moving cigar boxes this way and that, dusting, for a whole couple minutes.

"You must not knowed who I be."

"Course I do, lookin at your sorry face for near on five years."

More'n eight years. She pay more mind to them stogies than me.

"Reckon my new duds throw you off."

"Them not new. But that suit gonna look better with the new shirt I get you."

"You get me a present?" Big-city-fella feeling come back.

"Get new shirts for me, you, Little Joe, Big Jack and Clyde." She shake her rag in my direction. "We all wearin them to the revival in Glad Town next week."

Oughta knowed she didn't get one for only me. "Sittin in the middle of all them sweaty bodies ain't for me."

"You goin and you take Little Joe and Big Jack, I get Clyde with my car."

How I gonna track Big Ben with all them O'Haras in tow?

"Who learn you to tie that tie?" Jolene dragged out a chair. "Sit, let me fix that mess."

Plop down like a young'un she scolded.

Ain't no use talking Jolene outta something she got her mind set on. Leastwise, Jolene ain't dragging Lulahbelle long with her swelled up belly. Maybe I get lucky, Lulahbelle drop the baby same day, O'Haras forget bout the revival.

Jolene leaned over me. She undid the knot at my windpipe, flipped and folded nother one, did a good job a not touching my skin. She so close I feel her heat, smelled her clean white shirt. Wanna put my hands on her but that pistol in the holster on her hip in the way.

FIFTY-SEVEN

Folks swarmed to the revival like bees to a rose garden. Next to the last Saturday in March sunshine ain't too hot. In case some folks bring them paper Coca Cola hand fans the Chimney store give out free.

Baby ain't borned yet. Lulahbelle said she think nother week or so. Darn my luck. She didn't feel up for no revival.

Fellas stand by the tent, make sure nobody bring in no guns. Jolene grumbled, put her pistol under the seat of her runabout. Little Joe said, "Not gonna be no Harveys here leastwise. Them varmints not no religion types, sure enough."

We sneak in some whiskey, take swigs. No religion folk seen cause we stand behind Clyde, he taller than all us. Pretty soon people in robes start singing while a couple others played finger-harps. We take seats in the back. After the song a fella, a real gent, come from the side with a lady on his arm. He take her to a chair before he go behind the Bible stand. Little Joe elbowed me, whispered "Lookie her."

Clyde, Big Jack and Jolene hawk-eyed the woman too. Lotta fellas in the tent peered at her like she a storm cloud after a long dry summer. She got hair color of the sun, eyes color of the sky, a face that said she cared. Fine lady what deserved somma that romance stuff. Preacher got hisself a gem.

Preacher reeled in my mind with his words, smooth like dark likker. His sermon ain't what I reckoned. He didn't tell us how much we sinned, how we all damned to hell, like other religion folks I happened cross. He talked bout how we needed to give God thanks for everything, bad stuff to boot.

"He is your praise, and He is your God, that has done for you these great and terrible things, which your eyes have seen. Deuteronomy 10:21."

Tossed that idea round like dirt under a plow, furrow didn't quite go deep enough. What God gotta do with folks like Daniels and Cob getting shot, or other folks getting dead?

Heat picked up a bit. Folks flapped them Coca-Cola fans. But Preacher keep his sleeves buttoned, his tie tight to his windpipe. He didn't let a hair get outta place. He didn't sweat neither in his white suit.

When Preacher moved to work folks on tuther side the tent I spied B. J. Harvey in the crowd. Little Joe lose that bet. Peeked to see if them O'Haras spotted him. They too busy eyeing the Preacher's lady. Good thing I didn't draw a bead on no other Harveys.

After a while the harps played again, singers commenced to hum.

"the Lord talkin to me." Preacher put one hand on his head, one in the air. "Somebody here today in a lotta pain...and guilt. Shame for things not their fault, shame for death."

My insides buzzed like bees in there. He talking bout me? I ain't got no guilt.

"You know who you are. Come forward and be *healed*."

Singers hummed louder. B. J. stand. Bees in my innards stopped.

"Now everybody, get on your feet. Sing praises to the Lord." Benches scraped dirt. Everybody stand. Preacher raised his talk over the singing, crying, wailing. "Come forward all that want to repent. Leave your life of sin behind. Make room in the aisle for them what want to redeem their souls."

B. J. moved to the aisle. Jolene brushed by me on her way to the aisle on tuther side. Grabbed her arm. She shake me off. B. J. still in a bad way where he want a O'Hara clobber him? Lose sight of him in the herd at the front. Jolene glided her way front like she got wings, smile on her face like she seen a angel. Hit me she ain't seen B. J.. She gone forward for sake of her own soul.

Crying, wailing calmed down. Folks streamed outta the tent, some stayed up front. What I do? Go get Jolene out, way from B. J., or get Big Jack and Little Joe out so they didn't see him? I posta look for Big Ben, now I gotta worry bout this mess.

"We outta whiskey, sure enough." Little Joe get that hound dog look.

"Got more in my truck."

Outside by the cars and mule carts, me, Little Joe and Clyde drink more shine. Big Jack catch a nap in bed of my truck cause he run the still all night.

"Feel fet down, thure nuff." Little Joe wiped a drop of white lightning from his chin. "Fleacher didn't do no mirticles."

Miracles? Maybe a miracle O'Haras didn't see B. J..

Clyde looked one way then back real quick-like, stared out into clear sky. Acted like he seen somebody steal from the collecting plate. Peeked that way. B. J. Harvey get in a car with the Mitchell family what lived in Cedar Springs. Car headed to the road, passed Jesse driving a truck.

Put the jug in Little Joe's shaky hand. "Gotta take a piss, be right back."

Jesse parked by the building where they got the Cherokee show. At his truck door before he stepped out. "My pal Ace say to tell you 'hey'."

Jesse looked at me like I soap floating in buttermilk. "Done knows nobody name a Ace."

Nother one a them tall tales Ace tell. Oughta knowed. Wanna choke that fool. Followed Jesse round the truck. "Must not hear him right. Reckon you don't knowed a fella namea Big Ben, neither."

"Well, no." Jesse opened the door on that side. "But I do hears some tent meeting mens say who he be."

Glory take Jesse's hand, he helped her outta the door. Never think she come here after what happen to John Henry. Course made sense Glory wanna come spend time with her kind. Jesse and Glory make a nice couple.

"Over yonder, Big Ben, in a white suit, with his women."

Preacher and his wife stand where Jesse pointed. He that boss of all them speak easys? Think Big Ben probably a fella with nice clothes, airs like folks in them moving pictures. Never reckoned him onea them Bible thumper.

Lotta folks going to shake hands with Preacher and his wife so I go too. Jolene come from tuther way. We got to the back of the line at the same time.

"What you think you doin, fool?" Jolene pulled a mad schoolmarm face. "No way you gonna get in my way of becomin a legend."

FIFTY-EIGHT

"Tell Preacher how much I like his show, all I gonna do," I said.

"You enjoy that sermon so much, why you not go forward?" Jolene said.

"His words do me different." Made my skin crawl like waking to a mouse crawling on my face.

"I Bet. She not gonna give you one look."

Folks moved off. Preacher's wife open, Jolene moved in. "Lookin forward to baptizin tomorrow. What I gotta wear for that?"

"Outfit you wearin now look right nice." That lady run her fingers down the arm a Jolene's crisp white shirt. "No need to worry bout clothes. We bring robes for y'all to change into." She flashed her teeth.

Take a breath when my turn come to talk to Preacher. Before he seen me, he tilted his head, peered off into the sky like he listening to something far off.

"Enjoy your doins today," I said.

"For it is God who works in you, both to will and to work for his good pleasure. Philippians 2:13."

"Funny you say that. Work what on my mind."

"Would you like me to pray with you?"

Sweat trickled down my back like in the tent. "Pray for me, for my work. See I a comb seller, and I need to find more places to buy my combs."

"Hmmm." Preacher looked at me like I a truck tire stuck in the mud. "You come back tomorrow for the baptizin. Might be the Lord tell me about a place for you."

"I don't gotta get dunked do I?"

"Only if the Lord move you. You can watch with His flock if you wish." He put on a kind face. "Brothers, my heart's desire and prayer to God for them is that they may be saved. Romans 10:1"

"Uh, thank you." Ain't going nowhere near that water tomorrow.

Preacher shake my hand, his hot as a fire poker.

Jolene still jawed at Preacher's wife, I headed back to my truck. Little Joe sit on the ground, his head on one tire, mouth open, snoring. Too much likker.

"Where Jolene at?" Clyde's big feet stick out the window of her runabout.

"She gettin religion. Wantin to get baptized and all."

Clyde chuckled.

"Help me haul Little Joe into the truck," I said.

"Ain't my job."

Take some persuading but Clyde dragged his sorry behind outta the car to help. I go find Jolene.

Seen her outside by the main hall. "We gotta talk." She yanked Glory by the arm way from Jesse and couple other negre folks. Follow Jolene and Glory round the building. Hide by the corner so they didn't knowed I watched.

"Why the hell you let him touch you?" Jolene's face lose the glow from the revival.

"He treat me right. Done nit-pic at me, like some folks."

"I never nit-pic." Jolene slammed a hand on the log wall.

"He done tells me how to dress, how to act. He done just drink, he eat my cookin."

"You cook for him?" Jolene's cheeks go from raw meat pink to tomato red. "What else you do for him?"

"He not damaged inside. He let a body love him, not like some folk."

Jolene throw her fist into the side a Glory's head. Glory pushed her, Jolene shoved back, hard. Glory fall down in the dirt. Reckoned that the end of the fight.

Wrong. Glory scrambled to her feet. She got a rock in her hand. Looked like she got a knot in her gut.

Jolene roostered Glory into the wall, plunked hands on either side. "You not doin this to me."

"Dat what you say." Glory whacked Jolene in the head with that rock.

Blood trickled down Jolene's face, she stepped back, raised her hand again.

I run out trapped Jolene round the middle.

"Let go, fool." Jolene tried to loose her arms from my grip.

"I finish here." Glory tossed way the rock, headed to the kitchen door.

Let Jolene go. She spin, clobbered me in the head. "Mind your own damn business. And don't you dare get in the way a me gettin the baptism. Don't show your face in Glad Town tomorrow."

FIFTY-NINE

Dumped Big Jack and Little Joe off in front of Fresh Farms, reckoned they stumble home from there. Wanna drive, clear my head what still hurt from Jolene's fist. Passed the turn off for a roadhouse, too fast to stop. Think of pulling in at the O'Brien House. No, ain't in a mood to let my mind float in the clouds. Thumbed down the throttle all the way to Juniper.

"Your face like somebody fix you your favorite pie, then make you sit in it." Sammy Jean set somma that tea a hers in front of me.

Clutched the warm cup. Air outside cool now. "Tell you I fine."

"Problem that Jolene gal. I can tell."

"I seen a miracle today." Tell Sammy Jean bout the goings on at the revival. Leave out part where Preacher stirred up my innards.

"Give me that empty cup." She peered in at the leaves, pulled a face like she smelled pig shit. "Bewilderment. All I see."

"Knowed what I gotta do. Stay way from Glad Town tomorrow. Maybe B. J. onea them three blobs you seen in them last tea leaves."

"Don't see nonea that here this time." Sammy Jean go to a chest, come back with a cloth bag. "Stick your hand in this here. Bring out whatever you latch onto first."

My poor little sister cottoned to playing games. Did as she said.

She studied what carved in the stone I plunked down on the table.

"See more confusion. What must live in you."

"Me? I got my mind set. Ain't goin near that there baptizin."

"Pull nother onea these here." Sammy Jean offered me the bag again.

Blowed out air, draw nother rock.

"This one say healin sure as I holdin it in my hand." She sounded like Preacher.

"I don't need no healin."

"If'n you got bewilderment and you need to get healed, reckon you best go back to that there revival tomorrow."

"Ain't bewildered."

"Ain't what the stones and tea leaves say. I see the truth in your eyes. What you come here for? What you wanna hear from me?"

"This shit ain't nothin but foolishness." Flicked one a them stones off the table. "Jolene tell me stay way. That what I gonna do."

"Oh, I see, you fraida her." Sammy Jean pulled a lemon sucking face. "So much you lose out on more business."

"Ain't fraida nobody. Got me enough business."

"You love them greenbacks cause you bury more'n you spend."

"You ain't nobody to say what I love. Don't wanna be round when Jolene meet up with B. J. at the dunkin."

"You tell me God keep her from recognizin him."

Rubbed the sore spot over my ear. "Recognize. Where you get such a big word?"

Sammy Jean waved at some books by the bed. "Mason encourage me to read."

"Y'all do somethin sides readin, maybe you get you a bun in your oven by now.'

"Ain't your concern. You go tomorrow, face your devils, look em in the eye."

"Don't tell me what to do. You ain't Ma."

"Course I ain't. Ma so weak surprise me her head don't flop over." Sammy Jean crossed her arms. "Me and you gotta fight gainst that weakness. Mean you gotta find you some courage. Only way you get over your troubles, you gotta face em."

"You callin me chicken." Backhanded the teacup off the table, it break on the floor. Smashed pieces under my Brogans on my way out the door.

SIXTY

Turned in at Glad Town in the morning. Seen Jolene's runabout coming right for me. A fella with chubby cheeks at the steering wheel. He swerved last minute missed my truck by a inch. I recollected Jolene's runabout got a white top, that one got a black one. Her car nowheres round.

Grass round the springs in Glad Town like walking on feathers. The singers meow out "The Old Rugged Cross". Preacher wear a black robe with string sewed to the bottom that he tied round his ankles.

Spotted B. J. with the Mitchell clan. Singers switch to "When the Roll is Called Up Yonder".

Preacher strolled into the spring till water up to his waist. Reckoned the robe tied to his legs so the cloth didn't float. A repenter waded into the spring. Preacher put one hand on her back, with tuther he take her arm. He leaned forward, pushing the sinner back, her hand over her nose. When the poor wretch under Preacher yelled, "I baptize you in the name of the Father, Son, and Holy Ghost." Then he pulled her up slow so the water flowed off in sheets. Look to me like a dance people do in fancy duds.

B. J's turn come. Some folks whispered something bout O'Haras and shooting. Hold my breath like I the one getting dunked. No O'Haras fired at B. J.. Everybody clapped.

Ina Mae Mitchell shouted, "Thank you, Jesus."

B. J. come outta that water, his face peaceful like a sunny morning after a heavy rain. I recollected how the day he shoot Cob his face looked like a dark storm cloud.

Thunder rumbled under my skin. Worried myself sick bout what Jolene do when she seen B. J.. She didn't show. Get me a good mind to whip her behind for the fretting I done.

Swim through the pond of bodies round the spring. Get in my truck, pushed in the clutch before I remembered bout talking to Preacher. I go wait by the top of the meadow for my chance with Big Ben.

Hunted some more for Jolene in the group of worshipers. Maybe I missed her.

"You wont find her." Jesse come up to me. "Every man in dat crowd wonder where she at."

Make sense, others waiting for a O'Hara to shoot at some Harvey.

Jesse showed a lotta teeth in his grin. "Dat preacher wife got looks dat give a dead man wood."

Worked so hard watching for Jolene, I didn't notice Preacher's wife ain't round neither.

SIXTY-ONE

Preacher draw me a map, said go to that place if I wanna sell combs. I go off to find Jolene. Gonna tell her what for. She ain't at the O'Hara place when I stopped for bacon and cornbread. Lullahbelle said Little Joe getting to chores left from going to the tent meeting.

Find him with his feet in the creek, laying back on the bank, his arms folded over his face. Squatted next to him. "Real sorry bout not takin you to the baptizin."

"Don't wanna go. Ain't feelin good," Little Joe said. "Too much branch water last night, sure enough."

"Where Jolene at?"

"Who know. We gotta talk bout gettin them Gibbs boys set up with a still." He groaned, rubbed his eyes. "Wanna help clean chicken coops? Lullahbelle gettin nasty bout work not gettin done."

"Sorry, got somma my own nastiness to deal out."

Leave him to baby his headache, retch up whatever he got in his gut.

Drive by the O'Brien house, not even the goats seemed wake there, keep going. Next I tried some roadhouse by the river. Didn't see Jolene. Got a drink. The shine burned my gullet like the words I planned for Jolene.

Hit town when the heat working itself so hard I feel the sky sweat. Parked in front of the smoke shop. Peered in the window, seen nothing. Go round the back. Spied the runabout. Back door open. Take out a cigarette to calm what feel like white water running through me. A fan inside. Electricity a luxury of living in town. Glory got electricity but only for lights at night.

"You just gonna stand there blowin smoke in my window?" Jolene in the doorway. She got on her farm clothes, a union suit and overalls with the straps hanging loose, not her town clothes.

"You posta get you dunked today." Pointed my Camel at her like a gun. "Shoulda knowed you lyin."

"You blind? My tire flat." Law, if the runabout didn't lean low on one side. "Ed at the garage put a patch on tomorrow. Say he take me to the baptisin with them cept his wife don't let him. Thinks he wanna leave her for me." She funning me?

"You got a spare. Bet you don't knowed how to change you a tire." Stomped my cigarette out.

"You ignorant bout tires. That spare never last on them dirt roads over to Glad Town." She snuffed her cigarette on the brick wall. "Don't leave that Camel butt lyin round my alley." She tossed her Lucky Strike in a metal can. "Come get some lemonade."

Flat tire served her right. I feel outta air like that innertube. "Good thing you don't go. B. J. Harvey there. Get hisself baptize. He most likely drown you if you go."

Jolene pulled a pitcher outta onea them fancy cabinets with a heavy latch. "Ice delivery not till tomorrow but that icebox still keep this pretty cool. Onea the best investments I ever make." She take a pull from a glass.

Maybe she didn't hear me. "No other Harveys there. But B. J. look real happy." I sit in a chair, she sit on the cot she used for sleeping.

"I know you make sure to speak to the preacher's wife."

"Nope. She ain't there."

Jolene's glass stopped on the way to her mouth. "You wrong bout that."

"Surprise me too. Then Jesse tell me why." Take a long sip, enjoyed the sweetness of the drink.

"Well?"

"She gotta lay down. Heat too much in her condition."

Jolene set her glass down next to a box of nails, opened a drawer. "Condition?" She pulled out a bottle.

"She with child."

"Oh, I know that." Jolene stirred the likker in the lemonade with a spoon like the ones at the Cardinals Nest Cafe.

"I tell Clyde I need all the whiskey you run. Need a load sooner than yesterday. Reckon Preacher gonna give me some good business."

"Business, humph." She wiped her mouth with her hand.

"Gonna make me some good greenbacks, I reckon."

"Boy, you don't even read. You don't got no idea bout real business. What you do nothin like me runnin this smoke shop. Puttin on a poker game every Saturday night to sell whiskey. That not countin makin the coffin varnish, runnin two farms. Decidin what stocks to buy."

"Why you still call me boy? I probably older than Little Joe what got a wife and baby soon. Make me a lotta money too."

"You keep tellin yourself that. I Reckon you make a dime or two someday." She drained her glass. "You gotta learn to put it in the bank."

I leave. No use talking to somebody what didn't listen. Gonna show her I make something of myself.

SIXTY-TWO

Best looking colored lady I ever seen come to the door. Glory fussed bout how wild her hair got, this gal got hers cut down to her scalp. She lead me down a hall. Reckoned Preacher a smart man if he got a room called a study.

"You get here quicker than I think." Preacher waved me to sit. Feel his eyes on my city clothes, worried he see how sloppy I got the dang knot on my tie.

"My buddy Ace, he work on my truck. That fella, he fix aeroplanes in the Great War so he make things go mighty fast."

"Then you do good in this business. This job require fast drivin." Preacher slide what looked like a tattered Bible over in front of him. "Reckon you know the barbershops I got in mind not interested in buyin combs."

"Yes, sir. Gonna get a hair tonic sign for my truck. Tonic I sell ain't for hair."

"Good thinkin." He fingered the Bible. "Let me see if God got a message for you." He closed his eyes, flipped the book open, stabbed a thumb down. "Proverbs 1:5. Let the wise hear and increase in learning, and the one who understands obtain guidance. Hmm."

"What that mean?" Hoped he don't get like he did at that tent meeting.

Preacher stared over my head. "Means you smart but gotta learn more."

Poor fella touched in the head like my own little sister.

"I know how to drive, run shine, sell shine too. Know how to draw some too."

"Let's ask God what He wants to teach you." Preacher flopped open, poked at the Bible gain.

"Romans 8:1. There is therefore now no condemnation for those who are in Christ Jesus." He beamed at a cross on the wall. "Ah, you need to learn you're not condemned."

Tired of his game, his big words, his not looking me in the face. Leaned close to a frame on his table. The picture got the preacher, his wife, some older lady.

"My late mother-in-law," Preacher said. "Wonderful woman. We miss her a lot."

"She right pretty. Like your wife. Don't reckon I ever get me a woman that good lookin."

The colored lady come in with a silver tray. "Take heart, son," Preacher said. "You be surprised what some women might see in a man. That right, Sassafras?"

"Yessiree." Sassafras poured coffee with her smooth, long hands.

I enjoyed watching her backside leave.

Preacher opened a new map, added more lines. "Other than the barbershops, I need you to deliver to a couple brothels. That all right with you?"

"Done that before." Couple times Jolene tell me take a load fulla jars to the O'Brien House. "If'n you a preacher how come you dealin with shine and brothels?"

"Family business." Preacher looked to pictures of other folks on his walls. "My kin run the stuff. But like what happens to every good moonshiner sooner or later, they get caught. I thank the Lord for sending me you, pray you stay outta prison."

Tried not to think a prison.

"Ain't God gainst likker and harlots?"

"Also that everyone should eat and drink and take pleasure in all his toil—this is God's gift to man." Preacher touched his Bible. "Ecclesiastes 3:13. The Lord forgives man's weakness. Praise God for his forgiveness and relish your own desires."

Reckoned Preacher a right nice fella if he take to folks what drink whiskey and visited jenny barns.

The door opened. I hope to see Sassafras bring me more coffee. She make the best joe I ever drink. A large fella come in. He the one in the runabout with the black top almost run me down before the baptizing. "This the boy you tell me about?"

Preacher's eyes frogged from the fella to me and back. "Yes, he wants to start preachin the gospel soon as possible. I found him a sponsor family, soon as he through with school he can go to seminary." Preacher pointed his chin at the fella. "This here's my business partner Stanley."

When Preacher got up, I stand too.

"Thank you for coming, B. J.." Preacher's voice sounded different when he called me the wrong name. He telling lies to his business partner? Ain't like no preacher I ever hear tell of.

He pretending me B. J. Harvey? Thinking that make me feel like a glop a syrup with ants crawling in the mess.

SIXTY-THREE

"You look wrecked as I feel, sure enough."

"Sleep off last night pretty much." If I got my way, I sleep more. Cut my eyes to see the dirt road to Pine Gap in the headlights. Truck bumped long on the mule cart ruts, branches scraped the roof. Noise didn't do my hangover no good.

"What eatin you? You sellin more whiskey than ever before. You need more folks makin the stuff. We gettin them Gibbs boys set up tonight. In couple weeks they run you off some good shine. Mighty good shine."

"How bout the jack I put out for barrels and sugar? Don't like throwing money down a shithouse."

"Take that outta what you get for their first run." Little Joe dragged out a jug from under the seat. Nother drink, his answer to everything. "You gettin them boys a still ain't you?"

"Yep." How he talk me into that? "Some kid namea Popcorn say he learnin hisself to make stills, give me a good deal. But I don't like puttin greenbacks outta my own pocket when I got no idea bout the product I gonna get. That what Jolene call bad business."

"I gonna teach them boys whiskey makin myself. That shine come out good, real good, sure enough." Little Joe take a gulp from the jug. "Ain't tellin Jole nothin bout my plan and you better not neither."

"Jolene find out, she blame me." Maybe I turn back, get out now. "Johnny and that runt the only ones left livin with Lulahbelle's folks. Put together they ain't got the sense God give a beetle bug."

"They handle runnin a still fine. Runt say he fifteen now."

"I get bad product outta this here plan, I gonna break that there jug over your head."

"Take it easy."

"Gimme some a that there likker." Snatched the jug from Little Joe, take a swallow.

"Like you joinin me in a drink more often but I get the idea you doin that cause you got somethin bugggin you."

Passed him back the jug, didn't say nothing. Let him keep his ideas to hisself.

After a while Little Joe said, "Bet Fellas at them barbershop speakeasies badger you bad."

"Nah." Too tired to think of nothing else. "Preacher got me deliverin to somma them jenny barns."

Little Joe chuckled. "You ain't got no problem with them places. You like em."

"Yep. But them ones Preacher call dens of iniquity. Some folks at them there houses don't close doors."

"Ain't nothin. That jenny barn in Chimney got paper-thin walls. Hear everythin, sure enough. So that like not closin doors."

Wished he hushed up. He didn't knowed what I seen. How I tell what them dens like? "Some folks don't go in rooms, they do their business out in the open where other folks see." Ain't business neither. Some gal cornered me, didn't ask for no dough.

"Hmmm. Maybe next time you take me with you."

"Shut your mouth. You got you a wife." No way in hell he see what go on there.

"Man got a right to dream, don't he?" Little Joe take nother pull on the jug. "Damn! I drop the cork." Little Joe feel round the floorboard.

I seen headlights come from a side road. A dark colored truck pulled out in front of me. Make me think of Snake Harvey's truck. Hoped that ain't him. My foot go for the brake, something make the peddle stick. "That shit roll under my feet."

"Got it." Little Joe yanked the cork from under the brake, take nother gulp before he plug up the jug.

Slow down to let that fella get far head me. Didn't let on bout what I seen. Turned in at the Gibbs place.

Lamps lighted up the barn. Lotta fellas in there. They all clapped time, shouted. "Go. Go. Go."

Me and Little Joe go in. Fellas in a circle. In the middle stand a cow, the runt on a hay bale behind the cow. He pumped his hips, screwed up his face like he shitting out a hammer. The cow looked like she sleeping. The runt screamed, stepped back, pulled up his overalls. Crowd whooped and hollered. Cow didn't so much as moo.

"You look green," Little Joe said to me.

My head spin, leaned on the barn wall, get out my flask, take a long pull.

Runt jumped off the hay bale, older brother Johnny come up, slapped him on the back. "Good job! From now on we call you Bull."

"I gotta get outta here," I said.

"We gonna help Johnny and Bull setup the mash."

"Leavin. Them boys crazy with their tallywackers."

Dragged them barrels and supplies off before I crawled in the straw in the bed of my truck with the jug from under the seat.

SIXTY-FOUR

With Gibbs' whiskey added to my other suppliers, I got me plenty a product to deliver to the places Preacher send me. All that picking up and dropping off didn't leave me time to stop in Swift River. Looked forward to seeing Jolene at Thanksgiving but she stayed up to the Grady place with stinky ole Clyde, same thing at Christmas. When I said I going to see her, Little Joe said, "One more drink to celebrate."

In the end I stayed at the O'Hara place make faces at baby Buck to get him to laugh, show his two little white teeth. That baby looked more like Big Jack than Little Joe or Jolene. Little Joe said Buck gonna grow outta that.

One crispy Saturday afternoon in February I make up my mind. Tonight, I ain't gonna go to onea them brothels. Take a spin to Swift River, parked. Drink from a jar of shine, to keep the cold off, tell myself.

Pushed open the door to the smoke shop, bells jingled. Place cold as a cave. "You open?"

"That what the sign say." Jolene come in from the back. Her collar buttoned but she got the sleeves on her shirt rolled up. Not like her.

Boxes a tobacco on the shelves spread out, not stacked high like I recollected. "This shop quiet as a church on Monday morning."

"Reckon you know all bout church now. All that time you hold up at that preacher's house."

"Not too much time. How you knowed bout that?"

"Folks talk. I listen." She smug like a crow what steal a shiny coin. "Don't find time to come see me, what'cha do at that showy preacher's house?"

"Preacher teachin me bout prayer. And he like my drawin."

"You?" Jolene hen cackled. "Buck do better smearin grits. You a phony. You buy and sell whiskey, that don't go with prayin."

"Preacher say where you pray make all the difference. He tell me bout where to go, find me some peace." Ain't getting no peace in here with Jolene and her sassy mouth.

"What his wife think of him dealin with the likes a you?" Jolene poured a splash of shine in a jelly jar, slide the stuff to me, pulled out a pack a Lucky Strikes. "Want one?"

Patted down my pockets, didn't got me no Camels. "Much obliged." Downed what in that jar fast.

"You sure knock a drink back good." Jolene lighted her Lucky, give me the matches. Where her fancy silver lighting thing at? "Preacher's wife pop her bun outta her oven?"

"Sorry to say she did."

"Sorry? You fool. A baby a happy thing."

"This one ain't like no baby I seen before. She got a small head, flat nose, slanty eyes. Preacher don't touch her. Say they gonna send her off somewhere."

Jolene cut her eyes at me. Lines on her face I never seen before. "A baby not like a car. Nobody send their young'un off to get fixed. Man a preacher, he gotta do better."

"Preacher talk bout givin God thanks. He say different when talk come to that there baby." Pushed my jar her way, hoped she fill it. Itched my neck.

"What wrong with you? Stop your scratching."

Tapped the toppa my head. "This here haircut give me fits. Them barbershops I deliver to sell whiskey, don't cut hair worth a burned biscuit."

"Bad haircut, right. I oughta cut your hair. But I like that new suit you wearin. Make you look like a real gent."

Jolene barbering my hair sound mighty good, specially when she liked my city suit.

Outside I hear a roar like some circus tiger get loose in Swift River. Dark blue pickup speed down the street.

"Snake Harvey showin off." Jolene poured more in my jar. "Crow Tritt tell me Snake got him a girl in Pine Gap."

Pine Gap? Reckoned I right bout the truck I seen on way to the Gibbs place.

"Maybe I stay for the poker game tonight." Hoped Jolene happy bout that.

"Don't do them no more. Men don't come in like they use to. I make more money pourin drinks for Anna Marie. Come there tonight."

Studied the shelves. "You gotta restock soon."

"No money."

"Talk round say the bull market in New York City go belly up. Swift River Bank close too?"

"Mr. Pewtie what own the bank, he run off. Bastard leave me and most folks round here down a dry well. All gone. Every feckin dime." Jolene pulled a face like Buck when he dropped his teddy bear.

"Got some jack buried here and there. I get you some boxes of stogies." Waited for her to thank me.

Jolene turned cardinal red. "You don't got what I need. You think you fix thins? That money belong to me. Now a pack a Luckys set me back."

"Price a corn still good, price a likker too. Sell more shine, you make more dough." Gulped rest of the white lightning in my jar.

"Me loosin everything don't mean shit to you." She unbuttoned her collar, showed her scrawny neck.

"Hush up and listen. I wanna help."

"Don't you tell me to hush. I don't want your help. I do things my way. You go back to your prayin."

My blood perked like coffee on a hot stove. Jolene happy to see me then she talked bad bout my drawings. Now she throwed my giving spirit in my face. She think I ain't got no jack. All them years I worked the O'Hara and Grady farms, tending the stills longside tuthers. Didn't mean a damn thing to Jolene. What I miss not going to that den of iniquity that night?

Sweep my arm on the counter, send a box fulla lizard green cigars flying. "Close this shop for all I care. Never like the place no how." Stomped out. Slammed the door so hard the bells crashed on the glass. Wanna get loose of Jolene once and for all. In the truck I opened me nother jar fulla shine.

SIXTY-THREE

Every mean word Jolene said over the years rooted inside me, festered like a rattlesnake bite. Buried my mind in my work.

Some fella at onea them blind pigs tell me Big Ben wanna see me. While I waited for Preacher, Sassafras let me sit in the kitchen. She tell me bout the fighting Preacher did with his wife.

"Mr. Ben claim his pa say childrens like dis one be from the devil." Sassafras placed the cradle in a corner near the stove, not too close.

Baby sleep like a angel with her hand on her flat face. She ain't no prettier or no uglier than Buck. She borned different, that all.

"Where the missus at?"

"She gots to dolls herself up. Supper with outta town company tonight." Sassafras get a spark in her eye what die out quick. "Mr. Ben tells me keep dis chile hushed."

"You reckon Preacher and his missus happy ever gain?"

"Dat po'r little babydoll change everything." Sassafras plopped nother piece of fried chicken on my plate.

Bite into that juicy breast, licked my lips. Her fried chicken like heaven.

"You believe in happily ever after?" Used my napkin, not my shirt, so Sassafras see I a gent.

"Thinks I do." Sassafras studied the wall like she counting every bump and spot.

"There a place I knowed called Glad Town where some negres put on a Cherokee show then they gather out back for some fun of their own. Head negre there, he call hisself Jesse, he a palla mine." Mustered up some nerve before I go on. "Want I take you there this Saturday night?"

Sassafras looked at me like I asked her to cut off her right ear. "You tries to court me?"

"If'n I do, you willin to give it a whirl?"

"Ain't no good idea." Sassafras shake her head, pulled a lemon sucking face.

"You reckon Preacher ain't gonna like it? I ask him if'n you want. He say folks oughta do what make them happy."

"Nope." She get up, slapped more corn casserole on my plate with a wood spoon, sit back down. "I thinks colored and white ain't right for one nother. Most white folk good peoples, but I never wanna go with nonea them, in dat way."

Her corn casserole sat like gold nuggets in front of me. Her words kilt my hungry belly. "*Never* one strong word."

"Dat the way I feels. Ain't gonna change."

"Tell Preacher I sorry. I think of somethin I gotta do right quick like."

Get to my truck, scrambled for a jar. What I gonna do after that punch in the gut? Shine only thing on my mind. Didn't wanna drink by my lonesome. Knowed Little Joe up for knocking one back.

Didn't work out like I hoped. Little Joe get oiled early on, slipped off to sleep before Lullahbelle get Buck down for the night. I wandered up the path to the store.

Glory set on the lone wicker chair outside her cabin. She said for me to sit on her steps, offered me coffee. She hinted at a splash of whiskey in hers. I take my flask from my pocket. "Never go nowhere without a helpin or two."

That close to the road the creek rippling too far off to hear but I catch a whiff of moss now and again. Somewhere some owl hooted, over the house a bat shrieked.

"Jesse ain't here tonight?" I said. By then they jumped the broom.

"He only here couple days a week." Glory pulled her long sweater tighter.

"Why you don't wear that fancy coat Jolene give you?"

Take a minute before Glory talked. "Jolene gots a nice black wool coat. She never gives me one."

"She tell me the coat a gift for you."

"Ha!" Glory take a long pull on her cup. "What dat girl say and what she do, two different things."

Jolene ever tell folks she gonna give me presents she never give me?

Poured Glory nother splash from the bottle, take more for me too. The night critters played their music. Glory tapped her foot, reckoned to some song in her head.

"If'n Jesse white, you still marry him?"

Lamp light shine on teeth in her open mouth. "You thinks I gots a problem wid whites?" Glory let out a belly laugh. "My problem wid folk dat like to gives lovin, but turns round, say no, no when I wanna touch em too. Folks like dat fraida feelin somethin good."

My head spin like I caught in a waterfall. How Glory knowed bout my bad side? How she seen my innards, like Sammy Jean and Preacher do?

I stand, trees swayed. Stumbled off. Wondered where I gonna land.

SIXTY-FOUR

When I picked up whiskey squirreled away by the river, I didn't set foot in Swift River. Cedar Springs neither, cept to load shine.

Couple times I seen Little Joe to get his supply.

"Don't feel right with B. J. Harvey living so close, sure enough. He stay at the Mitchell place."

"Don't wanna talk. Got other things to do."

"Folks say he get religion. Gonna go to preacher school."

"Religion last thing I wanna hear." Recollected how Preacher pretended me B. J..

"How you reckon one them Harvey pigs run to that gospel shit? Snake one evil bastard, sure enough."

"B. J. and Snake different."

"You standin up for B. J. Harvey? Fella what shoot at me?"

"Ain't standin up for nobody." Maybe I oughta tell Little Joe he ain't the one B. J. shoot at. Opened a jar, gave Little Joe first swig.

"Wish that Harvey son-a-bitch get his ass outta Cedar Springs."

I wished Big Jack the one what helped me load their shine. He didn't say three words bout no Harveys nor no religion.

That how that year go. Steered clear of them O'Haras for the most part.

Day after wildflowers popped up at the end of the next winter I drive to Cedar Springs to get some mountain dew dumb ole Clyde posta drop. Dawn sun ain't showed her orange face yet. Mile or two past the Mill Creek turn off I slowed my truck.

A tree blocked the road. By the stump a car lie on its side. Tires all I seen. Stopped, leave on the headlights. Get out to look round. Car a runabout with a tan top, hood crumpled like a sleeped-in bed.

Seen a white shirt. Run that way. Grabbed a arm, turned over the body.

"Jolene." Hold my breath. She slit her eyes. "Thank the good Lord." Gotta act fast. Scooped her in my arms. She warm, gave me hope.

Speed to the O'Haras' like the law after me. Blowed my horn all the way from the road to the yard. Slide to a stop.

Big Jack and Little Joe run out.

Quick like a frog jumping in a pond I get Jolene outta the truck, back in my arms. She got cuts on her hands and arms. Most the blood come from her head, get some on me.

"I get Glory," Little Joe said. "She good with doctorin."

By lantern light Lulabelle and I lie Jolene in Big Jack's bed. Helped clean blood from her wounds. Worried with every groan she made.

Glory checked Jolene from one end to tuther. "Keep watch over her. Wake her every couple hours, make her drink dat water."

Did most the sitting myself first couple days, think on what life like if Jolene gone for good. Soon she stayed wake for a hour or two at a time.

"Gotta go off do me some buyin and sellin. Promise I come back soon." My hand on the door.

Jolene's face showed how all them bruises gotta hurt. Her eyes fixed on me. "Thank you." Her voice sounded like a itty bitty bird.

SIXTY-FIVE

Tell Preacher only praying I do, I do for my sick friend. He said he pray for Jolene too. Back to Cedar Springs by Saturday.

Buck galloped up when I get outta my truck at the O'Haras. "This young'un got legs like oak trees," I said.

Lulahbelle take clothespins outta her mouth. "Gettin mighty hard to keep track of him. Leastwise oak trees set tight."

Helped Lulahbelle get the clothes basket to the porch. Little Joe come outta the house bout the time Big Jack get there, pulled some greenbacks from his pocket. "Sell the runabout. Jole say to. Wood boy buying."

Recollected when Jolene buyed that car, her pride in the machine.

When Big Jack go in I asked Little Joe, "She recollect what make her crash?"

"She say somebody knock a tree down in the road so she crash." Little Joe squatted, catched Buck in one arm. Buck giggled, pulled way, run round the side of the porch. "We goin up to the store tonight. Glory celebratin her new electric coffeepot."

We go down to the creek. From where the runabout lie on one side, front bumper bashed in, looked like she run into the tree trunk. She don't hit the tree in the road.

"I don't drink too much of late," Little Joe said. "Done good, sure enough."

"Happy for you. Jolene say she worry bout you." Wished I cut down on my drinking.

"Jole and Lulahbelle both get after me. Hope you might need me to help with deliveries. We need the money, sure enough. Don't trust the price of corn to stick. Haulin shine to the city sound good to me."

Wondered when he get to begging me again bout taking a break from the farm. "Let me think on the idea." Some places I take that likker ain't no places I wanted Little Joe going.

"Promise to go light on the coffin varnish. Tonight different." He winked at me. "Got some celebratin to do. Lulahbelle think she in the family way again. Hope this one a gal."

Hoped Little Joe keep his promise to stay easy on the whiskey.

Moon ain't bright like couple weeks ago. Glory generous with the cream so we poured some on apple brown betty. Coffee taste real good too with plenty a cream and corn squeezins. Buck pushed on the lid to where Glory stashed the bait she sell. Little Joe said, "Get away from there now." Buck go chase after a big white moth.

The baby wear a black jumper fit him good. "Pretty spiffy duds he got on."

"We lucky, sure enough. Jole buy clothes he grow into before that there stock market go belly up."

Jesse up from Glad Town. He spend time with Glory when he can. Glory and Lulahbelle get the chairs, Big Jack and Jesse leaned on the porch poles. Hoped Jolene might come but she said she didn't feel strong enough yet. Me and Little Joe set on the end of the porch, got real used to the coffee with cream and likker.

"Gimme onea them," Little Joe said when I pulled out a pack of smokes. "What you got Luckys for? You only smoke Camels."

"This kind taste better."

"That moon sure somethin else." Little Joe settled back, blowed out smoke that looked like a haint to me. "Ever wonder what's up there in outer space?"

"Reckon they got all kinda pretty colors dancing every which way." I feel warm inside like sitting by a fire on a winter night.

Gazed in the clump of trees by the path what lead to the O'Hara place. Jolene stand in moonlight. Strip of cloth round her head to keep the cut clean. Wearing her town britches, a white shirt buttoned from the bottom to the chest, sleeves flapping open. Ain't like the spiffy Jolene what used to sit head table at poker games Saturday nights.

She gonna come join us? She swayed bit. Stared at something. Moved her hand to the pistol in the holster.

Followed Jolene's eyes to Jesse. She talked bad bout Jesse lotta times. She thinking she gonna shoot him?

Jesse ain't looking at her, he peered down the road.

Hear the engine, seen headlights ripple on the ground. Jesse run to the road, dive like a hawk after a rabbit. He bounced off a truck fender. Some pickup what looked like Snake Harvey's disappeared like Jesse never hit it.

Then I spotted what Jesse jumped for. We all rushed to the middle of the road.

Lulahbelle fall to her knees, wailed.

SIXTY-SIX

Little Joe and Lulahbelle didn't wanna talk bout what happened. Big Jack lay Buck to rest next to Jo Belle.

Go off to do my shine selling. When I got back wanna check on how Jolene feel, she nowhere round.

"The Grady Place," Big Jack said.

Get on up there quick. Jolene handed some bags from the mule cart to Clyde, he stand there like a dead tree.

"You doin better?" I said.

She got her Fedora on over her head bandage. "You carry that sack of can goods."

Picked up the bag, followed them inside.

"What'cha doin with all this here stuff?" My gut turned sour. "When you goin back to work at the smoke shop?"

"Never. No money for rent. Customers don't got no money neither."

Jolene take a bulging knapsack to the sleeping room.

Plunked the cans down on the table, hard.

Clyde looked at me like he eat the last piece of pie I got my eye on. "She moving back with me." He pulled some cans from that damn bag.

"Let's see how long that last." Moved way from Clyde.

Jolene come outta the sleeping room, unrolled a small quilt, folded it over the back of the rocker. She making herself to home when her kin in grief.

"We gotta do somthin." Words come out louder than I wanted. "Jesse say that there truck like the one Snake drive. That what I seen too. I talk to Sheriff Clayton, he don't like them Harveys."

"You and Jesse only ones what see." Jolene come closer to me. "Jesse's words in court mean shit. Plus Dove Tritt the judge, he on their side. I know you don't see Snake. You a liar, not a good one."

"If'n you go to the Harvey place I go too. Tween me, you, Little Joe and Big Jack we out number Stub, Snake and Toot. B. J. ain't there no more. Take Clyde too so we sure."

Chicken shit Clyde dropped a can of beans.

"Not goin near no Harveys." Jolene go to the fireplace, sweep the hearth with a little broom like she brushing off my words. "Ole Zeek step one foot on O'Hara land, my great grandpappy shoot him."

"You don't hear me say there more of us. Get Johnny and Bull Gibbs go long too."

Jolene hold up the broom like a hatchet she gonna chop my head off with. "Leave them nasty boys outta this."

"Want I fix some grub?" Clyde said.

"Go milk that goat. I not payin to feed no goat what don't pull her weight." Jolene pointed a finger at the door.

Enjoyed watching Clyde go out with his tail twixt his legs. "You gotta do somethin. Snake ain't gettin way with runnin down Buck."

"Damn right." Jolene fling down the broom, pushed up her rolled sleeves. "Got me a plan. One what work better'n your idea. Quit your rushin me." She plopped in the rocker. "I still got me headaches and dizzy spells."

Recollected how Glory tell us Jolene done concussed. Knowed she let me in on her plan when she better. Wished she do her resting some place other than where Clyde lived.

SIXTY-SEVEN

"Where Clyde at?" Grady place dark one summer night when I hauled Jolene from the O'Brien House.

"I tell him run off that double batch a mash I got brewing. Gonna keep him busy at the still till sunup." Jolene looked at me.

I shivered like somebody run a feather down my back. Me and her at the Grady place all by our lonesome sounded mighty nice to me.

"I gotta go change cause this heat squeeze down on me somethin fierce." Jolene disappeared behind the curtain to the sleeping room, come out in a blue nightshirt with no sleeves. What I think she don't got on under that nightshirt set me to sweating worse than I did all day.

She stoked the stove with kindling. "Gonna warm up somma this here rabbit stew. Not for me, for you, I don't take to vittles Clyde cook up. Glad I don't gotta hear his infernal banjo pingin."

Tasted the mess in the small bowl she gave me. Reckoned I didn't take to Clyde's vittles neither.

"Got a surprise for you." Jolene pulled a bottle outta her satchel.

"That the city likker I sell to Ana Marie."

"Ana Marie let me take this here one for poorin drinks there tonight. I wanna celebrate workin my plan gainst Snake soon."

"What your plan? Bet we gonna get them Harvey bastards good."

Jolene's eyes flashed in the firelight. "I let you know bright and early tomorrow. Tonight let's take things easy, set a bit." She poured us some dark whiskey, sipped from her cup, screwed up her face like she drinking weasel piss. "How you tolerate this? They let them barrels set round too long. Take mine. I gonna stick to good ole O'Hara shine."

I liked the city likker. Glad I didn't gotta share.

Recollection's a bit fuzzed but I remembered Jolene said, "I thinkin a makin Clyde stay down at the O'Hara farm. I like this place with him not round."

My mind drifted inside a dream where I stayed at the Grady place with Jolene, no Clyde. No nobody.

Waked in the sleeping room. Didn't knowed how I get there. Night before like a dirty windshield after a rain shower. Light showed through the curtains. Sunup some time back. Got a hankering for bacon. In the front room, Jolene nowhere in sight, Clyde neither. Drink my filla water.

Where Jolene get off too? O'Hara place? Reckoned I best drive down and see. Leastwise Lulahbelle probably got bacon on the sideboard.

Ambled down the hill. My truck gone. Shoved my hand in my pocket. No key.

Racked my head. Knowed I parked in the usual spot. Maybe I leave the key in the truck. My blood spin so fast I forget the pounding tween my eyes. No truck, no shine selling business. Tried to think of the nearest cliff to jump off.

Hear a chug-chug I knowed like my own breathing. Run to the road. My truck snail long, didn't kick up no dust. Water in my gut wanna come up when I seen Clyde at the wheel.

Truck stopped, Jolene stepped out her side. "You up earlier than I reckon, way you knock em back. I gotta pick you up off the floor, help you to bed."

Stomped up to the driver side door, stared in at Clyde. "You steal my truck."

Clyde climbed out, slammed the door. "She tell me to."

"I borrow," Jolene said. "All part of my plan. Gotta teach Clyde to drive."

"Ain't easy to learn on this clunker." Clyde knocked his shoe on a tire.

Think bout his bony behind in my seat made me wanna choke him. Wanna give Jolene a good kick. "You take somethin of mine, don't ask. That ain't right."

"You don't catch my point. Clyde gotta do the drivin. Me and you gonna ride in back. I got my pistol, you got your pistol."

"What you talkin bout?" Her words stabbed my aching head harder than the bright sun.

"I gather my facts good." Jolene leaned on my finder. "I hide in some trees cross from the road to the Harvey place, days and days. Seen Snake drive out at the same time every Wednesday. Alone. What I plan for us to do...like I say...Clyde drive, me and you in the back. When Snake head out we ready down the road. Clyde catch up, pull long side Snake on the left. Tween me and you shootin, we gonna kill Snake."

"Clyde ain't drivin my truck."

"Suit me fine." Clyde waved his arm, headed to the house.

Jolene come closer to me. "You a right good shot, better'n Clyde."

"Forget stinkin Clyde. Little Joe in back with you. Or Big Jack use my pistol."

"You a better shot than Big Jack." She take off her fedora so I seen her face up close. "He need specs."

"Little Joe good a shot as me. And he the one what got the one-uppin to do with Snake for runnin down Buck."

"I don't trust Little Joe to stay sober for this here job." She shake her head. "You know he got the moonshiner's curse." She grabbed my shoulders with both hands. "You the one I want help me with this here plan. I need Clyde too, but only till this over, then I toss him out with the bathwater."

SIXTY-EIGHT

Bad feeling creeped in my gut. Something bout Jolene's plan ain't right. Tried to conjure stuff Cob Turner tell me bout secret traps he set in the Great War, nothing come. Thinking a Cob make my innards worse.

No use telling Jolene we best take nother look at things cause she quick to say how I didn't knowed much. Reckoned I best put my trust in Jolene, after all she learned me lots too.

Backed my truck inside the hiding place Jolene find. Must say that one right good cover. Boulder on a curve with bushes long the road. Nice flat straightaway ahead. Maybe Jolene think this out better'n I first believed.

Leave the brake off. "You don't gotta touch no pedals, just the choke, starter and throttle. You hear?" Blocked my door, stared Clyde down.

"Ain't hard like you make it sound." Clyde forget I seen him drive. Jolene worked with him till he speed fast enough.

Clyde behind the wheel, I sat in the bed, Jolene in a tree over the truck. From up there she scouted the road. We waited.

Pistol I got when B. J. kilt Cob loaded, ready. Time grow real near. I got trouble gutting fish, how I gonna shoot at ole Snake? Truck what run down baby Buck looked like Snake's. I ain't all together sure that pickup his. Snake quick to put his knife to my windpipe. But he didn't cut me deep. I ain't never shoot at nobody before. I gonna be able to pull the trigger when time come?

Jolene dropped from her branch, landed with a thud in the hay by me. That the sign. Vowed to get one good shot in, do right by her.

Some engine passed us on the road. Clyde get the truck started, pulled out slow, speeded up.

"He ain't goin fast enough. Tell you Clyde ain't the right driver."

"He do fine." Jolene pounded on the back window. "Faster!" Clyde throttled down more. We gained on Snake. Reckoned Snake seen we after him cause gap tween us get wider. Putt, putt from my truck engine stepped up, beat like bees wings. We get closer.

"You sure that Snake? Seen couple pickups on this here road what look like that."

"Course I sure. I seen him in there." Jolene pulled her pistol from the holster.

Wiped sweat off my gun hand. Clicked out the chamber, bullets all ready.

My truck swerved. I grabbed hold of a wood slat on the side. Jolene clawed for a slat too. She missed, tumbled backward. Truck bumped to a stop in a ditch. Jolene banged her head into the back of the cab, fall in the hay.

Jolene laying like a ragdoll gave me a spark. Leap to my feet. Leaned on toppa the cab, squeezed off a shot. Gun jerked. Bullet make a spider web hole in Snake's back window. Reckoned Snake ain't hit cause he keep going.

Dropped my gun. Go to Jolene. Her eyes closed but I feel her warm breath.

Climbed the tailgate, jumped down. One front wheel on a rock in a hole. Yanked the door open, dragged Clyde out by the overalls. "You like to get us kilt." Shoved him so hard he bounced off the door frame.

He righted hisself. Punched me square in the eye. "A dog run across the road."

Didn't see no dog. Wanna beat Clyde till he looked like a messa rotten tomatoes. "Jolene out cold. We gotta get her help."

Lucky I got me a board in the truck. Leastwise stupid Clyde helped shove the board under the tire so we get outta that ditch. Front wheel wobbled, my eye swelled, but we make it back to the O'Hara place.

Knowed that plan ain't no good.

SIXTY-NINE

Jolene ain't got no cuts from that fall of hers but she groggy for nigh on a month. "Take me on up to the Grady place," she said.

"You gonna give stinky ole Clyde what for? Cause he mess up your plan?"

"Not his fault a blue tick hound run cross the road."

"Ain't no dog. He lie. Don't say what kind neither."

"You want Clyde kill a hound? How that gonna rest on your conscience?"

Something ain't right when she asked me to shoot at Snake then she worried bout some dog what never there. Then she believed dumb Clyde. Reckoned two bumps on the head inside a few months make Jolene a mite muddled. She stomped out the O'Hara house, sat herself in my truck so I gotta give her a ride.

"You say you gonna toss Clyde out. Somethin ain't right bout him."

"Yep, he pass that test."

"Test? What test?"

"Never you mind. I kick out Clyde, who gonna milk that goat? Not me."

Yep, her mind one straw short of bale of hay. She needed more rest.

Gravel crunched under my truck tires. Lucky I get the front wheel fixed by onea the Wood boys in Cedar Springs. Wanna get my pal Ace for the job but the poor fella in prison after his speak got raided. I never wanna go to onea them crowbar hotel places.

Waited a long time to tell her, this seemed like a peachy one. "I get off a good shot at Snake."

"What?"

"Soon as we land in that ditch, I seen you down, I fire off my pistol."

"You don't hit nothin. You terrible with a gun."

Before her plan she tell me I a better shot than all of them, cepting her. "Put a bullet through his back window." Waited for her to laud me.

"No. Tell me you don't do such a fool thing."

"What?" Take the turn after the bridge, headed in the direction of the Grady place. "You gotta be proud cause I let Snake knowed we mean business."

"Stop right here. I gettin out."

"Why you wanna walk up that there hill?"

"Stop!"

Pulled off the road, set the brake.

Jolene shoved her door open. "You fire a bullet in Snake's truck, you put me and my kin at risk."

"That your idea to shoot at him."

"My plan for Snake to die." Jolene climbed outta the cab. "He still breathin after gettin shot at. That sure to make him mad, go for vengeance."

"But if'n Snake get kilt tuther Harveys come after us."

"No." Jolene pulled a switch cutting face. "Stub too chicken. Toot dumber'n a doornail. B. J. got religion, livin with the Mitchell clan. Snake the mean one." She pointed a finger at me. "And don't you say us. You no O'Hara." She slammed the door. "If one O'Hara get hurt. I blamin you."

SEVENTY

"What do I owe the honor of this unexpected visit?"

Sat in a chair in Preacher's study, hang down my head, closed my eyes. Why Jolene gotta twist my tail bout that damn Harvey shit over and over? "Don't find me no peace at nonea them places you say go pray."

"Hmmm. Falls outside Walls of Water give off lotta harmony at twilight."

Opened my eyes. "Gonna try that there place today." Why I gotta go ask for something I don't want? Sundown gonna pour his blackness down on me.

Preacher slide over his Bible. "Let's see what words the good Lord will impart you at this lovely moment." He did his thing where he run his thumb over the gold-rimmed pages, flipped the book open, then stick a finger down without looking. "For God hath not given us the spirit of fear; but of power, and of love, and of a sound mind. 2 Timothy 1:7. Hmmm. You need to throw your fear out the window, embrace your power. Praise God for your smarts."

"First time somebody tell me I got smarts." A itch deep in back of my mind said that ain't true. No idea who might call me smart or when.

"You got you a good brain and you got power."

"Don't need no power."

Preacher keep looking at the Bible verse he already done read.

My hands twitched, pulled out a smoke.

"Use this ashtray." Preacher go in his desk, set out something what looked familiar.

"Somebody call that a clamshell at onea them brothels you got me deliverin to."

"I never been to nonea them, not one. Must've been somebody look like me."

"Ain't sayin I seen you there. No place nobody ought go. Ain't like no jenny-barn I ever seen. Them dark places, with no doors. Folks do nasty business out in the open." No folks round a good thing bout the places he tell me go pray.

"Thank the Lord for the power He doth bestow on you."

"That sound like I wanna hurt somebody." Wanna swig from my flask.

"Course not, some people like it when nother take control. Toss your guilt on the wind, drink to your God given rights." Preacher opened the cover on a hollow book, take out a flat bottle of good whiskey. "Take this. I don't drink myself."

How come Preacher so pa-like to me when he didn't touch his own little gal? Reminded me of something. "Got a gift for your young'un." A puzzle I buy for Buck, got no chance to give him that toy. Lulahbelle sure she got a bun in her oven, but a puzzle ain't no gift for a newborned.

"Don't bother." Preacher pulled a face like he stepped in a messa dog shit. "I'm sendin our curse away soon."

Knowed he do that before if his missus didn't fight him so hard.

"You gotta? Nothin else for you to do?"

"Doctor said it may never frolic like other children. Think what your life like if you never played tag, threw rocks at fish in the creek, built houses with sticks."

"Don't knowed if'n I ever do nonea them."

"Then what games did you play as a child?"

"How I posta knowed? Don't recollect nothin before I maybe ten."

"You must surely mean four or five, not ten, because that's not normal." Other folks said that, I didn't believe them neither. Preacher peered at something over my shoulder. Why he not look me in the eye? "After all the work we went through to have it, we must find our curse a different place. My wife is beautiful but holding it in her arms, people will not be drawn to us."

Forget my own troubles. Wanna do something to help that baby girl.

SEVENTY-ONE

"You want us to adopt a child what still got herself parents?" Sammy Jean set down her teacup.

"Like I tell you, her pa gonna send her way. But Sassafras say that one sweet baby girl. She only look funny."

"Don't see how a baby might look funny."

"She got a flat face, that all. Bet she grow outta that."

"Her pa a preacher and he don't want her cause she look different. He don't sound like a good man to me."

"Oh, he a good fella. He say his baby keep folks from comin to him to find the Lord."

"What bout your friend Little Joe and his wife?"

"Lulahbelle got a bun in her oven she gettin ready to pop out soon. Y'all ain't got no young'uns yet, knowed you want one. You and Mason right nice. I reckon this baby got your name on it."

"We find tryin for a child lotta fun. I got a feelin that time come soon when I find myself in the family way. Two babies gonna be more'n I handle good."

"Sassafras say this little gal never make no fuss. Reckon Sassafras wanna come here if the baby do. Pretty soon she growed outta her problems, Preacher say she come back. Leastwise you and Mason get practice."

"I see this mean a lot to you so I gonna give the situation plenty a go over." Way she fingered her teacup wondered if she gonna ask the tealeaves what to do. "I give this question up to the spirits, them and Dullsaine show me what to do. I gonna sleep on the question tonight, when I wake the answer appear in my head. That what I do when I need me some good advice."

"Mason gonna go long with what you say? Want me talk to him?"

"I know how to make Mason say yes." Sammy Jean get a twinkle in her eye. "You welcome to sleep in the shed out back so you here in the morning."

"Much obliged, but I got a delivery to make." Planned to go to onea them run-a-the-mill jenny barns, not nonea them nasty brothels.

Get me some hardy vittles and a quick pole-dipping. Sleep in back of my truck.

When I get back to Sammy Jean's I find her pumping the peddle on the contraption what she spin them clay bowls and plates on. Mason off trading for coal to fire up the oven to bake them clay things.

"You gonna be so, so happy when I tell you bout my wonderful dream."

"Y'all take Preacher's baby?"

Sammy Jean wiped her hands on a rag. "Better! What I seen, folks in a theater applaudin, clappin their hands like at the end of some Saturday matinee. I seen print, like in the newspaper, but it like to appear outta the air. Words, and pictures come to life in fronta my eyes, say wonderful things bout somebody. Don't recall the words. But a feelin wash over me, tell me this all gotta do with that little girl and the future. She gotta stay with her folks so they get the advantage of that."

Wanna get to Preacher quick-like, let him in on Sammy Jean's dream. This gonna change his mind. Sounded to me like his little one gonna be a legend someday, just like Jolene.

SEVENTY-TWO

Heavy door stand open. Made my way down the brick path. Fall leaves squished under my brogans. Preacher gonna get so happy when he hear the news. In the hall voices come from Preacher's study.

"People already starting to talk." Stanley in there. "A woman. What they gonna say next? Huh? You think of that?"

"God didst provide bread from heaven for them that hunger." Preacher like a mouse next to Stanley's bull voice.

"Pssst." Sassafras waved at me.

Kitchen smelled like cinnamon cookies. Sassafras shut her big brown eyes, breathed deep, opened them. "She gone. Take dat baby. He tell her go. He wont everybody be happy."

Feel like a windstorm inside my innards. "You gonna miss the missus somethin fierce, baby girl too."

"She wont me go too. I tell her I stay, take care Mister Ben. This bad for him. He done gots nobody now. She gots a new family."

Front door slammed. Stanley gotta be gone. Put a hand on Sassafras's shoulder. She tall as me. "Everything gonna be fine." I go to the study.

Preacher white like a new borned lamb. He take out a flask. I smelled the whiskey he poured hisself. First time I seen him drink. "Sorry to hear bout the missus."

He go to the cabinet under his books, opened a drawer. "Her happiness is my first priority. No matter that it gonna clear the smoke." He take out a small box like the one Ana Marie keep her white powder in. From the box he take out a pill, stick it in his mouth. What else he got in that drawer? Seen what looked like a pistol, smaller'n the one Jolene got. His hand rested in the drawer. He bring out something, opened his hand. "For you."

Wondered at the key. "What that to?"

Preacher showed me a map in a book, tell me where the warehouse at. "If a time come you can't get the product to deliver, you find some here."

"You stash some shine?" Stuffed the key in my pocket with the jack he gave me.

"I hid that supply from Stanley." He swallowed nother pill from the half-dollar-sized box, swigged from his flask.

"How come?" Seemed to me, Preacher like a still with no worm, no place for steam to go.

"Isaiah tell us not to question God. Go, my son. Now."

My neck twitched, reckoned God telling me to heed Preacher's words. Go on down the brick path. Stay by a willow on the corner. I gotta go back, tell him I ain't gonna keep that key.

Go back to the study. Hear Preacher screw the top on his flask. Swing open the door. Preacher stand at the window, pointed the pistol at his chin. If I dive for him, gun gonna go off. I gotta say something.

Sound of the shot bounced off the walls. Preacher crumpled to the floor like some ole mine caving in.

SEVENTY-THREE

Feel low like a ten-pound brick at the bottom of some well. Parked by the falls in Walls of Water, onea Preacher's favorite places. He never come here again.

Crawled in the hay in back of my truck. Keep drunk for couple days. Up chucked over the tailgate. Needed to load some shine jars squirreled away in the hollow tree by Swift River, supply some of them speaks. That gonna hafta wait.

Tried to get my mind to float way into the clouds. Didn't work too good. I oughta done something to stop Preacher from hisself. Stabbed a finger direction of the moon. "You oughta done somethin. He work for you, you bastard." God ain't no help.

For nigh on three years I drive round delivering to all them barbershops plus my regular places. Didn't do one lick of farm work for the O'Haras. Longest time I stayed at onea them farms I sat watch after Jolene's crash. Besides that, take her off my fire for that spell. Reckoned I best get back to what I customed to.

Two stops on my way to Cedar Springs. First, a roadhouse with vittles what bring my dried-up gut back to life and a gal what didn't go in for nonea that romance stuff.

Next stop I buyed something special.

Bout a mile from the O'Hara place, a horn honked like a goose needing to use a locked outhouse. Pulled up side the road. Red Chrysler with the top pushed down passed. Jolene driving, Big Jack next to her, Clyde in the rumble seat.

"Woohoo!" They all hollered. Speed up, get to the house right behind them.

"You get you a new car?"

What she do to gather up the money? Didn't wanna knowed.

Jolene get out. "Nah. Big Jack come get us at the O'Brien House, say Lulahbelle's time come. Course Ana Marie let me borrow her Roadster." Jolene patted the fender.

Good ole Ana Marie only needed Jolene for priming her customers with likker. Clyde go long to get time with Sadie, the gal what take care the goats.

We piled in the house. "Bout time." Glory sat Little Joe down in a chair, his face white. "Need yore help." She grabbed Jolene's arm.

"Oh, no. Not me." Jolene fixed her arm stiff like a tree branch.

"Dis no work for mens. Hold her shoulders, dat all. You done gots to look. I takes care of business where the baby come out." Glory stick her eyes to Jolene's for what seemed a long time.

"Gloooory!" Lulahbelle yelled from tuther room.

"Fine." Jolene go on in the room.

Little Joe swigged from the jug Big Jack bring him. "Don't like seein her work that hard, sure enough." Little Joe shake like a idling engine.

"Let's me and you get us some air." Didn't wanna hear the pain she gotta take on for a baby, didn't want Little Joe to hear neither.

We leave Big Jack and Clyde to sit, drink, not talk, listen to Lulahbelle cry out. Ambled down by the springhouse. Babble of the creek only sound. I gave him a Lucky.

"You look rundown like I feel. And you ain't been in no room with a wife cussin you up a wall, cross a roof and out a winder. My fault, say to Glory I wanna help."

Tell him what Preacher done to hisself. "One dern mess he leave. His head like somebody squish a tomato." Take a pull from the jug. "Sassafras gone, go live with the missus at her new home."

"Sorry, pal. Think you a mite sweet on Sassafras. But not gonna go nowhere, sure enough."

"Knowed that. For the best." Grinded the soggy Lucky with my shoe. "One good thing come of it all, I don't gotta go to nona them stinkin dens of iniquity no more." Patted my pocket. Jolene gonna like what I get her.

A bit later, Big Jack's howl come from the house, like how we signaled coming up on the still. Inside Glory hold the door to the birthing room open. Little Joe rushed in first.

Lulahbelle lay in the bed like she run a race with a freight train. Jolene got the baby. That little one wrinkled, red like she got too much sun, but mighty cute.

"This Lorraine." Jolene go to Little Joe. "Lorraine, this your poppa." Jolene stopped by us one by one. "This your Uncle Jack, your Uncle Clyde, your Uncle Rufus." She ended in front of Glory. "And this your Granny Glory."

Glory studied Jolene. "Granny?" They both cracked a smile at the same time. Glad Jolene ain't mad with Glory no more.

Jolene calling me uncle like the others made my innards more warm than drinking white lightning. Her calling Clyde uncle when they didn't knowed for sure he kin made me wanna spit.

Meet Jolene at the end of the path when she coming back from walking Glory home. Catching a smoke by the springhouse with this O'Hara different.

"Musta gotta vision bout tonight," I said. "Cause I bring you somethin fittin." Handed her the stogie.

"A Luxardo. Not bad." She run the cigar under her nose, put it in her shirt pocket, lighted a cigarette she called a Parliament. She puffed, eyed me in the lantern light like she counting every whisker on my face. "I gotta cut your hair. Make you look right nice." She blowed a smoke ring, showing off like usual.

SEVENTY-FOUR

Way 1932 go seemed like things back to normal. Then 1933 come long and it all slide downhill.

One night I got to the O'Haras hoping for supper and some good yarn telling. "Where Little Joe at?"

"He say he gotta help my brother Johnny with the still y'all got up there." Lulahbelle rocked pretty little baby Lorraine. She so sweet looking when she sleep.

Headed to Pine Gap. Parked in a hiding spot not far off the road. Make my way to a clearing where the Gibbs still at.

Somebody rustled in the woods. Stopped, listened. Nothing. Maybe a critter.

Get o the clearing where the still perked. Lantern light over yonder.

Boom! Orange everywhere. Blowed off my feet. Landed in a prickly bush.

Woods silent. Get my wind back. Smoke swirled with a smell like gunpowder. Scratches on my hands and face. Sting on my arm, sticky blood dripped down a gash.

In dim light I made out pieces of twisted metal all round. The damn still, gone. Pebbles stead of rocks lay where the furnace used to stand. Burned, crumpled stick of dynamite in the rubble.

Seen a fella on the ground. Metal stick outta his shoulder. Little Joe!

Recollected one time I seen Snake's pickup not far down the road, hear he courted a gal in them parts. He must find this setup. Little Joe hurt. This all my fault. Wished it me laying there. Rubbed my face, tried to think. Gotta help my best pal.

Go to where he face down. Touched the metal. He groaned. Leastwise he living.

"Hold tight. I gonna get you free from this dang thing."

Eased the piece out, pressed my hanky to his wound. Gotta get his shirt off, tie it like a bandage. Rolled him over. Take a gander at his face. That fella Johnny Gibbs.

Search round the clearing. Fetched the lantern to help. Little Joe nowhere in sight.

SEVENTY-FIVE

Lorraine growed strong. When she learned her to walk she didn't scamper round, mess in stuff like Buck. Give her a toy she cottoned to, Lorraine sat, played for hours. Blocks Little Joe made her with carved pictures on them her favorite. Lorraine didn't get sick much neither, cept a snot nose now and again. She getting over onea them summer colds one night when I at the O'Hara place.

After we eat us some butter beans, fried okra, and some mighty sweet watermelon, we set on the porch. Heavy heat of the day faded way, dark creeped in.

"Time for bed." Lulahbelle leaned on the door, wilted.

"Night, night Papa." Lorraine hugged Little Joe.

"Sleep well baby girl."

After Lulahbelle take the young'un in Little Joe jumped down, get something under the porch, come back with a jug. "I celebratin tonight."

"What you hidin that for?"

"Not hidin." He pulled a face like I catch him stealing my last piece of bacon. "Save this one for a special occasion. Done good not drinkin too much, sure enough. Tonight different, B. J. Harvey gone. Hope for good like when his ole uncle Rupert Harvey steal that gold watch, never come back to these here parts." He filled our cups, stowed the jug under a bucket. "B. J. sittin over at the Mitchell place here in Cedar Springs put a twist on my nerves. Hope that preacher school keep his behind."

"B. J. got the religion. Snake the one you oughta worry bout." Maybe I ought tell him he ain't the target when B. J. take his shotgun to Cob Turner.

"I don't worry bout Snake." Little Joe waved his hand like he tossing a ball.

Reckoned Snake happy wounding Little Joe's brother'n law in pay back for my bullet hole in his pickup window cause he ain't done nothing else. Little Joe lucky he fall sleep in the woods that night back then, didn't show till later.

Wished I round more. "With talk of this Prohibition endin I might be outta business. Need to come work for y'all on the farms like ole times."

"Prohibition not over yet. You gotta take me to the city with you gain. That train we seen go faster than anythin I ever seen before."

"The only warehouse I deliver to now outside the city. Whiskey not sellin good with this Depression on. Last time I go through the city the streets dirtier, the buildins got peelin paint. Lotta places plain close down. Swift River too. Smoke shop got busted winders. All them empty buildings make the town look sad."

"How bout deliverin farther way? Learn me to drive, I help you, sure enough. I like how your truck go so fast."

"Nope. After what happen back then with Clyde, nobody drive my truck but me."

"You no help." He get the jug from under the bucket. "Don't bother me none, not goin to the city with you. Got plenty round here keep me busy. Thinkin on puttin nother room on the house for Lorraine."

Put my cup out, he ignored me. "You gotta patch that kitchen roof first."

"Not you too." Little Joe throwed back his head, let his hands drop. "Tell Lulahbelle, Jole too, I fixin to get ready to get to the job. Everybody keep after me to do stuff. Too much to do. I need me a break, sure enough."

"When I get time I pitch in." Didn't make no money from O'Hara shine in them days. What I pay them didn't cover much more'n the rising cost of supplies.

"Wanna help? Let me do some deliverin with you."

"All that white lightin round gonna tempt you to drink too much."

"Tell you I done better. What you know anyway?"

I knowed he ain't doing that good. Little Joe still drink plenty. "Maybe someday."

"You one to talk." Little Joe leaned toward me, cut his eyes. "Seen you in the bag plenty times. Bet you get blacked out more'n me."

Couple times I wake in the hay in the back of my truck, didn't recollect crawling in. But that ain't no blackout. Onea them like me not remembering my life as a young'un.

"You pour whiskey in your coffee in the morning," I said. "I never think to do that."

"Bullshit, sure enough." He got a edge to his voice what made me think of Jolene. "Only when frost bite at my bones."

Big Jack stepped outta the door. "Lulahbelle want Glory."

Little Joe watched Big Jack go. "Reckon Lorraine's fever come back, must get bad." He take a deep pull, put his cup on the table slow like his arm needed some grease.

"Big Jack don't say nothin bout that."

"Ain't gonna lose nother baby." Little Joe looked at me, eyes all wet. "Nope, ain't gonna handle that."

"Maybe she want Glory for somethin else." Feel shame for him letting me see him cry. "Lorraine doin real good earlier." Little Joe ain't right in the head.

"No." He stand, wobbled cross the porch. "I got a bad feelin." He take the steps one by one. "Too much for me. Too much." He disappeared in the dark.

SEVENTY-SIX

"He back soon," I said.

"How long he gone?" Sammy Jean take way my teacup, forget to read the minty leaves, or she didn't wanna.

"bout nine months I reckon."

"What do his family say?" Sammy Jean gave me a look like she oughta take the revenuer job her man Mason quit years ago.

"Lulahbelle and Big Jack don't talk bout it." Take a bite of strawberry. "Glory say I right, he gonna come home."

"And Jolene?"

"She tell me Little Joe a fool for leavin and I a fool for thinkin he comin back."

"Might be she right. Nine months long time."

"Jolene ain't in a good way."

"I got somethin to tell you." Sammy Jean grinned like she a hen with a nice juicy worm. "Got me that bun in the oven you used to ask me bout."

"You sure this time?" That one treat to my ears. Needed me more good kin.

"Uh huh. I dream bout a nice healthy, strong baby boy." Sammy Jean changed back to a lawman face. "Now what bout you?"

"Me? I gonna treat my new nephew right nice."

Her face twitched. "Maybe I wrong bout the boy part."

"Bet you like you a girl. Maybe you get twins, a boy and a girl. Hear tuther day the Mitchell gal in Cedar Springs, she a Wood now, popped out twins."

"Not what I askin you. When you gonna settle down, get a girl and a family of your own? Most folk your age been married ten years with a whole pack of young'uns."

Moved my feet round. Wanna get up and run. "Ain't got enough money yet to make a gal take to me."

"Umph. What you got buried behind my shed?"

"No gal get that much of my interest yet."

Sammy Jean cut her eyes at me. What she thinking?

Ain't gonna tell my little sister I liked jenny barns cause I didn't gotta worry bout that romance shit. "Well, there Jolene but like I say she ain't in a good way. When she get back to herself reckon I try courtin her."

"Forget bout her. She shoo you way from her place more'n once."

"She say she gonna be a legend. I believe that true. Soon she get back to her ole self." Gotta figure out how I help her do that. "Got me a load of shine to haul."

Sammy Jean's dream come true. They named the baby Steven Starling after Mason's pa.

Prohibition over, folks still wanted cheap likker with no tax. Some moonshiners get nabbed by the law, throwed into prison, others popped up. Money ain't good like when Prohibition started. but I get by.

One day in 1935 when the corn taller'n me, ready for harvest, I delivered to some warehouse, catch me a nap in back of my truck. At daybreak I headed back to the hills. Spied a fella walking long side the road. Law, if he ain't Little Joe. Honked to get him to raise his head. Put on the brakes, swing open the door. He tilted his chin to the side, looked at me like he hear banjo music coming outta a fiddle.

"Get on in."

Little Joe eyed the road, then my truck. After a minute he grabbed the door with a shaky hand, pulled hisself in.

"You a sight better than a cold Coca-Cola on a hot day," I said.

"Got some whiskey?"

"Me? Nah, you askin the wrong man." I chuckled, pulled a bottle from under the seat. Put the truck in gear, get back on the road.

Cap on the bottle gave Little Joe a mite of trouble cause his hand so unsteady. He got the top off, take a long swallow, shuttered. He like a possum what crawled out from under the porch after a long hard winter.

Wanna cheer him some. "Lorraine doin real good. She still like them blocks you carve her."

He swigged from the bottle again. "Ain't tasted O'Hara likker in a coon's age."

"More where that come from. They all pleased as a half-growed boy in a jenny barn to see you. Gotta stop, get you some vittles first." He skinner than I recollected.

"Nope. Ain't goin back, sure enough. Not now." Little Joe gulped more whiskey. "Mind if I keep this?" He hold up the bottle.

"But I tell you, Lorraine nice'n healthy. She walkin and talkin up a storm."

"Reckon I know what folks say bout me." He pointed out the window. "Let me off at that train track. Learned me how to hop them freights good." He swing open the door, go to jump out.

Grabbed his coat. "You gotta come home."

"Let me go. Don't need your pity." He yanked loose.

"Wait!" Stepped on the brake. "Things be like they use to."

"No." Little Joe slide down to the road, keep on walking like he done when he leave Cedar Springs.

Watched him make his way to them tracks, amble long them rails. Stared till he nothing but a speck no bigger than a ant. Then that speck faded to nothing.

Part of me glad I didn't gotta take him home. Last time I to the house I get the feeling Lulahbelle done take up with Big Jack.

SEVENTY-SEVEN

"I told you, Sammy Jean, I'd mess up the job."

"Okay, Mason, I help you." She pulled a face like she trying to hold in a stinker. I got there only a minute or so ago. We still in the yard. "Go on in, Rufus. But don't lay a hand on Steven. He still nappin."

What she always worried bout? Steven two years old today. Come to celebrate his birthday. Sammy Jean acted more mother hen with Steven then Lulahbelle ever did with Lorraine.

Crib on one side of the sitting room. Mason said he gonna add nother room on the cabin but they ain't got the jack for lumber yet. I sat, take the present I bring outta the paper sack, smoothed the bag, get onea them pencils they got laying round. Draw the toy truck what looked a bit like mine.

A scraping noise come from the crib. Steven got the sleeping pad bent up so he can get his legs through the bottom, touch the floor. Law, if he didn't scoot that crib a few feet to a chair, crawled back in the bed, pulled hisself up over the rail so he landed in the soft chair. From there he climbed down, toddled in my direction.

"Why, hey, buddy."

Steven reached for the toy so I hand it to him. We sat on the floor and I showed him how to run the truck long the rug. "Choga, choga, choga."

Got some jack saved up. Reckoned stead of burring the stash I see to getting a car for Sammy Jean and Mason. Gave them a good price for the jugs I buyed from them but knowed that ain't enough. With this here smart young'un they gonna need more.

Sammy Jean come in looked at us like we on fire.

"I don't wake him, swear." Pointed to the crib by the chair.

"He start doin that a few days ago." Sammy Jean snatched Steven off the floor.

Steven stretched his arm down far as she let him. "Mama twuck."

My innards glowed warm cause the baby liked what I bring him.

After we eat some applesauce cake they gave Steven his other presents: a stuffed animal Sammy Jean sewed, a knit cap, some blocks what ain't nice as the ones Little Joe carved for Lorraine. Mason set the baby on the rug to play.

"Go get it," Sammy Jean said to Mason. He stepped outside, come back with three wrapped bundles.

Eyed the parcels he plopped in fronta me like they dropped from the sky.

"You and I never celebrate birthdays," Sammy Jean said. "Ma and Pa don't keep track when we born." She grinned real big. "So I want you to share Steven's birthday."

This better'n catching a fifteen-pound catfish. "Well…." Words stick in my windpipe. Never got me no presents cept for Christmas at the O'Hara place.

"Open them." Mason looked at me like he waiting for water to boil. "The wrapping presented me with difficulty so Sammy Jean helped."

Tear paper off big one first. "Blank pictures?" Wished I think before I said that.

"Canvases," Mason said. "I built those myself."

"This package next." Sammy Jean slide the gift to me.

Ripped that one open. "Paints."

"This here." Sammy Jean hold up the next parcel. "Got brushes in it."

"Y'all ought not spend nothin on me."

"These all homemade. Only money we spend go for the jars and the canvas. Not much more'n a dollar. I make them mule hair brushes." Sammy Jean put down the present, stick a finger on the paper bag where I draw the toy. "I seen you do lots a pictures like this here one. Now I want you to sketch on them canvases and fill in the lines with them paints."

Slipped the string off, unwrapped the brushes, set them next to the canvases and paints. Gonna make use of them first chance I got. What to paint first? Maybe Little Bear Lake at sunup cause Jolene said that a right pretty sight. Feel like I onea them there chicks pecking at the inside a some eggshell. "Much obliged. Mean a lot to me."

Spied Steven with one wheel off the toy truck.

"Oh, Mason," Sammy Jean said. "Get that before he swallow it."

Mason grabbed the tiny tire. "He's always figuring out how to take things apart."

"Always tinkering with stuff," Sammy Jean said. "Keeps me on my toes."

"Come here, Tinker." I waggled my fingers at the baby. "You and me gonna fix that there wheel." Wanna learn him everything I knowed.

The name stick. Nobody ever called him Steven again. They only called him Tinker, or Tink for short.

SEVENTY-EIGHT

Tree stump looked like a table stick outta the ground down by the river. Lay a canvas on the stump, plopped my behind on a milk stool, water canteen with a bitta shine mixed in at my feet. Sharpened a pencil with my pen knife, draw the outline of Little Bear Lake way I seen it in my mind.

Recollected first time I seen the site, day I followed Jolene up to the Grady place. She gonna get rid a Clyde but I said somebody gotta work the farm. She picked Clyde over me. Wished I never said them words cause maybe he leave. What Jolene do to make him stay this long? How he get the name O'Hara? He ain't like them other O'Haras with his long legs, arms, big ears.

Gotta get me a better eraser, better pencil too. This painting gotta come out perfect if I gonna give it to Jolene. She never said nothing good bout my drawings. Reckoned the canvas and paint make her take notice. Daydreamed Jolene lauded my work, made me feel like a army fella with a medal.

My mind fly to poor Little Joe. Why good folks take bad roads?

John Henry the piano player a nice fella but he go too far with a wild time. The way he take to Cob Turner the only thing what ain't right bout John Henry.

That steered me thinking of bad folks I knowed over the years. Daniels one mean cuss what get hisself blowed away, same way Cob did. Reckoned B. J. Harvey feel sorrowful for what he done to Cob but B. J. got hisself religion to get some healing.

Messed up a line on the mountain cross the lake. Tried four times to get it the way I wanted. Eraser smudged the canvas, hide that later with some paint. Didn't wanna leave room for Jolene to pick at my gift to her.

One bad fella never got his lot. Snake Harvey. Looked at the scar on my arm from where he cut me that time. That longer than the one I got when the Gibbs still blow. Tell Jolene I got a plan to get back at that weasel Snake for blowing up the Gibbs still but she said she didn't wanna hear it, that the Gibbs boys gotta do something, not us. Reckoned my idea to get back at the Harvey clan better'n the one she come up with when Clyde wrecked my truck. Problem how to get her to listen to me.

Drawing good enough for me to start with the paint. Saved that for nother day. Swigged from my canteen, pulled out a pack of Luckys. More smokes and whiskey left than I expect. Reckoned drawing keep my hands busy, off the drinking and smoking.

Nigh on a week I worked on that painting, least till I trusted the dang thing good enough for Jolene. Let the paint dry for a couple days. Night before I take Jolene the picture, I go to the O'Hara still what Big Jack hide up above a gorge. Helped him run off a batch.

We take some samples to make sure the stuff good quality. Wobbled into the woods to take a piss, gotta take care not to fall off that cliff. Lay on my back by the furnace while the last jug filled, drifted off.

Wake to dim light. Hear somebody in the woods moan. Big Jack on tuther side of the furnace, mouth open, breathing like he a kettle ready to boil over. Nother moan come from somewhere.

Shake Big Jack. "Wake up. Somebody out there."

He raised hisself on one elbow like he come outta two day sleep.

Cranked up the flame on the lantern. Go to where nother moan come. My legs like lead. Through the trees I seen something white. A night dress. Looked back to Big Jack, he stumbled to his feet.

Closer, hold up the lantern. Light shine on a face.

Big Jack clutched my arm. "That there Lulahbelle."

Why Lulahbelle come up here? She rested on a tree, tried to stand, she ain't steady on her feet. Big Jack pushed past me. "Hold tight baby."

Run to help too.

Lulahbelle slipped, snatched at a tree limb. Branch snapped with a crack. Big Jack reached out. Think he gonna catch her. She tumbled over the side of the mountain. Her night dress fly like a haint.

Big Jack dropped to his knees. I sat me down in the dirt. Tried not to let the tears come, that didn't work out too good.

On the road to the Gibbs place, drink corn squeezings. How I gonna tell her kin the news?

Come near the house, seen Bull Gibbs by some ole Model T. A little gal a couple years older'n Lorraine in the car.

Waved at Bull to come over to me. Tell him what I knowed. Take me and Big Jack a while to climb down that gorge. When we got to Lulahbelle we seen why she come up to find Big Jack, why she so weak. "Big Jack say she with child. She musta lose that baby, lose lotta blood."

Bull pulled a pricked with a needle face. "Ma gonna wail right mournful when you tell her. Sure she fall and flop all over the floor."

"Reckon this best come from you cause you kin and all."

"Nope. You go on in the house." Bull looked toward that car like a hungry fella looked at a apple. "Gotta take Johnny's daughter someplace special. She waitin for me."

"How Johnny doin alate?" Feel bad cause Johnny get hurt when that still blowed. My bullet hole in Snake's pickup window what make Snake target the Gibbs setup.

"Ha!" Bull said like I spit at his feet. "Johnny claim he don't hear worth shit. Say his arm so bum he don't gotta pull his share of work. He dynamite that still damn good."

"What you say Johnny do?" Twisted a finger in my ear.

"Reckon runnin dog piss too much a chore for my big brother cause I seen him with a sticka dynamite that day."

"Snake brag all over the place bout how he do that blowin up. Why you don't spill this back then."

Bull keep his face hard. "Yeah, Snake Harvey say he the one what set that dynamite, I don't believe him."

"Why Johnny wanna get his own self hurt?"

"I think Johnny only wanna wreck the still. He get lucky two times. One cause Snake say that bullshit and two cause Johnny get outta workin hard. Nobody believe what I seen so I think other ways to get back at Johnny for his fat ass dead weight." Bull peered back at the Tin Lizzy.

Snake some coward to spout off bout something he didn't do. That get my hackles up. Promised myself to talk Jolene into using my plan. Soon. Ain't gonna take no for a answer. Wanna see Snake dead on the ground.

SEVENTY-NINE

"That the craziest plan I ever hear tell of," Jolene said. "But I gotta hand it to you for gettin your brain to churnin."

"Paintin this here seem to loose my mind." Hold out my picture for her.

"Some big holes in that plan."

"No holes." I shake the canvas. "I do this for you."

"Put that thing over there." She flicked her hand at tuther side of the room. "You bring me good information. I put that to use. But I gonna tell you how this gonna go down, when I say the time right."

Stick the picture in the corner where she said. Hope neither that canvas nor my plan gather dust.

Go to the O'Brien House on a Saturday night. Fellas liked the place cause it seemed homier than most jenny barns. Even got indoor plumbing.

Jolene behind the counter they used for a bar. Her sleeves rolled up, pinstripe vest open, her hair stuffed under her fedora. All kinda bottles, pitchers of tea, bowl of mint on a shelf behind her.

Pondered what to drink. On occasion I enjoyed me a Bees Knees: honey, lemon juice, orange juice, white lighting. Honey go good in O'Hara likker cause they sometimes use the stuff for distilling when sugar too expensive. Seen they got ginger beer, decide on a Mule Kick: ginger beer, twist a lemon, snake oil, white lightening.

Jolene pushed a jar at me. "Drink that."

Peered at the red drink like it a boil on a dog's behind. "I wanna Mule kick."

"I give you a kick. What'cha want onea them for? Got a hangover? This here tonight's special." Jolene tapped the glass. "A Carolina Kiss. O'Hara whiskey, strawberry puree, maple syrup, lemon juice, soda. Make this one a little weak for you. Think you already got a snootful."

Over on onea them couches with the carved roses on the trim, Crow Tritt talked up onea them gals, glasses bout empty. Swigged from my drink. "Girl, you call this a drink," I said to Jolene. "Whatcha do, squeeze a cardinal in here?"

"Suck down the damn thing and shut your mouth." Jolene pulled a face like she gotta clean a dirty outhouse. Outta the corner of my eye I seen Ana Marie take Crow's gal aside, whispered to her. Gal go back to Crow with a grin what covered her whole face. Crow ordered new drinks.

Bout the time my jar drained Jolene come my way with nother of them red drinks. She stopped at a fella I knowed a mill worker what come up next to me. "This Carolina Kiss for you. On the house." Jolene winked at the mill worker, set the jar in front of him.

"Right nice of you, honey." He take a gulp. "Reckon you sweeter than this here concoction."

Jolene fingered the scar on his wrist. "Oh, that musta hurt somethin fierce." She never did that to my scars.

"I got plenty worse." Mill worker looked at her like she a rabbit bout ready to step in his snare. "Splinters still comin out where a log the size of a freight train knock me over ten year ago."

"You po'r thang." Jolene put her hand on his shoulder. "Here?"

"Nah, over here sweetie." He take her hand in his big mitt, moved her fingers down his chest.

Knowed my time come to say something. "Don't touch her."

"You hush up," Jolene said.

"Tired of you makin eyes at every fella in this here place." Banged my glass down.

"You not my husband, you not even my beau." She gave me a stare like I pissed in her vegetable garden.

Didn't wanna say the words. "You ain't onea them workin gals, but you sure act like one."

Catched the mill worker's Carolina Kiss full in the face. Jolene hold the jar like she might throw that too. "Git! I don't ever wanna see your ugly face or your pitiful self gain."

Lighted a smoke in the yard. Through the window seen folks getting back to business after the hullabaloo we make. Tried to smoke slow, waited.

Pretty soon Crow Tritt come out, rolled his tobacco with a white paper. "Quite a spectacle you and that whiskey bitch make."

"Sick of her. Way her talk all bad. Way she treat folks." My words come out like a hurt young'un.

"Doin business with her." Crow shake ash off his smoke. "Ain't you?"

"Ain't no more after what happen in there." Looked through the window. "She still all over that mill fella. I make do not sellin O'Hara likker."

"If'n that true, I might got nother moonshiner for you." He ambled way from the house where the dark blacker, I followed. "Snake Harvey got trouble findin places to sell these here days. Don't reckon you wanna buy from him."

Hear more'n once Crow try to help find places for the Harveys to sell.

"Shit howdy I do. But, if that true, what I don't knowed it to be, he ain't gonna sell to me."

Crow throw down his smoke, grinded the butt with his boot. "After I tell him what I seen tonight, he might give in."

"That gal get me madder than a whore what draw a stinky fella that don't pay his bill." Find Crow's eyes in the dark. "I wanna buy from the Harveys and I want Jolene knowed I do. You work that out I buy all the shine Snake got."

"How that whiskey bitch gonna know you buyin from Snake?"

"Let me tote somebody long to the drop."

"Nah, you teched in the head. Nobody Snake gonna let you bring long."

Tuther side of the window I seen the gals working their magic. "Hey, what bout Ana Marie? Hear Snake a mite sweet on her at one time."

Honked, revved my engine, honked again. Somebody stepped outta the door onto the O'Brien House porch. In the light from the open door I seen the dress tight round the hips, the high heel shoes with strap to show off the curve of her leg, the small hat with the veil over the eyes. She pulled on her coat, shut the door, rushed to my truck fast as them shoes let her. Soon she in I take off for the gorge near Glad Town where Crow tell Snake to make the drop.

Smelled powder and perfume on her, whiskey too. Reckoned she need courage for tonight. "How you...uh...fill the...uh...toppa the dress?"

"Ana Marie help me stuff scarves in her brassiere," Jolene said. She added this part to my plan. I reckoned she wanna hide out in back of my truck, Jolene got herself her own ideas.

Made good time, passed Cedar Springs in bout half hour. My back tingled. "Sure you wanna do this? What if Snake don't wanna do a ole time shootout?"

"He will," Jolene said. "<u>The Virginian</u> play in Swift River for months. He gotta seen it, wanna be onea them cowboys, just like me."

"Ceptin you make that dress look better than Gary Cooper do."

"Hush up." No meanness in Jolene's words. "I best check my gun." She pulled at her coat, reached in the pocket. "This not my pistol. This a big bottle a that toilet water. I grab the wrong coat." Her hardness back. "We gotta go back, get my gun. Your fault for rushin me."

"Ain't goin back. No time. If'n we don't meet Snake he don't wait long." Sweat dripped down my face. "My pistol under the seat. I keep the thing clean."

"Don't got no practice with your gun." She growled like a hound keeping a watch over a bone. "Don't got no choice."

"Maybe the sighta you in that there dress befuddle Snake."

Snake pulled upside in his pickup he painted yellow after what happened to Buck. I go round to get the door for Jolene, dressed like Ana Marie. Door of the pickup opened, out slipped Toot Harvey.

"Where's Snake?" I said.

"My big brother under the weather. I got your shine. You got the cabbage?"

Toot never done nothing to nobody, far as I knowed. Snake the one what hit Buck. Toot much younger than Snake, younger than B. J. too. Hear Toot get hisself hitched to some gal that year.

Helped Toot move boxes a shine from his truck to mine.

Before we finish, Jolene said. "Hear that?"

Listen. Something hissed.

"Sound like a cop car to me," Toot said.

Hear the siren then.

"Run!" Jolene jumped in her side, I hopped in, flipped the key, choked the starter. We didn't move too far. Tires go thunk, thunk. Didn't get more'n fifty yards when the headlights and siren come down on us. Looked back, seen Snake lean on the pickup next to his brother, he wiped his bowie knife on a hanky, laughing like a mule.

Ain't nothing to do but get out, hands up. The car a black one, a federal fella, not Sheriff Clayton, what hated the Harveys. "Buyin tax free whiskey, are we?" The revenue fella tipped his big hat back. "This here a dry county. You gonna do some time fer this."

Pointed my raised fingers at the Harveys. "They the ones sellin, you gotta haul them in too."

Revenue fella unscrewed one a Toot's jars, take a sip. "This water." He pulled a bait stealing grin. "But you think you buyin shine, that make y'all liable. Harvey boys the ones what tell me where to find you."

Snake come up beside the revenuer. "That one there," Snake nodded to Jolene. "Say she let me slip her the bone for some bacon."

"He lyin," Jolene said.

Revenue fella patted her down, find him my pistol, long with a box of white powder.

CHAPTER EIGHTY

That sneaky Snake laughed like a clown smoking reefer when that revenue fella hauled us off. My blood boiled. Didn't get no chance when me and Jolene gotta go up before judge Dove Tritt, what got ties to the Harvey clan. They take my truck, everything in it. Money I got on me all go to pay fines. Both me and Jolene go to prison, her to one for gals.

Prison dirtiest place I ever seen. Peeling paint never bothered me but that place got black stuff growing all over them gray walls. Place smelled like a hundred farts. They gave me clothes what hang on me. Get baggier in time cause food like hog slop, some stuff I didn't knowed what it posta be. Didn't feel much like eating.

Guards with big keychains marched us to the showers, made us strip down to what we born with. Tell my mind to go to the clouds for them five minutes two times a week.

My cellmate named Jerry. He come from up North to hide out, get caught selling some sorta powders like what Ana Marie wanted all the time. Hear he kilt somebody one time but he didn't seem the type, he kinda scrawny.

"What'cha writing?" He said.

"Ain't writin, drawin." Showed him my picture.

"Not bad. Nice Lake. That your home?"

"Close enough." I missed that place something fierce. "Ain't easy goin this long without seein a tree or smellin the moss in the creek."

"You should learn perspective." He chuckled. Reckoned cause he seen that word didn't mean nothing to me. "Mother sent me to art school." He gave me some ideas how to make my pictures better.

Lotta letters come to me. Looked at one, tried to cipher what it said.

"What's happening at home?" Jerry asked. "Must not be good."

Think hard on what to tell him, shrugged.

Jerry take the letter. "Here, Let me read that to you." Jerry read all my letters for me. They come from Sammy Jean and Mason, Glory, short notes from Big Jack. Jolene write too. Hers said "You don't know how to handle yourself" and "All your fault." Jerry good bout reading them over and over to me, didn't tell nobody bout me not reading neither. He helped me write back too. He tell me bout letters he get from his wife and young'uns.

"How I ever gonna thank you for all you do for me?"

"Oh, I'll think of something?"

We out in the quarry smashing rocks ten hours a day, six days a week. Off on Sunday when they let us convicts out in the yard for a couple hours. Some fellas tossed baseballs, some sat and smoked. Keep to my lonesome for the most part. Guards watched us, ready with rifles if somebody made trouble. Jerry talked up the guards, made them laugh. Sometimes Jerry walked the walls of the yard with three pals of his.

One Sunday when spring sunshine warmed up the chill I seen Jerry with only two fellas cause the tuther one got release. They come up to me. "I think of a favor you can do me."

"Why sure." Happy to do something to thank him.

"Come with us."

Followed them to a place behind a locked shed where the prison stowed tools.

"Guards don't like us back here." Didn't see no guards from there, reckoned they didn't see us. Ain't a good sign.

"The guards working today on my payroll." Jerry looked at me like he owned that prison.

Onea his pals grinned at me with broke teeth, his name Jeb. Tuther one with a square head, his name George, pulled a you-ain't-nothing-but-a-animal face.

"Ready to show your gratitude?" This here ain't the Jerry I knowed.

"What you want?"

Jerry eyed his pals. Jeb and George leaned down to their boots, stand back up, showed knifes. Small but sharp.

Spring air warm, not too hot. Sweat run down my back.

"Don't worry. This won't hurt." Jerry lifted up his shirt. "Unless you fight. But no reason to do that." He unbuttoned his britches. Slipped out his tallywacker.

No air. Gonna fall. Jerry's goons moved in. Knife points close to my windpipe.

"All you gotta do's get on your knees and do me a little favor."

Trusted this fella. Now he got the noose round my neck.

Shake my head. No words come.

"This don't go no further than the four of us. Get to it. Get this over with." Jerry looked to his goons.

Blades pricked my skin. Do what he say or die.

I gonna die in prison. Sounded like the right end to my life. "No."

One knife stick harder in my neck, gonna cut out my breathing.

"On your knees, boy."

Get set to leave this world. Then I hear Preacher in my head. "Some people pray on their knees." Recollected how Sammy Jean said sometimes Dullsaine take over her mind, showed her things from the beyond.

Opened my soul, let Preacher move in. Tell myself, if I prayed, Preacher the one doing the deed, not me.

EIGHTY-ONE

Jerry acted like nothing happened. Eat me up inside staying in the same cell with him.

"Hey, you got a letter. I'll read it" Jerry hold up the envelope I knowed from Jolene cause of the size and color.

"Nah."

"It's from that dame you like." His fingers on her letter make me wanna lose my supper. He read Jolene's words. "Clyde use to tell me you dumb. Now I see he sure right."

Same ole thing. When Jolene get a bone to chaw she didn't let loose. How I ever gonna get her to speak to me again?

Recollected how she tell me stuff Clyde said. Maybe she made up stuff to tell Clyde I said. She wanna see us fight. How I might do that in here. Got me a good idea.

In the chow line I whispered to Jeb how George complain bout him smacking his lips when he eat. In line for the toilet I mumbled to George how Jeb said his feet stink worse than skunk cabbage. Every chance I get I tried to think like Jolene, planted them little seeds.

One night at supper Jeb and George sit at the end of the table cross from one nother. We all still got chains on our forearms till we get back to our cells.

"That a joke, stupid," George said.

Jeb throw some burned toast, hit George in the eye.

George tossed a glob a gray meat at Jeb.

They jumped up. Jeb clobbered George in the gut. He let out a groan, shoot a punch what split Jeb's lip. They grabbed one nother's shirts, twisted round like they dancing. In a blur of black and white stripes, George get him turned round. By the time guards come George pullred his chain tight, choke Jeb's windpipe.

Them two got hauled off. Jerry don't got him no muscle no more.

Next Sunday Jerry come up to me in the yard. "Well, the screws put it to our pals." He tell me George got hisself two days in what they called The Box. "After that they move those two to opposite sides of this joint."

Didn't feel sorry for them fellas none, after how they helped Jerry. "That okay. We still have us some fun."

"I knew you'd figure out how things work in the slammer," Jerry said. We walked the walls round the yard. "With those thugs gone you're now my righthand man. We can enlist some help for you. Then the next rube that comes along, we make him the patsy."

"You think me a rube, a patsy?"

We come to the tool shed, slipped behind.

"That's not what I mean. You're new to this life." Jerry lay a hand on my arm.

Snatched the front of his stripped shirt with both hands, shake him. "You ain't gonna touch me nor nobody else ever again, ya hear?"

Jerry pulled a shit his pants face. "You got this all wrong."

Take one hand off his shirt. Slammed a fist into his pickle nose. Blood dripped down his mouth. He tried to get his chain over my head. Learned from what I seen in the super table fight, stepped back. Jerry come at me. Tried to cover my face, knocked his ear good. His fist come up under my jaw like a firecracker. Pain flooded my mouth. Spit a bloody tooth at him. Swing at his head like I swing that sledge hammer at them rocks. Shoved him back. He tumbled like a pilea bricks.

Somewhere guards yelled. Kicked Jerry in the ribs. "You dirty son-a-bitch." Kicked him over and over.

Guards hit at me with clubs. Take three of them to wrassle me to the ground.

They give me four days in The Box. Nothing but a dirty cot with no pillow, a bucket in the corner. Tiny cell got three windows but they the size of matchboxes. Two times a day they slide in a nasty boloney sandwich and a cuppa water. No coffee. No smokes.

"Gonna get a few months added to your sentence," the doughy guard said when he tossed me in there.

My head ached where Jerry and them guards hit me.

Nothing to do but think and sleep. Dreamed I did what Jerry made me do. Fella in the dream ain't Jerry, he over a foot taller'n me. At one time he nice, I trusted him, not now.

"Don't you want me to learn you growed folks stuff?" He said.

What right, what wrong? Gotta do what he said. Tasted sweat, smelled something the like of hogs. Looked up. He grabbed onea his arms, choked out a moan, go limp.

Opened my eyes. I in a bed at the Grady place. Reckoned I blocked out the rest of prison, get me release. Stepped into the front room, rubbed sleep outta my face.

Jolene there. "All your fault."

"How I posta ..."

"He dead cause of you."

Dropped in a chair at the table.

Jolene stand over me, pointed her finger. "You kilt him just like you kilt Jerry."

Waked up in The Box, my heart beating fast.

EIGHTY-TWO

Jerry ain't dead. When I get outta The Box he still in a place they called the infirmary. After that I hear they moved him to stay with the prisoners what clean the joint.

Fellas treated me different. Reckoned cause word get round that I beat somebody up right bad.

New cellmate I get like a mouse in a house fulla cats, didn't look at or say nothing to nobody. Pretended I staying at the Grady place with Clyde.

Go over the old letters, recalled Jerry reading them, knowed what each said by memory. New letter come on blue paper from Jolene. Opened the envelope feeling bad with nobody to ask to read. Studied on words. Recognized a few from the old papers. Law, if I didn't figure out what the letter said by my lonesome.

When I in there I run the place. Bet they got you on some chain gang. That where you belong.

Now I home for so long we got a barn full of shine again. I got to find me more places to sell the stuff. That your fault leaving us in this fix. How I going to sell all this whiskey? Well, you no help. You mess everything up good.

Asked a guard to let me see a newspaper. Twixt the pictures and the words I knowed I read somma the news.

Wanna write a letter of my own. Ain't ready to send one to Jolene. Reckon I write Tinker cause he too little to care what I said. Go through the letters, picked out words, copied them on some paper.

You be good. Do what your ma and pa say. They good folk.
Some day I take you to see some thing what go mighty fast.

Draw a locomotive picture to go with the promise.
Never did get my penmanship good like Jolene's.

EIGHTY-THREE

My turn come for release. Prison gave me clothes and enough money for a bus ticket to Juniper County. Hiked to Sammy Jean's place.

The shop got all sorta clay pots in every shape, size, color a body imagine. A few of them statues too, Mason made them with a mold. Nobody there, I headed up to the house not far behind the shop. Couple hens pecked at the grass in the yard. Sammy Jean grow roses and some other pink flowers round the porch. She come outta the door holding a broom. The braid down her back seemed longer than I recollected.

"Lordy, you skinnier than I ever seen you." She bearhugged me, dragged me inside. Mason and Tinker out picking berries in the woods but Sammy Jean fixed me some vittles right off. Biscuits covered in a creamy vegetable stew.

"This sure tasty." Anything good after what I eat in the joint.

"Did you see the cabin behind our house?"

"Oh, that? I catch a peek." After Mason added on Tinker's room, reckoned he didn't wanna stop building.

"You welcome to stay there." She pulled a what'cha gonna do face.

"I got me a business to put back together."

"You goin back to bootleggin after what happen?"

"That all I knowed."

"Them federal men take your truck and all your money."

"What I got on me at that time. Need to borrow me a shovel."

Sammy Jean crossed her arms. "If you get caught again they might keep you longer next time. That place no good for you. You not only skinny, you got dark circles under them eyes of yours."

"Bad dreams haunt me of late." Stared down at my empty plate.

"See, I told you." She jabbed her finger three times on the table. "You gotta stay outta prison. What kinda nightmares? You know I read me some dreams."

"Just bout some evil fella." Looked her in the eye. "I ain't never gettin caught no more. I gonna do my bootleggin like I use to, with no funny business. Folks count on me to sell their shine."

"You not a bad fella. I sure of that now." Sammy Jean put her hand over mine. Feel like hers come right off the stove, think she gonna burn me.

Snatched my hand way. "Now? You think me bad."

"No, no, no. Not bad." She inched her fingers closer. "With a family like ours, one never know who learn nasty stuff or what."

"I knowed right from wrong." Hide my hands under the table, didn't want her to touch me again. "Some folks got more wrong than our kin." Think on the Gibbs boys.

Sammy Jean settled back like a snail crawling into his shell. "You a nice man. So why you gotta go start up bootleggin again?"

"Jolene. She write me, say she gotta find more places to sell her shine. I gotta eagle-eye the blind pigs I knowed, sniff out new ones."

"You don't gotta do everythin that woman say." Sammy Jean whipped my plate off the table, take it to the sink. "You put too much stock in that girl. She don't do nothin for you, but treat you like yesterday's trash."

"Jolene make the best shine I ever taste, folks pay a dear price for that grade of whiskey."

Sammy Jean planted her fists on her hips. "That work land you in prison. Your drawin better now. Paint more pictures, sell them in our shop. Stay in that cabin we build for you. Don't let that woman slap you round."

Jolene never lay a finger on me. Sammy Jean didn't knowed nothing bout the O'Haras or the shine business. Maybe now I read, Jolene might find more use in me.

"Much obliged for the offer. But prison learn me how to handle them what give me trouble. Jolene gonna see me in a new light." Scraped my chair way from the table. "Gotta get back to business."

Dig up a metal box I buried in the woods behind Sammy Jean's house. In the box enough money to buy me nother truck. What left I gave to Sammy Jean and Mason to pay back what they spend on wood for that cabin I might stay in someday. Ain't enough jack to buy whiskey to sell. Planned to talk Jolene into giving me her shine on credit.

EIGHTY-FOUR

Buy supplies at a mercantile: soap, razor, fishhooks, that sorta stuff. "Damn!" Go back in for something important I forget.

Get used to driving the new truck on the way to Cedar Springs. Odd working the speed with my foot, not my thumb. This engine got more horse power, go mighty fast. Spied my face in the mirror. I lucky the tooth that bastard Jerry knock out on the side, not the front. I looked older, more like a big city fella, not a country hick. Jolene gonna see that, think of me in fresh light. She over what happened when we get nabbed by now. This shiny Ford gonna put a spark in her eye.

Stopped by to say 'hey' to Glory. She glad to see me, tell me Jolene live at the Grady place, reckoned as much. Maybe she send Clyde packing by this time. Climbed on foot the trail not wide enough for the truck. New overalls feel stiff, new brogans raised blisters. Gave a howl at the top. Fireflies sparkled round the yard.

Opened the door. Dumb ole Clyde, on wobbly legs, stacked clean supper dishes in a cupboard. He picked up his banjo, sat in the rocker like he didn't see me.

"Where Jolene at?"

"Out back." Clyde got him one hecka shiner.

Sat at the table where I used to, put the stogie I buyed at the mercantile where I knowed Jolene like to sit.

Clyde fixed hisself a big drink when Jolene come in, her hair wild round her face. She didn't pay me no more mind than Clyde did. "Pour me somma that nitwit juice too." She sipped at the cup he set down by her.

Before Clyde tinked on his banjo gain I called over to him. "You in a fight?"

"No."

"Hmph," Jolene said. "Some folks don't heed no when they hear it."

Glad Clyde on her bad side tonight, gave me a leg up.

"She...no...fun." Clyde slithered into the sleeping room with his banjo. Hear him in there plucking out "Salty Dog" pretty good. He played better when he oiled up.

Waited for Jolene to say something to me. She didn't so I said, "Come take a look at my new truck."

"I know what a truck look like."

"Reckon I miss supper."

"Eat that rabbit stew, Clyde make the stuff, I won't eat none. But don't you touch that biscuit no how, that mine."

The stew not bad but not good like Big Jack make. Washed the vittles down with fresh spring water, lots better than water in the slammer. Jolene quiet while I shoveled in the chow, she didn't offer me no corn squeezings. Stogie I put by her place gone. "Now I outta the joint, I scoutin spots to sell whiskey. You wanna supply the shine, I in the market."

"We got some to sell. Got the dough on you?" Jolene poured her nother drink.

"Well, not on me. You give me the whiskey, you knowed I good for the jack."

"Got enought to buy you a truck, not enough to pay for my likker?"

"Ain't gonna haul the stuff in a mule cart. Them days gone for good. Make good use of the money I got. You knowed I turn that there shine over right fast."

"You bury cash in more'n one place. Dig up what you need for my goods now." How she get wind of my other stashes?

"If'n I got that much, you think I come here in overalls? Wanna buy me a city suit, look nice'n spiffy. Stead I only get what I need to do business."

"Some businessman. You get us drug in by the law." She take a swig from her cup. "When I in there, I run the place."

"Earn me some respect in the joint too."

"What?" Jolene hooked her thumbs on her ragged overall straps. "You beat somebody up in there? That make you feel like a big man?" She waved a hand at me. "That nothin."

She in a prison for gals, she didn't knowed what I gotta do.

Headed for the door. "Reckon I get me some shine on credit from onea my other suppliers."

"Fine. Take you a load, but you best bring me my money in twenty-four hour. And after tonight, Clyde supervise you packin up so I know how much you take."

EIGHTY-FIVE

"Tell Jolene I buy me a new truck, she don't wanna see it." Coffee Glory served me warmed my hands. "Now I gettin me back on my feet right good." Paid Jolene what I owed pretty close to them twenty-four hours. "She ain't far behind. She back to her ole self real soon, feel that in my bones."

"Dat girl shore let herself go. Miracle gonna happen before she sees her way out." Glory clanked stuff round on the shelfs, wiped them down clean.

"I don't blame her none givin into sadness. She lose all her jack, they run her outta her smoke shop." Watched Glory with her dust-rag. "How you feel if'n that French lawyer fella come long, pull this here store out from under you?"

Glory let out a belly laugh. "Jolene never tells you the truth?"

"Tell me what?" Set my coffee on the counter with a thud, heat on my face.

"Mr. Cormier done own this store. He my cousin. He helps me buy this store for myself. Money all mine, but we lets folks believe what they wants."

Seen Cormier one time. Shake my head, tried to fit the pieces in place. "But he...."

"Yep." Glory chuckled. "He as white as my granpappy."

"Your grandpa white?"

"Not everythin as it seem." Glory pulled a I-hook-me-a-big-one face.

My head liked to sprout wings. Glory got white kin. What other things might not be like I think? "Why you reckon Jolene let Clyde stay at her house? He stinks at farm work."

"She hate him." Glory slapped her cleaning rag on the counter.

"That wrong. Don't make a licka sense."

"Some folk sit more easy with ones they done take to than ones they do. Way I sees things, Miz Jolene done took to misery." Glory poured me more coffee. "She not gettin no better lesson somebody real strong drag her out by her heels."

"You right, Glory. And that somebody me."

"Fraid some dark parts of Miz Jolene never be fixed." Glory stared at the counter.

"I gonna tell Jolene I drivin her to the O'Brien House this Saturday night so she mix up drinks like she use to. That mean she gotta spiffy herself up, dress nice."

"Cain't do that. Miz Ana Marie closin down her house."

Feel like my supper fall in the fire. "Why she go and do that to such a nice place?"

"Miz Ana Marie gonna jump the broom with some rich fella, move to New York City. She givin the house to the county cause they good bout not slappin her with too big of fines. Somma the long time girls still there, Mary Jo and Sadie, they gonna retire, help the county run the house as a home for orphans."

"That tale nothin but a load a what they plow into fields to make the corn grow."

"Plenty of folk come in my store, flap their gums if nobody else in here."

Find it hard not to believe Glory. She tell the truth bout part of Jolene broke inside. Nothing wrong with that. Jolene tell me right to my face I damaged. If we both like that, reckoned I got me a duty to help her.

If Glory recollected the story right, Sadie the goat gal still at the O'Brien House. Clyde get wind of the news yet? If I played my cards right, I get rid of Clyde for good.

EIGHTY-SIX

"Hey, Clyde. You ever tire a doin every little thang Jolene make you?" Most times when Clyde helped me load whiskey we did the job with no words, today I got me a plan, talked loud so he heed what I said.

"You right, she one bossy woman. But this my idea to oversee so you don't break no jars."

Knowed Jolene ordered him keep watch. But he said I right? Hm. "Speakin a breakin, Jolene bust up bout Ana Marie's news?"

"Oh, Ana Marie show up not long ago. Jolene jump at a ride in Ana Marie's new car. Talk for days about that shiny machine."

My hackles go up cause Jolene turned up her nose at my new truck. "So she don't tell you?"

"Jolene don't keep no secrets from me."

"How she feel bout Ana Marie movin to New York City?"

"That a load of hooey. Never gonna happen."

"Ana Marie marryin some rich fella. Reckon Jolene ain't happy bout that."

Clyde pulled a shitting-a-pinecone face. "That why her mood so dark after Ana Marie leave."

"Them gals gonna retire. Sadie ain't gone yet, but reckon plenty of fellas in line for her hand. She snatch her up a husband real soon."

"Sadie ain't gonna marry no man but me."

I laughed. "Pretty gal like Sadie never gonna give her hand to the likes of you."

"I know she will."

"You ask her?"

"If I do, she say yes."

"Wanna bet?"

"Bet everything I got on that."

"Got a fiver what say she tell you no. I drive you to the O'Brien House right now if'n you that sure."

Waited for Clyde to knock or turn the doorknob to the O'Brien House.

"If'n you change your mind, give me the five smackers and I haul you back to Cedar Springs."

Clyde go on in. Ana Marie packed some boxes in the parlor.

"Look like you ready to go," I said.

"Day after tomorrow." She pointed a red painted fingernail at Clyde who stand looking up the stairs. "What he doin?"

Clyde take the first step of his climb.

"He aim to ask Sadie to marry him."

"Him too? Sadie one popular girl today."

"What?"

"Nother one up there right now talkin to Sadie."

"Askin for her hand?" Floorboards creaked over our heads. "That might mean trouble." Scurried upstairs, Ana Marie ain't far behind.

Seen Clyde grip the knob. "Wait."

Two shots ring out behind the door. Clyde busted in. Sadie on the bed. Blood on the headboard, the wall, the floor. Clyde run to her.

I chokehold the fella from behind. Gripped his gun-hand like I tearing a bone from a hound.

"Let me go." He wriggled like a slippery trout. "She say I don't really love her."

Ana Marie covered her flour white face with her hands.

Pulled harder on the fella's windpipe. He coughed, dropped the pistol.

Clyde on his knees. "Sadie! No! Not again."

Fella sputtered more so I loosed up a bit.

Red blood spread cross Sadie's yellow robe.

On his feet, Clyde hauled off and socked that shooter in the face so hard he fall back, knocked us both into the wall. Wrassled the limp fella to a chair. He blinked. I picked up the gun hold it on him. Clyde gone.

Ana Marie stretched a blanket over Sadie. "She gone." Black tears dripped on Ana Marie's face. She meet my eye. "This crazy son-a-bitch like to shoot us all. You a hero."

Not far before the Mill Creek turnoff I spied Clyde, he sat on some rock. Pulled off the road, go to him. "I take you to the Grady place."

"No." He rubbed his wet face, wiped snot on his sleeve. "Why again?"

Gave him a jar fulla shine from my coat pocket, sat on the cold ground. "Again? What'cha mean?"

"When I a kid I run away from home. Never survive on the streets if she don't take me in. Her name Rose."

"Ain't that what you name your goat?"

"Go to hell." Clyde gulped from the jar. "She like Sadie but she work for herself. Twice my age, teach me lots, let me stay." He take nother pull. "That day I bring her a painting of flowers somebody toss out. She love that pretty picture like I know she would, and she hang it in the sitting room. Our deal that I stay out late while she entertain her customers. One night I get home to find coppers. Hide outside the window. A knife in her chest. Hear a cop say to look for a skinny, blond kid with big ears. Get my ass far, far away from there."

"Nobody gonna say you do nothin to Sadie. Me and Ana Marie hand that fella over to Sheriff Clayton."

"I ain't gonna talk to no sheriff name Clayton."

"What you got gainst the sheriff? You ain't never met him." Seen now that Clyde's big ears a lot like Sheriff Clayton's.

"Look for a sign for me to leave for a long time."

"But Jolene…"

Clyde waved a hand in the air. "I no farmer. You fit to take care of that woman. She talk all sorts of good about you. Treat me like bad cabbage. I on my way, away from Sheriff Clayton and Jolene."

Reckoned that why he so quick to take the bet. "Where you gonna go?"

"Talk of the draft with the war in Europe. I gonna join up."

"You too old for the army."

"Lie about my birth year as good as I lie about my name. When the states jump in that shit over there, they gonna need every man they get."

Find a five in my back pocket. "Here. If'n Saddie didn't get herself kilt, she marry you."

EIGHTY-SEVEN

Reckoned the job fall on me to tell Jolene bout Clyde taking his leave. Grabbed onea them hamburger sandwiches at Stewarts, a café on the line twixt Cedar Springs and Mill Creek, gave me time to think on what to say.

Leave Stewarts still not sure how to break the news to Jolene. Half mile down the road, hear a knock on my back window. Looked over, seen a hand. Tried to keep my heart from jumping outta my chest. Somebody in back of my truck. Got all them jars fulla shine back there. Not the law, please Lord. Pulled off the road, go round back to the tailgate. What I gonna do if they throwed me back in prison?

Fella what climbed outta the hay, jumped off the truck, ain't no sheriff. He older, taller, pudgier, but he still B. J. Harvey.

Darted in behind some trees, B. J. followed me. I turned on him. "What the hell you doin? You like to land me in a load a pig-shit? Word get to Jolene that I give you the time of day, she show me the door faster than a bullfrog catchin a fly. I oughta not be on the Harvey side of the road to boot."

"That's what I wanna talk to you bout."

"Why you here? In Cedar Springs? You leave long time go."

"I'm the new preacher at the Cedar Springs Community Church."

"Preacher? They got a Harvey for a preacher?"

"I wanna end the feud. I'm not like my pa, not one bit like stupid Snake neither. God seen me fit to get saved."

"You crazy. Ain't nothin for me to do bout that there feud."

"Talk to Jolene. Say I don't shoot at Little Joe. You the only one know I don't do that."

"Nope. I ain't tellin nobody why you kilt Cob Turner."

"Say I do in that bastard cause of money. I need Jolene to make a truce."

"Why you so rile up bout this now?"

"Snake a poor excuse for a man. Evil drunkard run down that O'Hara baby sure as Jesus turn water to wine. But I don't think he aim to. I think when ole Will O'Hara kilt my great uncle Zeek, that a accident too."

"Y'all don't even feud. I hear tella folks over in Kentucky what shoot lotta bodies and you only got two, and them you call accidents."

"Three. Three bodies."

"Three? Your Uncle Zeek Harvey and Buck O'Hara that make two."

"They never tell you bout their ma?"

"O'Haras never say shit bout their ma. Reckon one bad sickness take her from this world."

"No sickness. My cousin Annabel Lee."

"A cousin a yourn? A Harvey? A gal Harvey shoot Jolene's ma?"

"No shootin. When I bout six-year-old we all go to the county fair. Cousin Annabel Lee don't know Mrs. O'Hara enter the jelly and jam contest too. Annabel Lee always a bit tetched in the head. When Mrs. O'Hara win the blue ribbon Annabel Lee so durn sure she gonna win, she get mad as a bear with a bee in his ear. She crack Mrs. O'Hara over the head with a shovel."

Feel like that shovel hit me in the gut, I feel so bad for Jolene, Big Jack, Little Joe.

"They never tell you."

Looked way from B. J.'s brown eyes drilling me. "So your kin got one up on them O'Hara's."

"Don't say my kin. They nothing like me. I know that when I seen Mrs. O'Hara in the dirt on that fairground. Then and there I vow I wanna end the feud."

Circled a tree, tried to think, come back, stared B. J. in the face. "Then your pa spout off bout you shootin at Little Joe."

"I block out the feud. But I seen Mrs. O'Hara's limp face in nightmares of late. Her face melt into nother bloody one, not clear to me. You gotta talk Jolene into seein me. God above tellin me that if I don't speak with her somebody else gonna die."

I knowed bushels bout bad rememberings coming in dreams. "Ain't hat easy. Where y'all posta meet? Got no clue what I gonna tell her."

"Tell her come to the church. Or I sneak over to the O'Hara place. I'll give you a week, you go discuss this with her. After that, if I don't hear from you, I slip over to the O'Hara's anyway."

EIGHTY-EIGHT

One week. I got me one week to talk Jolene into meeting B. J.. How I posta do that? After what I heard bout her ma, made the job harder. What if the face what ain't clear in B. J.'s dream his own face?

Meanwhile, reckoned I best sell off all them shine jars before I get me nother scare. End up in the city with a wad of jack in my pocket. Clouds looked like they gonna spill rain. Buyed me a slicker. Picked up a newspaper and a couple special treats too. Got a haircut and a shave. Gotta look good. Jolene ain't got no Clyde, no poker playing town fellas. This time she gonna sit up and take stock in me or I show her how.

At a filling station I scouted out the fella what run the pump. Seen legs sticking out from under a pickup, knocked on the fender.

Law, if the fella what slide out ain't got a handlebar mustache like…Ace. "Why, hey, pal."

Ace pulled hisself to his feet. "You still in the same business?"

"Yep." Slipped out a flask for him. "This some pretty good hooch."

"No thanks." Ace hang his wrench on a tidy tool board.

"You don't misplace things no more."

"Don't smoke reefer no more."

"Good, but this here whiskey ain't reefer. Try some."

"No thanks. Since my time in prison I kick botha my habits."

"Me, I gotta drink to forget prison."

"Guess I got lucky. I play along with whatever games go on in there, get out and find a job doing what I love. Keep off the drink and smoke, feel better than I ever do in my whole life. That a new truck? Let me soup up that one like I do the old one."

"Sure. I want my truck fast as a hound chasin a rabbit. But no way I give up whiskey. Haulin shine the job I love."

"You don't gotta drink it. Hear that preacher you bootlegged for, poor fella, never touch the stuff. Me, I like waking up with no headache, remembering the night before."

Somewhere far off a train whistled. Where Little Joe at? Hoped he safe, hoped he live. Maybe Ace got him a point.

Find coins in my truck to pay Ace for the gasoline. Some nickel dropped, rolled clean to the sidewalk. A tall fella in a wide brimmed hat and a brown coat picked up the nickel, come my way. He got a ole folded piece a paper stuck in his pocket. Look like the hindend of a goat drawed on that paper. "This your buffalo head?"

"Much obliged."

"They got a map here? I need to find a place called Cedar Springs."

"Goin there right now. Look like you need you a ride with that knapsack a yourn. Not to mention the rain storm comin in."

"Thanks. Hear Cedar Springs kinda small. You know Sonny Harvey? He my brother. My name's Rupp Harvey."

"Harvey? Uh, no." Got me enough of them Harveys with B. J. and his story bout his aunt and Jolene's ma.

Ace clicked out the gasoline hose.

Ain't sticking round. Dropped coins for the gas on the ground. Jumped in my truck, get the hell outta there.

First chance I get I swigged from my flask. What the drawing on that paper remind me of?

EIGHTY-NINE

"That there some steak." Put the package by the sink.

Didn't see Jolene take the stogie I leave on the table. She like a mouse stealing cheese outta a trap. Where she stick the cigar? Maybe in the holster with her pistol. Seemed like she never take that thing off.

"Clyde do the cookin. I don't touch them pans no more."

"He gone. Ain't comin back."

"You cook."

Me? Slapped the meat in a skillet with potatoes and onions. Crossed my fingers the stuff didn't burn. Turned out pretty good, if I do say so myself.

Jolene eat a couple potatoes, no onions, maybe one bite of steak, that all.

"Wash up them dishes lickety split, try my new batch a whiskey." Jolene pushed back her tangled hair.

Rain stopped for the time being. We sat by the crackling fire. Remembered what Ace said. Drink the white lightning slow.

"You don't ask me where Clyde at?"

"Who? Oh, him. Seen this comin, him slinkin off like a skunk with its tail tween its legs."

"Leastwise you gotta wanna hear the story."

"Nope. He worthless, that it. Here's the jug, pour you some more." Jolene turned down the coal oil lamp.

"Still got me some. Remember them electric lights in that smoke shop a yourn?"

"Top off your cup. Kills the chill." She pushed the jug my direction, pulled her granny sweater tighter. "My town days done for good."

"Times much better now. Lotta places in town what close down open gain, new ones too. You get money soon to open the smoke shop back up. I help."

"That never gonna happen. I done with that shit business. You don't like this batch of shine? Try some more."

"Nah." Covered my cup with my hand. "You posta become a legend, remember? How that gonna happen with you up here on the farm?"

"I messed that up long time back. That day I don't go get baptized the day I know I never gonna become a legend."

"You ever hear B. J. Harvey get hisself baptized that day?"

"No religion gonna suck the evil outta no Harvey." She added more corn squeezings to her cup. "Too bad you no good at plowin. We gotta start plantin. Your rows never come out even. Lucky you don't gotta grow your own food. You starve."

"Done some farmin in my time." Tossed back what left in my cup. "How come you never tell me your ma go down in the feud?"

"Nothin to tell. We put her in the mule cart take her home to the buryin yard. Nonea us like to use Ole Abe or that cart after that." She take a big swallow. "Nother lucky thing, that sister you got gonna take care you. That revenuer she marry don't haul you in first" Her laugh rubbed my ears like sandpaper.

"Mason ain't got nothin to do with the ATF for a coon's age. You make any pies lately?"

"Funny. All this time he waitin for the right time to arrest you."

Nother splash of shine sound good by that time. Just my luck, Jolene take her cup and the jug to the kitchen. She didn't sway or stumble like a drunk but she talked slower.

"Clyde not here, you sleep in the big bed."

"I make my way to my truck."

"No, I smell more rain comin. You hole up indoors."

Reckoned staying that night get me one step closer to settling in for good.

NINETY

"Lookie them damn clouds out there." Jolene poured coffee, stirred in shine from the jug. "Nobody do no plantin today."

Spied ads in the newspaper open on the table. "We goin to the city."

"The city? What fool reason we got for goin to the city?"

"Gonna see a movin pitcher show." Tapped the newspaper. "Remember when we seen that there *Jazz Singer*? That fun. This time we see *The Wizard of Oz*."

"I don't wanna sit in no stinky, dark movie house with screamin young'ns."

"Why not? Gonna be dark outdoors by the look of that weather. This truck do good in the rain, she got wipers."

Jolene sipped her coffee. She looked like she bout ready to confess a crime.

"Hear some folks talkin bout that *Wizard of Oz*," I said. "They say the movie got color."

"Color. Humph. Movin pitchers in color? No such thing."

"You a bettin woman, so how bout I bet you this one in color?"

"What kinda bet?"

"We work that out later. First we gotta see the movie, see who win." Go to the door. "Get yourself doll up."

In my truck I find clean britches, mite wrinkled but good enough, a suit coat, a tie too. When I go back Jolene wiping her pistol down with oil. She wear a shirt beneath her overalls, her hair stuffed under her straw hat, old coat. Reckoned she let Ana Marie keep her nice coat when she get her gun back after release from prison.

"Fill your flask," Jolene said. "I got mine but we gotta stop in Chimney, buy me a pack a Camels."

When the movie start Jolene whispered, "See, tole ya." Then when the house crashed in Oz Jolene muttered, "Shooooot."

On the ride home Jolene talked bout the show. Seemed like she enjoyed the movie. "You win the bet. What'cha want?"

"Let me think on that." Roads ain't too wet. Reckoned the dark clouds passed on by.

"Just don't go askin for somethin you not gonna get."

"Haulin some corn squeezins tomorrow. Tell you when I get back."

"I gotta do the plowin tomorrow." Jolene swigged from a flat bottle. "I gotta get the mule from Big Jack. Drop me at Fresh Farms. I wanna sit a spell with Glory."

Go over the bridge, headed into Cedar Springs like Jolene said. Her wanting to visit a good sign. Slowed when the store come in sight. Lorraine sweeped the porch, she to the age where she did her share of work. She talking to some fella. Braked hard. Recollected the fella by his wide brimmed hat and brown coat. He take off in tuther direction.

"That Harvey fella." The words slipped from my mouth.

"Harvey? What?" Jolene twisted the lid shut, let the bottle drop on the floorboards.

"Say his name Rupp Harvey." Drive the last few yards, stopped in fronta Fresh Farms.

Jolene outta that door like onea them flying monkeys. Marched up to Lorraine. Didn't hear much a what she said. Something bout "how dare" and "talk to some worthless Harvey."

Sucked in air when Jolene slapped Lorraine's face. Jolene jumped back in my truck, slammed the door. "Get me outta here. Take me to my house."

Thanked the good lord she didn't ask me to run after that bastard.

"Lorraine must not a knowed, She only a little gal." I said.

"What bout you? You talk to that pig-shit Harvey?"

"No. Hear him jawin with somebody else."

At the Grady place Jolene didn't go near the cabin. "I goin up to the still. Alone."

The house feel strange by my lonesome. No Clyde, Jolene off in the woods. Tried to make myself to home. Think bout bringing my belongings up from the truck. What Jolene gonna say bout that? After all, I do win our bet.

NINETY-ONE

Jolene come in when I drinking my coffee. She get her some, stirred in whiskey. "Gotta add some taste to this mud you fix."

"You sleep atall?" Didn't think she did by the look of her.

"I got the mule from the O'Hara place. Gonna get to the plowin today come hell or cold water." She picked up onea my stone hard biscuits, dropped it.

"Reckon I gotta learn me some cookin," I said.

When Jolene go outside, I looked at the jug, think bout a splash in my coffee. Recollected what Ace said, reckoned I better not.

Followed her out, go down the porch steps. Why Jolene standing in the yard? What she looking at? White clouds hang over the trees like snow. Patches of blue sky bring hope for a clear day. Then I seen who coming.

"Hole up right there," Jolene hollered, pulled her pistol from the holster.

"Looking for somebody." Rupp Harvey called to her. Looked like climbing that hill take the wind from him. "Just wanna talk."

Jolene go down on one knee. "Get off my land." She hold her gun with two hands. Her trigger finger shake.

Rupp stopped. "Listen." His face showed he didn't know what else to say. He take one more step.

Crack. Smoke come off the end of Jolene's gun. Rupp fall like a tall tree in a wind storm. Stink of gunpowder hit my nose. Jolene get to her feet.

Ain't Snake she shoot. She ain't got nothing gainst Rupp. Knowed how Dorothy feel when the curtain pulled back showing the plain ole fella, not no wizard.

Blood trickled from a hole in Rupp's head. His hat lay not far off with graze marks on the wide brim.

Jolene grabbed one leg. "Help me drag him to the house."

We get the body up the steps to the front room.

"Get me jugs from the shed."

I didn't move. Rupp's open eyes dead stared at me.

"Now."

Bring the whiskey like she said.

She snatched them from my hands. "Get more."

Maybe she gonna drink way what happened. Reckoned not with that dead Harvey fella in the house. Set the jugs on the porch.

Jolene shoved papers at me. "Take them deeds to town, get Big Jack's name put on. Take this." She hold out her gun. "Hide this where nobody find it."

Cranked up my truck, the pistol on the empty seat. Where I gonna hide that damn thing? Seen my rain slicker on the floor, recollected how Little Joe made me think he drown hisself at the swimming hole.

Drive down the hill, smelled fire. In the side mirror I seen a dark gray cloud grow over the Grady place.

NINETY-TWO

Next few days I feel like a stone sinking in the river. Everything moved slow like underwater. Didn't sell no whiskey, didn't do nothing. Stayed way from Cedar Springs, Swift River too.

When my belly rumbled I reckoned I best get me some vittles cause it been while. Stopped at The Redbird Diner in Juniper. Shuffled the eggs and taters round on my plate. How I posta eat when what Jolene do eat at my innards?

Spied a tellyphone booth in the corner. Slide open the door, dropped in a nickel, asked the operator for Fresh Farms Country Market.

"Gots some real bad news." Glory sounded like she trying to swallow a pepper sprout. "Miz Jolene place catch fire. Some mill workers seen the smoke, theys up there later. Theys sayin musta bin lotta whiskey in the house. Fire burn so hot, only somma her bones left."

"Them fellas find only one body's bones?"

"Uh huh."

Spinning in my gut stopped.

"Guess you done hears, Clyde leaves for good."

"How you knowed bout Clyde?"

"Onea the mens that drink at Glad Town seen him waitin for a bus."

Glory ever figure out who Clyde really be?

"This so sad bout Miz Jolene. Bet you in shock. The news gonna hits you real bad later."

"Be strong, Glory." Set the earpiece on the hanger next to the part you talk into.

"You look like your dog up and die." Sammy Jean by the counter when I leave the tellyphone booth. Her face reeled me outta my swamp mood. Feel like I waked from a three-day sleep.

"Somethin like that. What'cha doin here?"

"Come to town for some sewin items, seen your truck out front."

"Sammy Jean, food in this dump like ole shoes. You mind if'n I come by your place for supper? Maybe stow some stuff in that shed you got out back?"

"Why sure." She got a twinkle in her eye. "You sleep there too, if you like, long as you want."

I did stay, leastwise most times. Got better at drawing and painting. Sammy Jean sell somma my pictures in that shop they got for selling them clay pots. A fella payed fifty dollars for one I painted what showed a goat eating purple morning glories.

Get Ace to soup up my truck. Everything Ace learned me bout that engine I passed on to Tinker cause he always asking what this and that do. He take to learning like a dry field soaking up water after a long hot summer. By the time Tinker fifteen he built his own car from what he find in the junk yard.

"Crank it up."

I pulled the starter. "You got her runnin nice'n smooth."

Tinker slide shut the engine cover. "Thanks to your help."

"Me, I don't help so much."

"I never get this car done if not for what you show me. You my hero, Uncle Rufus."

"Hero? Don't go that far."

"I really look up to you. You got your own business you built all on your own."

"Got me some help. Your folks got their own business with that there shop."

"But that just right here. You go all round the state doin what you do."

Not so much no more. "Gotta feelin you gonna do right good for yourself, Tink."

On my way to pick up a load of shine from Big Jack I think on how Tinker called me a hero. Wished I feel like that honor one I lived up to.

Seen a fella walking in the direction of Cedar Springs. Something bout him seem familiar. Snake Harvey? Not sure, cause I only seen his back. Beeped my horn, fella stopped, turned.

He Snake for damn sure. Stomped down on that gas pedal. Snake looked ready to mess his pants. Nothing but rocks to the side of the road. Nowhere for him to run but down the road the way he headed before. Them long skinny legs no match for my truck. Catch up to him in seconds.

Front of my truck gonna plow him down. I ain't like Snake. I ain't like Jolene. Turned the wheel when he ain't more'n a inch or two way. Feel a bump under one front tire. Snake screamed.

Slowed, checked the mirror. Snake moaned, rolled on the ground in a cloud of gasoline smoke, hold one leg with both hands. He gonna live but he gonna limp bad.

Feel more like a hero than I ever did before.

NINETY-THREE

My heart beating fast as a freight train when I parked at Fresh Farms. Store ain't open. I forgot it Sunday. Ambled down the path to the yard by the O'Hara place. Recollected the first time I go down this pine tree lined path with Little Joe all them years ago.

Seen a squat fella get in a ole car drive way.

"Uncle Jack ain't here." Lorraine meet me at the door. "He at the still runnin the batch you come to get. With all the rain we get of late the mash don't turn till today."

"I come back tomorrow."

"Stay. Look like more clouds rollin in. I got us hot coffee on the stove and I bakin cookies."

"That Bull Gibbs I seen skedaddlin from here?"

"Oh, yeah. Uncle Bull don't come round here much, like when I a young'un."

Lorraine leaned over me to pour my coffee, her leg brushed mine a bit. Never noticed before, she done become a woman.

"Bull ever do funny stuff to you?"

"You so sweet to worry bout me but I handle him fine."

"You sure he never do nothin to you?" Studied Lorraine's face. Her soft curls make me recollect Ana Marie, give me a glow inside.

"He only come here for whiskey." She waved at the jug by the sink. "Want you some?"

"What bout you?"

"Nah, I never take to the stuff."

"Like your pa in the early days. You must miss your pa, ma too."

"I lucky I got Uncle Jack and Granny Glory. Folks ask me if I miss my aunt Jolene what burn up in that fire years ago. I say I do, but tell you the truth she ain't a nice person what I remember. She slap me real hard one time. You recall that?"

Done good keeping Jolene outta my mind the last few years. Rain pounded the ground outside, wished that rain wash her name outta my head.

"Did you say you want some?" Lorraine hold up the jug.

That a hard question, like if she asked me if I know what going on with that war over in Korea. Shake my head. "I hear Bull ain't no nice person."

Lorraine sit next to me at the table. She smelled like the gingerbread she got in the oven. "Don't you go worryin bout me and him."

"If'n Bull make you do something you don't wanna, I make him one sorry...."

She wrapped her pretty fingers over my hand holding the coffee cup. "What get you all riled?"

"Got me onea them uncles what push me to do bad stuff when I a boy."

"Oh, no. I so sorry. You get back at him for that?"

"Don't recollect cept what I seen in bad dreams."

"Where he at now? I help you give him what for."

"He die way back then. Piece that together from them nightmares."

"Oh dear, you think you there when he die?"

"More'n one night I wake in a pool of sweat after I seen him in a dream. He grab his arm, gulp air like a fish outta water, fall over."

"What a brave soul you got. You deserve somethin good."

Feel comfortable in that kitchen I know better than no other kitchen. Talking with Lorraine reminded me of talking with her pa, with Jolene. Lorraine looked a mite like Jolene, in the same way Ana Marie looked like Jolene.

Sleep good that night. Go back to the kitchen to light the stove. Sat by my lonesome, out the window the silver sky got brighter. Bout the time I think the water gonna boil the porch creaked. Then nothing. Back of my neck prickled.

After a spell I gave into the nagging in my gut. Opened the door. Right outside sat a little wooden box like the ones at the ole smoke shop. Bring it inside, opened the lid. Six cigars, two hand rolled. Seen them all before. Every time I bring her onea them stogies I hoped she happy to see me.

Take that cigar box inside, plunked my behind down on the hearth. Stoked the fire with couple of branches. Lay my find on top. Flames licked at the box, then it catched. Smoke from them stale stogies roared up the chimney and far way from me.

Please check out my website and join my email list at
whiskeyandoldstogies.com

Acknowledgements

I feel listing names of individuals in this space an impossible task. So let me offer up some of the organizations that help me along my author's journey:

San Luis Obispo NightWriters
Cambria Writers Workshop
Santa Barbara Writers Conference
Riviera Writers Workshop
Southern California Writers Conference
Toni Lopopolo Literary Management
Writers and Publishers Network

CPSIA information can be obtained
at www.ICGtesting.com
Printed in the USA
LVHW040431200821
695741LV00016B/639

9 781737 047407